About Bucking Time

A SWEET COWBOY ROMCOM

MARIKA RAY

SYLVIE STEWART

First Edition: January 8, 2026
Cover Designer: Sylvie Stewart
Illustrator: Sylvie Stewart

Ebook ISBN: 978-1-947853-96-6
Paperback ISBN: 978-1-947853-97-3

To every woman in her "coming of rage" era... we see you.

No woman wants a pity proposal.

Just because I'm turning forty, dealing with peri-menopause, and recently dumped another loser doesn't mean I need rescuing—especially not by my best friend.

But when Dallas Gamble blurts out that we're engaged in a very public attempt at protecting me, there's not much I can do but play along. Bless his dumb, beautiful heart.

The man has always been impulsive. Protective. Flirty. And able to fill out a pair of Levi's like nobody's business. In no time at all, he slides a ring on my finger, moves me into his house, and swears it's no big deal.

But then things get complicated.

Because suddenly, he's trying—as in, *really trying.*

And even though every clumsy romantic gesture ends in disaster, it's getting harder to pretend this isn't real.

Dallas Gamble was never supposed to be my happily ever after. If we do this, I risk losing my best friend.

And if we don't… I might lose the great love story I've been chasing my whole life.

But I'm starting to think it's *about bucking time* we go for it.

About Bucking Time
Playlist

Rumor - Lee Brice
   Butterflies - Kasey Musgraves
   We Danced - Brad Paisley
   Sunshine & Whiskey - Frankie Ballard
   Body Like a Back Road - Sam Hunt
   You're My Best Friend - Queen
   A Million Things - Old Dominion
   Company You Keep - Maren Morris
   I Can Help - Charley Crockett
   I Wanna Let You - Lost Saints
   How Country Feels - Randy Houser
   My Best Friend - Tim McGraw
   Strip It Down - Luke Bryan

To listen to the full playlist, click here!

Prologue

THERE AIN'T A POT TOO CROOKED THAT A LID WON'T FIT

TWENTY-FIVE YEARS *Ago*

"See you tomorrow!" the neighbor girl calls as she splits off from Shelby and heads for her own house.

Shelby lets go of her backpack straps long enough to wave, her heart thudding with tension. The whole day has been filled with stress. The first day in a new school and a new town is enough to make even the most extroverted kid feel sick with nerves. At least her neighbor, Charlene, is in her grade and helped her find her classrooms. She also told her which mean girls to stay away from and which boys were the troublemakers.

Shelby checks the mailbox, but it's just a few pieces of junk mail for her parents. A loud noise from behind makes her spin back to the road. She can barely believe her eyes. A fully grown black and white heifer trots down the paved country road like it has every right to be there. She grins, her love of all animals already well established at fifteen.

She clicks her tongue and holds out her hand, hoping the cow will come closer. It does, its tail swishing back and forth like a dog. She's just about to scratch its broad head when a loud rumbling noise spooks the poor cow. It bellows something fierce, its eyes going wide as it dances away from her hand. A truck and trailer barrels down the road going entirely too fast for a residential area. It screeches to a halt just past her with a high-pitched wheeze, and the driver slides out the door, his blue-jean-clad legs and dusty cowboy boots eating up the asphalt.

"You steal my cow?" the boy asks in a sexy drawl.

Shelby's mouth drops open at the accusation.

And at the way his upper body fills out a T-shirt.

"I didn't steal your cow! She was lost, running down the road!"

The boy grins, and Shelby's heart pounds. He's too handsome for words. Baby-faced still, so clearly young. Maybe even her age. Definitely too cocky for his own good. He winks at her, and she feels her cheeks flame red.

"Well, I do thank you for stopping her." He holds out his hand, and Shelby stares at it. "Dallas Gamble."

In slow motion, she finally lifts her hand, and he shakes it, oblivious to her reluctance. You see, Shelby just spent twenty minutes walking home from school with Charlene Russell, who spent nineteen of those minutes discussing the Gamble twins, namely Dallas. She knows exactly what a flirt he is.

His smile only amps up in the face of her silence. He doesn't let go of her hand.

"This is where you tell me *your* name."

"Oh, um, Shelby Sweet." She tugs on his hand, and he finally releases her.

"Well, Sweetness, I gotta get this girl in the trailer before she starts eating Mrs. Perkins's flowers again."

Shelby doesn't know who Mrs. Perkins is, but as Dallas rounds on the cow, the frightened thing rears back. Dallas claps his hands, but that just startles her more. Rolling her eyes, Shelby puts her hands out gently and speaks in a low tone, murmuring sweet nothings to the animal. Dallas stares at her like he's never seen someone sweet talk a cow, but it works. The dang thing comes closer to her, finally nudging its head against her hand. He gets a rope around her head while Shelby distracts it with pets and soothing words. Together, they get the poor thing in the trailer, and Dallas closes the back. He dusts off his hands and turns to the new girl.

"Thank you for your help. You live here?" He points to Shelby's new house, the one her parents just bought to be closer to her grandparents.

"Yeah. Just moved in."

He grins at her. "Well, come on then." He starts walking. Not toward his truck, but up her driveway. Shelby scurries after him, having to almost run to keep up with his long legs.

"What are you doing?" she manages to ask right as they mount the porch steps.

He turns to her, that smile making his golden eyes twinkle. She notices the twinkle. And everything else about this boy that makes her stomach feel funny.

"I'm walking the new girl home. It's what we do in small towns, Sweetness."

"That's…that's not my name," she stammers.

Music streams from the house, stealing Dallas's attention as he pulls open the screen door. Shelby grabs his arm to stop him from entering, but he's determined to see what's happening inside. Shelby already knows her parents are home unpacking their moving boxes and doesn't want Dallas to meet them. Fifteen-year-olds never want parents to be involved.

Dallas trips over a giant sandwich board wishing everyone a most glorious Labor Day and then ducks down behind the couch that Shelby's always hated. Its giant flower print is too loud and too…turquoise. He pulls her with him, peeking over the top of the couch into the kitchen where two adults are in each other's arms, swaying back and forth to the song, "We Danced."

"Are those your parents?" His face is just inches from hers.

Her skin feels like it's on fire where he's touching her. Her cheeks flame. "Yeah. They like to dance. It's so embarrassing!"

Dallas's grin intensifies. Shelby feels like she's staring into the sun. "I think it's nice."

They look back at the adults just in time to see Shelby's father dip her mother, then pull her upright. They're smiling at one another like there's no one else in the world.

"Are you going to introduce us to your friend, Shelby?" her mother calls out.

Shelby rolls her eyes. She swears her mother can see out the back of her head. Dallas suppresses a laugh while Shelby climbs to her feet. "Hey. This is Dallas. He lost his cow."

Dallas marches right past Shelby, his hand outstretched. He shakes her mother's hand, then her father's, charming them both in a matter of seconds. They're talking about cattle and land and breathing fresh air.

Her dad finally puts his hand on Dallas's shoulder. "Now, Shelby's new around here, son. You take care of this girl and don't take liberties, you hear?"

Shelby's cheeks can't possibly go redder. "Daddy!"

"I won't, sir. You can count on me." Dallas shakes her father's hand again, winks at her mother, then heads for the front door. "I'll pick you up just after eight tomorrow for school, Shelby. Don't be late!"

And then he's gone, leaving her dazed and confused.

Shelby's mother puts her arm around her shoulders, steering her into the kitchen, the resemblance between the two almost making them look like twins. "He's awfully cute. Seems like fun." Since the color on Shelby's cheeks makes a response unnecessary, her mother continues, "Just watch yourself, okay? Good-time guys are great, but you don't want to set your heart on one. Save your heart for the real thing, and it won't get broken." Her mother nods toward the living room where her father is unpacking boxes and humming along to the radio.

When he notices them looking, he straightens and puts his hands on his hips, smiling broadly. "Look at my girls." Shelby's heart melts, and she's pretty sure her mother's does too.

———

Senior Year of High School

"Your turn, cowboy."

"Do you even have to ask?" Dallas spreads his arms wide, taunting the crowd of tipsy teens assembled around the bonfire. "It's always dare."

He's got a worn shearling jacket on, but no shirt underneath, showing off his impressive muscles. The weightlifting requirement to play football has been good to him, and so has Mother Nature. He's grown four inches in the last two years.

Jeremy, a fellow senior on the football team, snorts. "You're gonna die one of these dares. Would it really hurt you to choose truth for once?"

A stiff breeze tumbles all the girls' hair. The horses over by the trees start stirring. They don't like being out here when a storm's approaching, but they're used to the midnight rides on the weekends. Teens in Big Knob have been obsessed with middle-of-the-night horseback rides for decades. Parents look the other way because the alternative is worse. Can't be arrested for drinking and driving if you're riding.

Dallas chugs the rest of his beer and tosses the empty can into the raging bonfire. "I prefer action to words."

The boy has more swagger than is good for him. Several of the girls around the fire—girls who know exactly the kind of action Dallas likes to take—bat their eyelashes at him, despite boyfriends by their sides. Shelby rolls her eyes, shifting closer to Dallas for extra heat. She hates Truth or Dare with all these people. Real life is scary enough without these made-up games.

"Okay, fine. I dare you to skinny dip in the river." Jeremy smiles like he's won. He knows how dangerous it is to step foot in that river in the winter.

Dallas also smiles, unhurried as he stands and strips off his jacket and cowboy hat. A few girls hoot at his naked torso, which only eggs him on. "You wanna see me naked, Jer?"

"Shut up," Jeremy mutters, kicking dirt at Dallas's boots.

"Dallas, don't," Shelby murmurs to his back. He ignores her, bending down to pull off his boots.

"What are you doing, man?" Houston, Dallas's twin, releases his hold on his girlfriend, Josie Mae, and stands up to put his hand on Dallas's chest. "Don't do it. Jeremy's an idiot."

"Hey! He chose dare!" Jeremy shouts in his defense.

Dallas pushes Houston's hand off his chest. His skin is already pebbled with goose bumps. "I'll be in and out. Don't worry." He swaggers away from the bonfire, stripping out of his jeans when he hits the riverbank. His thumbs go into the waistband of his boxers. "Avert your eyes, you perverts!"

And then he's dashing into the river, naked as the day he was born. Shelby leaps to her feet and races over to the river with several blankets. Dallas resurfaces with a whoop and crashes out of the water, hands covering the goods. Shelby wraps the blankets around him before he's fully out of the icy water.

"Are you okay?" she urgently whispers, rubbing up and down his arms to generate warmth.

Dallas tosses his head back and howls at the moon while Jeremy cracks up. Houston flips off his brother and settles back in front of the fire.

"D-dang, that was c-cold," Dallas whispers to Shelby, who's shaking her head at the idiot.

They both sit down, Dallas as close to the fire as he can get without burning himself. The game continues and so does the drinking. At one point, Shelby catches Houston watching her from across the fire. She narrows her eyes. Houston looks pointedly at Dallas and the way his arm is draped around Shelby's shoulders. She makes a funny face, as if to blow off the whole thing. Everyone knows how affectionate Dallas is with everybody, but especially her since her parents died in a tragic car accident.

Houston suddenly speaks, cutting in line when it isn't his turn. "I've got one. Shelby, truth or dare?"

Shelby feels all eyes shift in her direction. A tingle of warning slides up her spine. She doesn't like the seriousness of Houston's gaze. He looks so much like Dallas, but there's no easy humor with him. He's always so damn dead intense.

Normally, Shelby would choose truth. But not now. Not with Houston looking back and forth between her and Dallas. She will never, not ever, confess to having a crush on her best friend. She'd rather strip naked and slide into that icy river never to get out again than tell her truth.

"Dare," she answers more confidently than she feels.

Houston grins, and her blood runs cold. "I dare you to kiss my brother."

Shelby's cheeks flame hot, and she can't blame it on the bonfire. She knows in an instant that she needs to put on the performance of a lifetime to get out of this with any dignity. Josie Mae slaps Houston's arm, but the challenge has already been issued.

Shelby stands confidently, even flips her hair over her shoulder. She narrows her eyes at Houston, but when she turns to face Dallas, he smirks just like he always does. If he can act like nothing is serious, so can she. She plops herself right down on Dallas's lap and loops her arms around his neck. His eyes go wide, probably stunned she's going through with the dare.

Shelby plucks the cowboy hat off Dallas's head and holds it so that no one can see her kissing Dallas on his cheek.

The teens laugh and jeer, thinking she kissed Dallas. Only she and Dallas know their lips never touched.

"Thank goodness. I was worried for a second," Dallas whispers, then tosses his head back and laughs.

Shelby joins in, but her heart's not in it.

And when she sits back down, Houston is still studying her.

———

Early Twenties

"This is seriously the dumbest pose you've ever had us do, and there have been a lot of dumb poses!"

Shelby climbs onto Dallas's back as he creates a steady base on the ground on all fours like he's giving a horsy ride to a toddler. Except he's in leather chaps with a fake rifle lying next to his hands, and Shelby's in a barmaid outfit with layers and layers of lacy ruffles.

"For what it's worth, the camera loves it. You two might be the poster for the Knockers County Fair next year," says the hippie photographer with the low ponytail. He waggles his eyebrows and both Shelby and Dallas crack up.

They collect themselves and pose with matching serious expressions, Shelby riding Dallas's back with her feet flared out to the side, showing her ankles. The camera flashes repeatedly, capturing the cheesy western moment in all its sepia glory.

"Hey, at least our tradition isn't Glamour Shots," Dallas says wryly as Shelby climbs off his back.

Shelby grins and checks that all necessary part are still inside the barmaid costume. "Are we done here, Dally?"

"I have an idea!" the photographer calls out. He looks excited, which doesn't bode well for Dallas and Shelby. "I got a new sheepskin rug."

Shelby makes a slicing motion across her throat behind the photographer's back, but Dallas loves shenanigans more than he fears his best friend's wrath. With Dallas sitting on a hay bale, the rifle propped against his hip, and Shelby on her side on the sheepskin, her torso draped across Dallas's legs, the photographer is finally satisfied. Her neck is craned back so she can stare into her friend's twinkling brown eyes, while her long hair covers her cleavage as it tests the boundaries of the costume.

"Perfect!" the photographer calls out, snapping picture after picture. "Now sink your fingers into her hair like you can't spend another moment without touching her."

Dallas's lips quirk into a laugh, but he reins it in. His fingers lightly trail across Shelby's soft skin before delving into her hair. He has to bite back a moan as he grips her hair with his strong fingers. Shelby's so close to him now, they're sharing the same air. They stare into each other's eyes, forgetting for a moment that anyone else is in the tent with them. His fingers flex, kneading across her scalp. Shelby's eyes flutter shut, and he can feel her full body shiver. His nose slides against hers, and he forgets to breathe. Heat licks at his skin. If Dallas doesn't release her soon, he fears he'll cross a line by kissing her finally.

His head shifts, his lips grazing her cheek toward the corner of her mouth. For one heady moment, he thinks she might just welcome his kiss. That all these years of friendship could lead to something a little different. Like, friends with benefits.

"Is this like one of those book cover photoshoots?"

Jeremy's obnoxious voice has Dallas and Shelby jumping apart. Shelby flutters her eyes open to see their group of friends barging into the photo booth.

"Come on, it's our turn!" Josie Mae and Jeremy, now married, start flipping through the rack of costumes. "Honestly, you two look exactly like my grandma's romance novel covers!"

Dallas clears his throat and stands, offering his hand to help Shelby up. She pulls on the bodice of the dress, trying to cover up her cleavage, to no avail.

"That's what we were going for!" Dallas chirps back, not missing a beat. "Think we can sell the pictures?"

"Not without my fee, you dig?" the photographer drawls without much humor.

Dallas pays for the photos while Shelby ducks behind the partition to change into her jeans and tank top. Josie Mae follows her with a gunslinger costume in hand.

"You two looked…" She smirks at her friend. "…friendly."

Shelby commands her cheeks to stop blushing. She rolls her eyes. "Whatever. You know we do this every year. It's a joke."

Josie Mae straps a fake gun and holster around her hips. "Didn't look like a joke to me."

Shelby brushes past her, standing on the other side of the tent from Dallas while their friends get pictures done. When they're kicked out by another group who wants their western pictures taken, Dallas suggests they head over to Knockin' Boots for cheaper beers.

He throws his arm around Shelby's shoulders and pulls her in close, walking hip to hip back to his truck. He's been more touchy-feely since his mom died. Shelby feels guilty for liking his physical touch so much when she knows he's grieving. He talks to her about his mom. He won't talk to anyone else about her. She knows she should treasure their friendship, and she does, but she can't help wondering what if.

"Can't believe Aaron broke up with you on your birthday.

What an idiot," Dallas mutters as they drive back to Big Knob.

"Can't believe Sharice dumped you the day after your mom's funeral because you were too sad to take her out. Now that's an idiot."

Dallas grunts, not saying a word until they park at Knockin' Boots. He turns off the engine and swivels to face her. "She didn't break up with me because of that."

Shelby frowns. "She didn't?"

Dallas shakes his head slowly. "No. She broke up with me because she said I spent too much time with you."

Shelby snorts unattractively. It makes Dallas smile. "We're best friends!"

He shrugs and looks out the windshield. "That's what I told her." He sighs, his thumb tapping out a rhythm on his leg. "You know what I think?"

"Huh?"

He looks back at Shelby. "I think we should get married if we're both single by…I dunno…forty."

Shelby stares at him. Then throws her head back and laughs.

Dallas has always been the class clown. And that one might be his funniest joke yet.

CHAPTER

One

RIGHT CHURCH, WRONG PEW

DALLAS

For forty years, women have captivated me. Tall ones, short ones. Redheads and brunettes. Lord have mercy, don't forget the blondes. Smart women, funny women, and quirky ones too. The ones who smile so sweet you forget your own name particularly light me up. Older, younger, quieter, or louder. Doesn't matter. They all make the blood thrum in my veins the moment they sashay through my life. It's like the swing of their hips and the flick of their hair pulls me right into their web. I've rarely met one I didn't like.

But as of this moment, I know that women will also be the death of me.

Well, one woman in particular.

"Come on, Nelly!" My holler brings my chocolate lab running to the truck, dirt and foxtails decorating his lean legs and underbelly. He leaps into the passenger seat and assumes his position as I close the door, his head out the window and tongue dangling from the side of his mouth. "She ain't here."

Nelly barks once, agreeing with Violet at Rockers 'n

Knockers General Store when she said I just missed Shelby. At this point in the evening, Shelby should be done making her rounds, visiting all the livestock she treats as the only large animal vet in the county. I've been raging across town, looking for Shelby for an hour now, always one step behind her. If I didn't know better, I'd say she's purposely avoiding me.

Ah, Shelby Sweet. My best friend. The one woman in all of Big Knob, Oklahoma, who can make me madder than a cat getting baptized one minute and laugh my butt off the next.

Dust flies behind my dually, the tires eating up the road as I head for the ranch, my destination less about finding Shelby now and more about needing someone wise to talk me off the ledge. My father has always been the voice of reason in my life, and I thank the powers that be every day that his heart's still ticking.

The giant fireball of a sun setting over Honeyhole Lake doesn't even register. I've seen these gentle rolling hills all my life. Never felt the need to leave Oklahoma like my twin brother, Houston. But all I see tonight is rage and annoyance out my windshield.

Nelly whines and stops licking at the breeze long enough to give me a doleful look. He hates it when I'm in a tizzy, mostly because it doesn't happen often. Quite frankly, it only happens when Shelby dates someone stupid. And they've all been stupid, every last one of them. I think my canine might have more discernment of a man's character than Shelby.

"You think you can talk some sense into her, bud?" My thumb taps out a rhythm of irritation on the steering wheel.

Nelly's ears perk up. Right before he slumps down to the passenger seat, defeat lining his posture. Even my dog knows there's no talking sense into Shelby about men.

At the four-way stop where I'll make my right to head to Big Ridge Ranch, our family's operation for five generations, I have to wait for Mrs. Perkins, the elementary school librarian.

She looked old back when I went through school, so she has to be positively ancient by now, as confirmed when she doesn't see me try to wave her through the intersection. Instead, she creeps forward at a snail's pace, sucking on her dentures and squinting her eyes at me. When she finally recognizes me, she slams on the brakes and causes her boat of a Buick to lurch back and forth before coming to a stop in the middle of the intersection.

"That you, Dallas? Or is that Houston?" she hollers through the rolled-down windows.

Nelly covers his eyes with his paws, a whine I wish only dogs could hear leaving his throat. I lean out my window and wave, knowing there's nothing for it. The old people around here can't be rushed. My mouth quirks to the side, thinking of how my own son, if he were with me right now, would make a wisecrack about me being part of the "old folk" now that I celebrated my fortieth birthday.

"Dallas, ma'am!" I holler back. "You seen Shelby today?"

Her eyebrows nearly hit her pure white hairline. "I ain't seen her in a month of Sundays, but I seen that worthless boyfriend of hers!"

"Ex-boyfriend," I answer back immediately, irritation about the whole situation rubbing like a tag on a new shirt.

Mrs. Perkins's face scrunches up, her eyes and dentures disappearing in the many folds of aging skin. "What's that now?"

"Ex-boyfriend," I shout, then lower my voice as I realize shouting at an old lady is a new low for me. "Sorry to rush off, but I gotta get home to Ryder."

Her face morphs into a sweet smile at the mention of my eight-year-old son. "Ah, Ryder. He's a good boy, that one."

"Thank you, ma'am." Despite the anger that fueled my afternoon, hearing praise regarding my son will always puff out my chest with pride. That boy is the one thing I've done right in the world.

Mrs. Perkins beams a little brighter like she always did when us kids remembered our manners. Then her Buick chugs out of the intersection as she waves out the window, leaving me room to cross. I don't look back, and I don't observe the speed limit as I race toward the ranch.

It's not long before my truck bounces along the potholes that line our long driveway. My brothers and I keep meaning to fill the holes, but at this point, it wouldn't feel like home if you didn't have to test out your suspension to get there.

Pops and Ryder are on the wrap-around porch, wildly waving their arms in the air. I grimace, wondering how long Pops has been out in this heat placating Ryder. My son's current obsession is swimming, despite showing very little aptitude for the competition of it all. There's no telling what he'll get his mind set on, but as long as he's happy, I'm happy.

A plume of dust greets me as I brake a bit too fast and exit the truck. Nelly hops out and darts between my legs just to make me mad. I steady myself and follow him to the porch where I pull my sweaty son into my side and ruffle his sun-bleached hair. He's quick to hug me back, his little boy scent reaching my nose.

"Hey, Dad! Wanna practice flip turns?"

I look over at my father in time to see him sink into an Adirondack chair and swipe a handkerchief across his brow. A sweating glass of sweet tea sits on the small table beside the chair.

"I can give it a go for a few minutes before supper," I answer, knowing it'll give Pops a reprieve. I mutter out the side of my mouth to Pops, "You know, you can say no to him."

He smiles despite the exhaustion, pausing to take a long drink of iced tea before answering me. "I can, but I never will."

I copy the moves Ryder makes, pretending we're in water. Nelly barks his fool head off, thinking we're playing some fun game. I've had this same argument with Pops for years. He's been watching Ryder a few days a month since he was born. Every time I worry about Pops getting overworked for his age, he brushes me off and says he'll never tell his only grandson no.

It's sweet. But I also fear it'll give him a heart attack one day.

I open my mouth to ask the same question I've been asking all afternoon, but Pops beats me to it, holding up a thick, scarred finger.

"She ain't been by, and you ain't gonna stick your nose in her business." He lifts an eyebrow, reminding me of all those times growing up when we thought we'd gotten away with something, and somehow Pops always knew.

And just like all those times, I slide right into an innocent expression that no one's buying. "I wasn't going to stick my nose in it. I was going to offer my support to my best friend."

"Mmhmm."

"Incoming!" Ryder hollers, drawing my attention back to the corner where he's gearing up to "swim" the length of the porch after an impressive flip turn. Gosh, that boy is cute. His skinny arms become a blur of motion, and he looks pretty ridiculous. Speaking of ridiculous, one of Meemaw's Silkie chickens launches itself off the porch railing and into the face of my son as he swims by. Ryder screeches, Nelly barks, and my boots pound out an SOS as I race over to the fray.

"Dang it, Meemaw," I mutter, disentangling the fluff ball of a chicken from Ryder's flailing limbs. It squawks off back to the porch, feathers in a twist, like we're the ones to blame. I haul Ryder to his feet and inspect him for scratches. Meemaw pokes her head out the screen door.

"What's with all the racket?"

I point to the offending animal, ignoring the fact that Pops is laughing his head off now that Ryder appears safe. "These chickens are a nuisance, Meemaw!"

The screen door slaps shut behind her as she turns to me, hands on her bony hips. Her dark eyes are snapping like one of them death turtles. If I missed that detail, I certainly couldn't miss the way two red spots have appeared on her weathered cheeks. Well, crap. I've gone and angered Meemaw. Nobody disrespects her Silkies. At least not to her face. Thing is, she's as unpredictable as her prized chickens when she's mad.

She inhales, ready to let me have it, but gets cut off by my little sister, Frankie, with her face pressed to the screen door.

"Give him some grace, Meemaw. He's mad at Shelby again and isn't in his right mind."

Meemaw exhales without tearing into me but gives me the stink eye before turning to Frankie. "What happened with Shelby?"

Meemaw loves Shelby. So does my whole family. Which is why Frankie takes it upon herself to spread gossip about her. It ain't gossip if you're praying for them, is what Frankie always says.

"I heard from Sue Ann—who was seated one table away, so this ain't gossip, it's just eye-witness reporting—that Shane flipped out on their big date at the Buttery Clam last night. He lit into Shelby right in front of everyone." Frankie snorts. "The dummy ordered the seafood special for them both, not remembering that Shelby is allergic. Of course she had to turn away her plate."

Meemaw smacks her lips while my whole body goes rigid with rage. I heard there was a scene and a breakup, but the details are worse than I thought. Everyone knows Shelby's allergic to shellfish. What was he thinking taking her on a date to a seafood restaurant? Never much liked him, but now I know he's also an idiot.

"I guess he got embarrassed about her turning down his romantic gesture and stormed out, calling her ungrateful. They got outside, and he rounded on her, lifting his fist. This bit I got from David Jr. who was trying to load up a plant his wife bought from The Dirty Orchid across the street. Shane punched the brick wall by her head and then moaned about the potential broken hand being Shelby's fault. Poor girl started shaking, and David Jr. had to give him a talkin' to."

Meemaw gasps. Pops stands up faster than I've seen him move in ages. And as for me? I've already pulled out my keys to go find that jerk despite the curtain of red that's taken over my vision. He's gonna die tonight.

Frankie pushes open the screen door and snags my arm as I stomp by. "Now hold up, big brother."

I turn on her, tamping down the irritation that seeps out of me like sweat from fixing fences in the summer sun. "For your own safety, take your hand off me, Frankie. I have a score to settle."

She smiles, snug as a bug in a rug. "I figured you'd say that, which is why I already invited Shelby over for supper so we can get the real story." She looks past my shoulder. "If I'm not mistaken, that's her now."

"Shelby!" Ryder abandons his pretend swimming to race across the porch. If there's one thing he loves more than swimming, it's Shelby Sweet.

My heart pounds, watching her ancient Chevy bounce over the driveway at a speed even Meemaw could out walk. Her shock of curly brown hair becomes visible the closer she gets, the copper highlights more pronounced in the golden hour light. All that adrenaline that was aimed at her ex is now squarely aimed at her.

"Easy now," Frankie purrs as if I'm one of the family horses.

My sister tries to reason with me, but I'm not in the mood for reason. I'm spoiling for a fight. It's been a long time since I've raised my voice, and I'm due. A man's gotta let out some steam every now and again.

Shelby's questionable vehicle finally pulls up to the house.

I've begged her for years to get rid of it and get something more reliable, to which she's ignored me. She claims that barge of a Blazer could stand up to a speeding train.

I watch as she gets out of the car and faces me. Her lips are slicked with a rosy gloss, but they aren't smiling like usual. In fact, her sky-blue eyes are bloodshot and wary, a look I hate to see on her pretty face. Half of the anger pulsing through me is replaced with something I can't identify and don't want to examine too closely.

"Dallas," she says calmly.

"Shelby!" Ryder barrels into her in his typical single-minded focus. Shelby sweeps my boy off his feet and twirls him around, obviously just as happy to see him.

I don't miss the way her jeans hug her full hips like white on rice. She's insecure about her hips thanks to a careless comment from a boyfriend senior year of high school. Thankfully, she has equally impressive curves elsewhere that she is proud of. I don't like to objectify my best friend, but I do have eyes. Sadly, so does every other man in this county.

Shelby sets Ryder down and he's already asking her to swim across the porch with him. I step forward, putting my hand on his shoulder. I don't take my eyes off Shelby, though.

"Maybe after supper, bud. Right now, I need to speak to Shelby. Adult talk."

Shelby's eyes narrow just a hair.

"Everybody inside, please," I say louder through clenched teeth.

"Aww, man," Meemaw whines like a child, but she goes, beckoning Ryder and Nelly inside with her.

Once I hear the screen door slap shut for the last time, I take one more step toward Shelby. We're close enough she has to hinge her head back to hold my stare. And hold it she does. This girl has a spine of steel—at least around me. I wish she'd show off that spine around these weak boyfriends of hers.

"You've been avoiding my texts. And my calls," I drawl,

careful with my tone.

Shelby folds her arms across her chest. Any lesser man would get deterred by the look of irritation on her face, but I have a bone to pick and manage to stay on topic.

"Didn't know I needed to check in, *Dad*."

Ignoring her sass, I dive right in. "Did you kick Shane to the curb after his little stunt last night?"

Her eyes well up with tears, and I feel like an ass for bringing it up. But someone's got to. How many of these boyfriends have turned out to be losers? Twenty? Thirty? Dang, I've lost count.

The thing is, I know Shelby. I know her to her core. She's a good woman. The best there is. She just doesn't possess the ability to pick someone who deserves her or who's going to treat her like she needs to be treated. And since her daddy's not around anymore to knock some sense into these man-babies, it's up to me to do it. The man asked me to take care of her, and I take my promises seriously.

"Why do you care?" she snaps. The tone is cold, but the tears in her eyes, along with the wobble in her lip, give her away. It's the wobble that hits me right in the chest. Shelby's the strongest woman I know, and yet this man has made her question herself.

I reach into my back pocket and pull out my wallet, blinded by fury and protectiveness and a sense of duty that's careening out of control. Years of pent-up frustration have reached a boiling point. Enough is enough.

Shelby's eyes follow the movement, confusion clear on her face. I pull out the thing I've kept in my wallet for longer than I've had Ryder's picture in there. I hold it up for a brief moment, the ends fluttering in the evening breeze, then slap it down on the hood of her stupid truck.

"I care..." I lean in close enough to count the freckles spanning across her nose. "...because this here piece of paper says I'm your fiancé. And no one treats my woman like that."

CHAPTER
Two

WHO SLIPPED A BURR UNDER YOUR SADDLE?

SHELBY

It's time Big Knob got its own otolaryngologist because, despite having my hearing checked at my yearly physical last week, I could swear I just heard Dallas Gamble call me his fiancée.

What in the world is going on? He's not even supposed to be here! I've done a dang good job of dodging him all day, and Frankie promised he wasn't coming by for supper. I'm pretty sure my defenses can withstand the rest of the Gambles, but Dallas? Not right now.

"You been gettin' into Meemaw's weed, Dally? You know that stuff knocks you on your butt," I quip, despite feeling the furthest thing from lighthearted.

The last twenty-four hours have been one giant mess, and I don't have the bandwidth to deal with my best friend's fire-breathing dragon imitation—*or* this "my woman" nonsense he's going on about.

If I had my way, I'd be home in bed crying my eyes out or distracting myself with my favorite kind of book—an old-fashioned bodice ripper. But since that's the first place Shane will come looking for me, it's not an option. Shane Conover can kiss my gorgeous booty and fall face-first off a cliff for all I care.

Dallas hits me with a scowl liable to drive permanent troughs into his forehead. The man is stupid handsome, with thick sun-kissed hair he doesn't bother to hide under a hat most days and a tiny cleft in his scruffy chin that makes a girl want to press her finger there just because. So, I'm sure a few more lines on his forehead to match the ones fanning out from his golden-brown eyes would only make him hotter.

Not that I have a habit of checking Dallas out myself, but other women in town make a part-time job out of it. Always have.

"Shelby, I swear…" He trails off, clenching his jaw tight, as if the power of his voice might knock me over should he continue.

I honestly don't know what he's so worked up about. *He's* not the one whose boyfriend humiliated her in public and then slammed his fist into a wall when he didn't get his way.

Dallas silently jams the index finger of his free hand into the paper he's just slapped onto the hood of my Blazer. I choose to humor him since I'm starving, and I really don't need Dallas stroking out before supper. He knows I get hangry, especially when I'm stressed out like I am today.

"Okay, fine," I allow. "What are we looking at here?" I realize now it's a paper napkin—the kind they use down at Knockin' Boots, the lone bar and dance hall here in Big Knob. But this napkin is falling apart and covered in ink.

Instead of responding, Dallas taps the toe of his boot impatiently on the dirt and gravel beneath our feet, so I move closer to get a better look.

And then the breath leaves my lungs.

Because resting innocently under his hand is a napkin I

recognize. In fact, I can't believe I didn't know what it was the second he waved it in front of my face just now.

But...but how does he have it?

My mouth drops open, and I have to shake my head before stuttering, "Wh-where did you get this?"

If possible, my question sharpens his scowl even further.

This is not the Dallas I know. The Dallas who's been my best friend for going on twenty-five years now doesn't scowl. Well, unless it's at one of his brothers—or any of my lame boyfriends.

No. The Dallas I know is as carefree as they come and never met a situation he couldn't laugh off or a problem he couldn't solve with a cold beer and an out-of-tune rendition of a Willie Nelson song.

"Never you mind." His aggravated tone is lined with more gravel than the drive beneath us.

I blink rapidly, my eyes struggling to focus on the words spelled out in blue ink on the nearly shredded tissue beneath his finger. And there it is…

"I, Shelby Melissa Sweet, do solemnly swear that if I am not in a serious and fulfilling relationship by the decrepit old age of forty, I will marry Dallas Beaufort Gamble."

The words are written in the familiar messy scrawl of my best friend, but the neatly curved signature at the bottom is undeniably mine.

When I reach for the napkin, Dallas allows me to pick it up, only releasing his hold when the paper is secure in my hands. I flip it over with gentle fingers, the single word and signature on the back causing a quiet huff of laughter to bubble from my throat.

"Ditto.
Dallas Beaufort Gamble"

"Don't matter where I got it. The point is that I have it, and *you* signed it," he inexplicably continues.

My eyes flash to Dallas's, expecting the return of his usual eye twinkle now that he's played his joke in what was surely an attempt to distract me from my Shane troubles. He must have found this napkin in some random drawer and was saving it for a rainy day to bust my chops.

But, to my surprise and not a small degree of dismay, there's nary a twinkle in sight—just the same simmering irritation. And something else I can't for the life of me identify.

The only possible response in the face of this absurdity is a sweeping eye roll. "Very funny." I pat one of his pecs and hand back the napkin as I skirt around him, intent on reaching the house and the armor of familiar faces waiting inside. I really hope Meemaw made fried chicken.

But Dallas is too quick, one of his muscular arms snaking out to snag me around the waist and pull me close enough that I have to strain my neck to look up at him. He smells like wood shavings and sweat. "This ain't no joke, Sweetness." His voice is quiet now, but no less intense, as his golden-eyed gaze skips across my features.

What in the hell is he playing at here? If I didn't know better, I'd say he's looking at me like he's...hungry. And not for fried chicken.

A familiar flush begins creeping up my chest, but I tamp that traitor down.

Nope.

Sure, there was a time when I harbored a crush on my bestie like every other girl in our high school—and probably some of their mothers if we're being honest. But I've always prided myself on my intelligence and practicality, and it didn't take long to recognize that Dallas Gamble and his flirty winks spelled nothing but heartbreak. Just like my momma said.

Not to mention he's the furthest thing from my type.

I used to joke that we were friends because I was the only woman in Big Knob who didn't want to sleep with him. That, and we're both members of the unofficial Dead Moms Club.

But our friendship works because we get each other. We fit. He helps me cut loose and fly my freak flag when I need it, but he also instinctively knows when peace and quiet and a strong shoulder are the only things that will keep me upright.

In turn, I prevent him from ending up in jail or a fistfight, and I give him the space to just be himself and not have to be the life of the party or the "fun twin" all the time. Maybe most importantly, I don't take his flirting as anything more than it is. Casual instinct.

Which is why Dallas Gamble calling me Sweetness never sparks the least reaction in my ovaries like it might a more naïve—or self-delusional—woman.

"Chow time!" Frankie's voice shatters the weird-as-hell tension like a sledgehammer to an egg, and Dallas's arm drops from my waist.

I stumble back on a boot and clear my throat before shouting toward the house, "Be right there!" Then I hurry to the porch, giving Dallas a wide berth so he can't rope me back into his circle of intensity.

Today is not the day for flirting—nor is it the day for pulling out some marriage contract from eighteen years ago that we both signed after a few beers and nursing a couple of half-broken hearts.

And just when I wrap my fingers around the screen door handle, thinking I've escaped the bizarreness of the evening, my best friend's voice calls from behind, "We're not done talking about this, just so you know!"

Fan-freakin'-tastic.

———

"Pass the potatoes, would you, darlin'?" Pops asks thirty minutes later as I set my iced tea down next to my empty plate.

I send him a warm smile and hand him the bowl. I'm pretty sure this is his third helping, not that I blame him. Meemaw cooks up some of the best food in the county (and isn't shy about making it known).

It's always a treat dining at the Gamble family table. Not only is the food consistently excellent, but the company's far from boring.

At the head of the table, we've got the family patriarch, Emmett Gamble, who everyone from here to both coasts calls Pops. To his left is his mother-in-law, Francis Ridge, known as Meemaw far and wide. Next to her sits Frankie, the youngest and most well-adjusted member of the Gamble family. And then Frankie's wife, Morgan Proctor, a librarian who's the spittin' image of Barbie. When they got hitched, Morgan somehow talked Frankie into hyphenating their last names in the most head-scratching way to make them the Proctor-Gamble family. Neither of them appears to notice when people raise their eyebrows at that one.

I'm seated on Pops's other side, with Dallas's adorable son having claimed the chair next to mine, leaving Dallas on Ryder's other side. The seating arrangement has worked in my favor so far, evidenced by the fact that the words "marriage," "fiancé," and "my woman" have yet to be uttered.

We're short a slew of regulars at the worn oak table tonight, though. Ridge, the oldest Gamble offspring, and his wife, Tiff, are MIA. That last one I don't mind much, but Ridge is good, solid folk, if a bit grouchy. We're also missing Dallas's big sister, Skye, who's probably off rescuing a goat she'll inevitably beg me to come check out tomorrow. I don't mind, though. Animals are way more predictable than people, and Skye is one of my best friends.

"Save room for Morgan's pie, Pops!" Frankie scolds her

father as he heaps another giant spoonful of potatoes on his plate.

Dallas coughs into his fist, and I stifle a grin because, as usual, I know exactly what he's thinking.

And I'm not the only one, it seems, since Ryder interjects with, "Morgan's not very good at baking," in the most matter-of-fact tone you've ever heard.

All eyes dart to Morgan, where she sits slack-jawed and sputtering, her tanned skin turning red with embarrassment.

"Ryder!" Dallas scolds. "That's…" He trails off and then shuts his mouth entirely—because, well, it's not like the kid isn't speaking the truth.

I find myself choking on a suppressed laugh because I'm confident there's not one person seated at this table who doesn't recall the great "Garlic Cake Incident of 2024." Pops is still probably paying off that plumber bill.

Frankie, ever faithful, jumps to her wife's defense. "I disagree wholeheartedly, Ryder." She lays her hand over Morgan's and gives it a squeeze. "Morgan is very talented."

"Not at baking, she ain't," Meemaw murmurs under her breath. Or at least I assume that was her intention. Due to her crappy hearing, however, it comes out just under the volume of a megaphone. See? We really do need an otolaryngologist in Big Knob!

Frankie and Morgan both gasp while Pops chokes on his potatoes, trying to stifle his laughter. Ryder beams at Meemaw before sending Dallas a challenging hitch of his eyebrow and saying, "Tell me I'm wrong."

Dallas's eyes dart from his son to Pops, to Frankie and Morgan, and then to me. His mouth does its best imitation of a goldfish as he grasps for the right thing to say to smooth things over with his sister-in-law without throwing his son— or himself—under the bus.

What he ends up with is unquestionably the last thing

anyone expects, most of all me, when he blurts out, "Shelby's movin' in with me!"

I'm seriously starting to wonder if he got kicked in the head by a horse this morning.

Silence falls over the table, broken only by Ryder talking casually around his mouthful of dinner roll. "You can sleep in Dad's room, Shelby. I need my own space. And, besides, my room smells like farts."

It's now my turn to be the goldfish. But before I can gather my wits to respond to either Dallas's insane declaration or his son's sleeping arrangement plans, the doorbell rings, followed by a series of insistent rapping.

Nelly takes off for the hall, barking his furry head off. My back goes ramrod straight at the same time Dallas lunges to his feet so hard his chair falls over behind him. The hairs on the back of my neck stand on end, and I'm suddenly having trouble catching my breath.

What is wrong with me? Even if it *is* Shane on the other side of that door, it's not like he's any real danger to me. I could take that jerk in a fight. Maybe. I just don't want to see the man, that's all.

Dallas, on the other hand, moves with purpose toward the hall like he'd take Shane's appearance as his most cherished birthday and Christmas presents wrapped in one. Sweet mother of Mariah Carey! I need to stop this insanity.

I spring from my chair as everyone else does the same—I should have known my business had reached every ear in town by now—all of us chasing after Dallas, intent on keeping him from committing homicide on the front porch.

"You'll run if you know what's good for you, Conover! I'll even give you a head start!" Dallas snarls as he swings the door open, nearly tearing it from its hinges in the process.

But it's not my ex-boyfriend standing on the other side. It's a terrified-looking delivery driver who may or may not have just pissed his pants.

"I…uh," he stutters, "need a…s-s-signature for this package. Th-there are hazardous materials inside." He extends the signature device, and Dallas grabs it, shifting his eyes to glare at Meemaw before scribbling his name.

Meemaw darts her gaze to the ceiling, scanning every inch as if it holds not only the secrets of the universe but next week's winning Lotto numbers as well.

"Dang it, Meemaw," Pops grumbles. "How many times do I have to tell you to stop ordering stuff online when you're smokin' your medicinal weed?!"

She dips her chin to give him the dirty eyeball before prancing to the door and snatching the package from Dallas's hands. "At least I know how to have fun!" she calls over her shoulder as she escorts the shaken delivery guy back to his truck. Oh, good! His pants are dry.

My lungs having recovered to their normal level of life-sustaining function, I hustle back to the table, hoping to quickly help clear up and avoid any more drama for the evening. There's a book titled *His Lordship's Unbuttoned Desire* waiting for me on my bedside table and a deadbolt keeping any unwanted guests out of my house. It's time to go home.

Based on past experience, Dallas will be back to his happy-go-lucky, mischievous self tomorrow, and life will move on as it always does. I'll lick my wounds from another dating disaster for a couple weeks, and Dallas will forget about his misguided mission to "avenge" me for my own crappy taste in men. We'll meet for BLTs at Butter My Biscuit Diner and laugh about Morgan's baking fails. We'll hike down to Beaver Hollow Falls to watch the blue herons that gather there this time of year, and he'll fish while I read a book on a blanket in the grass. Everything will be the same as it's always been.

"Oh, no," Morgan mutters from behind me.

"What?" Frankie asks as I turn to see Morgan staring wide-eyed down at her phone.

Her gaze lifts to meet mine, and I don't like her panicked expression one bit. "Norinne Kuntz just texted that Shane left Knockin' Boots drunk and saying he's on his way to your place, Shelby. She doesn't have your number and wanted me to warn you."

My heart drops to the bottom of my gut as my butt hits the seat of one of the old oak dining chairs. Well, crap.

"He's likely to be disappointed then since Shelby'll be at *my* place," Dallas practically growls from where he's taking up the entire entryway to the room, chest puffed out like a gorilla at the zoo.

"Now, son," Pops interjects, hands extended in a placating gesture.

But he's cut off by Meemaw as she ducks under one of Dallas's beefy arms, brandishing two handfuls of brightly colored fireworks and proclaiming, "I've got *just the thing* for your housewarming!"

CHAPTER
Three

SHE'S AS NERVOUS AS A LONG-TAILED CAT IN A
ROOM FULL OF ROCKING CHAIRS

DALLAS

"I don't want any ice cream, Dallas."

I shoot Shelby a look over Ryder's head. He insisted on riding on the bench seat between us, which is probably a good thing based on the way Shelby's got her arms crossed over her chest like a petulant child. She's just mad I conned her into getting into my truck after supper while Frankie and Morgan schemed to drop her car off at my place in the morning—just to keep Shane from knowing where Shelby was.

"Since when does a woman not want ice cream after a breakup?" I drawl, to which Ryder snickers.

"Mom likes Rocky Road and that movie, *War of the Roses*, when she and Bowen have an argument," Ryder adds helpfully. "Says it scares my bonus dad into an apology real quick."

I can't help but chuckle despite the tension in the truck. My ex isn't wrong. It might surprise some people that I actually like and respect the woman I coparent with, but I do.

Hallie is a good mom, a kind person, and absolutely not the woman for me. We figured out real quick we had physical chemistry and nothing else. However, after the breakup, she peed on a stick and got two pink lines. We decided being friends and raising a child together was entirely possible. So far, we've done real good, if I do say so myself.

"Sure you don't want some mint chocolate chip? My treat," I sing-song, knowing it's her favorite flavor.

Shelby opens her mouth but hesitates. Ha! Got her.

"Well, it *is* National Ice Cream Day," Shelby drawls slowly.

With a smirk, I swing the wheel toward Afternoon Delight, Big Knob's one and only ice cream shop, and Ryder pumps his fist. I see Shelby fighting a smile out of the corner of my eye. She can never turn down a national holiday, no matter how small, just like her momma.

We find a parking space right outside the front door, order quickly, and are back in the truck, headed for Shelby's place in a span of fifteen minutes. Hopefully our little detour not only gets Shelby in a better mood but also provides some time for Shane to stop by her house, see she's not there, and head on home to sleep off his intoxication. I don't want to have to bloody a man's face in front of my kid, but I'll do what I have to do to keep my best friend safe.

Shelby's hands are twisting in her lap, her no-nonsense unpolished nails turning white as she grips them even harder the closer we get to her place. My gut takes a nosedive, seeing her this nervous. No woman should ever be fearful of her boyfriend. I may not be the world's best boyfriend, nor have I experienced the trap—I mean, privilege—of being married, but I would never treat a woman like this jerk.

Thankfully, the coast is clear when we pull up to Shelby's building on the edge of downtown Big Knob. Her vet clinic occupies the bottom floor while she lives in a bougie apartment above. The jerk's truck with the oversized exhaust pipes is nowhere to be seen on the street below.

Shelby and Ryder climb the stairs on the side of the building, and she unlocks her door. I command Nelly to stay in the truck bed and follow after. Ryder heads straight for the old PlayStation Shelby keeps on hand just for him. With ice cream all over his face and his attention redirected, I follow Shelby, only stopping short when I see an old picture of her and her parents on the wall in the hallway by her bedroom. There's a crack right across the glass that wasn't there the last time I came over.

"Did that guy do this too?" I hiss, not wanting to alarm Ryder, but needing to know the extent of this guy's issues.

Shelby freezes, her stiff shoulders acting like earmuffs. When she doesn't respond or turn around, I have my answer. I clench so hard my jaw shoots pain across my skull like the fireworks Meemaw threw in the bed of my truck as we drove away from supper.

"You gonna follow me into the shower too, Dally?" Shelby snaps from the middle of her bedroom, finally spinning around and plopping a hand on her hip.

I like the attitude. It means the scared is fading away.

"I will if that's what it takes to get you to come back home with me, Sweetness." I lean against the doorway and try not to inhale too much of the perfumed scent of her bedroom. Shelby is all woman, evidenced by the pink and white floral bedspread, refurbished shabby chic furniture, and the girly touches everywhere the eye can land. It's enough femininity to make a billy goat puke.

I watch in real time as her cheeks get heated, and her blue eyes start sparking. She holds up a hand, counting off on her fingers. "I'm not going home with you. I'm not moving in with you. I'm not your fiancée! Jeez, Dallas. What's gotten into you today?"

Despite my better judgment, I step farther into the room.

Shelby and I have been just friends for longer than I've sported chin hair, but I tend to stay away from her bedroom if I can help it. I have the problem of falling into bed with women, and I refuse to let Shelby be one of my mistakes. I care too much about her to do that.

"Listen, it's for your own safety. This guy is a powder keg just looking to be set off. You've been on your own for too long, picking these stupid man-babies with zero substance underneath their fragile egos. It ain't working, Sweetness."

Shelby opens her mouth to let me have it, but I cut her off, needing to get this all out on the table before she goes scorched earth on me.

"Let's try a new tactic. You use this temporary move-in to get Shane to leave you alone. He'll get distracted soon enough. Small brains can't stay focused. I should know. Then I'm gonna take the reins for a moment in the dating department and find you the perfect man."

Shelby scoffs, the sound astonished and bitter at the same time.

Stepping even closer, I cup her elbow and sweep my thumb across her arm. "I know you don't want to marry me, so I won't hold you to our agreement. Even if that napkin *is* legally binding." I shoot her a wink before sobering. "I know you want a man to sweep you off your feet and feed you grapes and read you poetry. You also deserve a man who'll handle his emotions like a fully evolved adult male. In case no one's told you lately, you deserve it all in a partner, Shelby. You deserve a man who'll give you the Bridgerton romance you've always dreamed about."

Shelby's eyes fill with tears. She pulls her bottom lip into her mouth and clamps down on it with her teeth. A few sniffles later, she drops my gaze. "I loved the Bridgertons long before they made the books into a series," she says pitifully, refusing to address anything I've just laid out.

"I know, Sweetness." I pull her into a hug, letting her face cradle into my chest. She fits there perfectly, her curves giving the kind of hug a man can sink into after a hard day. The scent of horses, sweat, and sweet perfume hits my nose, reminding me of no other woman on this planet but Shelby.

Would it really be so bad to be married to my best friend? I mean, I'm not sure I'm up to being celibate for the rest of my life, but I'd certainly give it a try. I've had plenty of years to sleep around with whomever I wanted, and I've definitely tried my best to spread my signature Dallas Gamble cheer as far and wide as possible. Maybe it's time to retire the Casanova lifestyle and save Shelby from all the crazy jerks and losers out there.

I kiss the top of her head and continue to rub up and down her back. "And if that doesn't work out either, we'll get engaged for real and live together growing old as best friends."

Shelby stiffens in my arms and then pulls back, her fist connecting with my pec muscle so fast I don't see it coming.

"Ow!" I howl from the pain, cupping my pectoral and stepping back. "What the heck was that for?"

Shelby lifts an eyebrow, looking cute as the devil all fired up. "That's for being an idiot. You really think my daddy left this green earth thinking that's how his one and only precious daughter would be proposed to?" She contorts her face into something comical. Her voice comes out high-pitched and mocking and like I lost half my brain cells recently. "If no man on the planet will have you, I'll suck it up and marry you, Shelby."

"I don't sound like that," I snap.

"Yes, you do."

"No, I don't!"

"Are you two going to fight all night? Because I really need to get good sleep for my swim practice tomorrow morning. Coach says sleep is as important as practice."

Shelby and I zip it real quick, looking over to see Ryder

innocently standing in the doorway, head swiveling between us.

I point at my best friend. "Shelby's getting her things together, bud. Women just take a little longer to get ready."

Shelby gasps, but I ignore her, walking over to Ryder and putting my arm around his skinny shoulders. With both of us looking at her expectantly, and the cracked picture frame behind us, her shoulders fall in defeat.

"Fine. I'll get an overnight bag." She shoves her pointer finger in the air. "For just one night!"

My triumphant grin is instantaneous. She growls at it but spins around to yank various articles of clothing out of her dresser and toss them on her bed. Ryder and I wisely get out of her way.

When we're back in the truck, Shelby's bag stowed in the bed with Nelly, Ryder starts chattering about exact hand placement between several strokes. I love my son, but he just might lull me to sleep if he keeps on about the finer details of swimming.

About five minutes from home, Shelby puts her arm around Ryder and pulls him into her side. "That big brain of yours needs some rest, little Gamble. What do you say we make my famous blueberry pancakes tomorrow for breakfast?"

Ryder grins up at Shelby like she's made of chlorine and swim lanes. The two fall silent, snuggling together in a calm way he never manages with me. By the time we get home, he's out cold, looking more like the toddler he used to be, all dirty and exhausted from a day of running around the ranch.

I reach over and pull him into my arms, savoring the feel of him boneless against my shoulder as I carry him into the house. There'll be a day very soon when I can't hold him like this, and I hate that it's coming. I lock the front door behind us, something I wouldn't bother with normally, but Shane the idiot might make a late-night appearance, and I don't like my sleep disturbed.

Shelby lifts up on her tiptoes and smooths Ryder's hair from his forehead and kisses him. "Night, my little G."

"Night, Shelbs. Love you," he whispers back, apparently not as asleep as I thought he was, the little trickster.

Shelby and I grin at each other over his head. She nods toward the stairs, and I move in that direction, careful to step over the toys and clothes dotting the floor. I would have put them away if I knew Shelby was coming over. She's forever giving me a hard time about being a slob. But since I have yet to find a way to make cleaning up fun, I rarely do it.

I set Ryder on the bed and pull his shoes off before he rolls over and is lost to his dreams. Nelly curls up in the dog bed next to his dresser, tail thumping quietly.

Back downstairs, I stop short when I see Shelby bent over the couch in the living room, clad only in a pair of short shorts and a matching tank top thing. The thin cotton with a dusting of blue flowers across it doesn't leave a whole lot to the imagination.

"Oh boy," I mutter under my breath, tearing my eyes away from her to focus in on why she's putting sheets on the couch.

She spins around, clutching the top sheet to her chest. "What?" she asks, blinking innocently.

I wiggle my fingers around in the darkness between us. "Where are the rest of your pajamas?"

She looks down at herself and then back at me with a little shrug, dropping the sheet onto the couch. Now my eyes are searching for anywhere else to land except for her. "It's summer. It's hot. I don't like to sleep in warm clothes. If I'm 'living here,' I want to be comfortable."

I don't like the way she used her fingers as air quotes. I latch on to the irritation and ride it through the wave of lust that shouldn't be there. Not with my best friend. Sadly, I'm a guy. And when we see breasts, we notice.

"Do my pajamas bother you?" Shelby's struggling to hold back a laugh.

"You know they do, you little tease."

She bursts out with a shocked laugh like she doesn't believe me. Even knowing it's at my expense, I love to hear it. I lunge forward, making her shriek and move out of the way. Snatching the sheet, I plop my butt on the couch and cross my boot over my knee like her half-naked appearance doesn't affect me in the slightest.

"Get your exposed self to my room, woman. What kind of man would I be if I made you take the couch?"

Shelby's smile turns sad. "You certainly wouldn't be the kind of man I date. That's for sure."

With that sad pronouncement of her dating history, she walks down the hallway and disappears into my bedroom. I tilt my head back and remind myself that we do not lust after best friends.

Even if they have the nicest curves this side of the Mississippi.

CHAPTER

Four

BEWARE: A DEAD SNAKE CAN STILL BITE

SHELBY

"I feel like this is an existential question." Daddy grins at Momma in the passenger seat of the sedan as the radio blasts "Who Let the Dogs Out" by Baha Men. It's my favorite song of the summer.

Momma laughs with her signature crooked smile on full display. Daddy says its imperfection makes it all the more beautiful, and I agree. Momma is undeniably gorgeous, inside and out.

"Shelby, your daddy's thinking way too hard again." Her wavy russet hair falls over her shoulder as she winks at me.

I laugh because that's nothing new.

"Hey!" Daddy pretends to be offended, and I grin back down at the latest edition of *Jane* magazine resting in my lap.

"Oh, Shelbs, I forgot to tell you," Momma starts, but when I look back up, she's gone. And so is Daddy.

All I can see is a speeding truck coming right toward me through the windshield. I slap my hands over my eyes and scream like there's no tomorrow.

"Shelby!" A shout hits my ears, and I feel someone shaking me. "Sweetness, it's me!"

I gasp for air, my eyelids fluttering open, only to be blinded by a bedside lamp. It takes almost a minute to steady my breathing and bring my heart rate down as I frantically repeat to myself, "It was only a dream. It was only a dream."

It takes another thirty seconds to fully realize where I am and that Dallas has been stroking his fingers up and down my back while holding me to his bare chest, my head cradled in his other hand. I inhale one long, shaky breath through my nose, filling my head with the clean scent of plain old bar soap and a hint of cardamom and amber from Dallas's favorite shampoo.

"Shhh," he murmurs, never breaking the rhythm of his strokes as the bed creaks under us, and he adjusts to rest his head against the wooden headboard.

I squeeze my eyes shut, determined to keep the memories and tears at bay. Despite the sweat from my temples wetting Dallas's skin and the beginnings of embarrassment that I know will flow like lava from a volcano in the morning, I can't make myself move. Or apologize. Or explain.

It doesn't take long for the steady beat of his heart under my ear and the hypnotic brush of his hand along my spine to lull me back to sleep. The nightmare is gone, and for once, it doesn't come back.

Two heavy weights pin me to the mattress when I drift back to consciousness—one over my hip and the other across my shoulder and arm. I open my eyes to get my bearings, only to see unfamiliar olive drapes framing a bright blue morning sky.

Confused, I look down my body to see that it's not some supersized weighted blanket plastered over me, but two very tan, *very* firm body limbs belonging to one Dallas Beaufort Gamble. I'd know that scar on his right knee anywhere. A light dusting of hair covers both his arm and leg, the latter thrown over my hip like I'm a horse he's attempting to mount.

My first thought is that I don't hate waking up like this.

My second is that I must be an idiot, and I need to get my butt out of this bed as soon as humanly possible. This is a road my head does not need to be going down, especially after that nightmare—and also given that I might have myself a stalker waiting on my front porch this very minute.

Oh-so-slowly, I slide Dallas's arm off my shoulder and begin to flatten onto my stomach to inch away. But before I gain even a millimeter, the arm that was a limp, dead weight a mere moment ago curls around my waist and pulls me back into the hard body behind me.

Dallas groans in his sleep, his limbs banding around me even tighter, like a koala trying to climb its favorite tree.

"Crap," I mutter under my breath before freezing in place. I track his breathing to make sure he hasn't woken, all the while ignoring the fluttering in my belly.

Newly determined, I twist onto my stomach and carefully slither my way out from beneath him. But the man's thigh is as heavy as a Buick, so my legs get trapped while my top half slides off the side of the bed until I'm supporting my weight with both hands on the hardwood floor.

"Crap," I repeat in another whisper.

Blood is pooling in my head now, so I do the only thing I can and jerk my knees forward in one quick movement. The move works, dislodging my legs from beneath Dallas. However, the force propels me forward where I complete some crude version of a somersault and land flat on my back, limbs splayed and pride a little worse for wear.

So, of course, that's the moment Dallas's scruffy, sleep-softened face appears over the edge of the mattress. "Mornin',

Sweetness." His grin is lopsided to match the laziness in his tone and the tangled mess of hair atop his head.

I open my mouth in the hopes that a perfectly snarky comeback will magically spill forth, but before my tongue can even begin to form a word, Dallas points a finger at my tank top and shoots me a casual, "Might want to fix your shirt."

I look down at all the cleavage on display, proceed to go into cardiac arrest and die on his beautiful hand-hewn wood floor.

Not really, but I consider it.

———

"This towel has a tag on it," Ryder announces twenty minutes later as he descends the staircase wearing yellow swim trunks and nothing else.

I'm sipping coffee on one of the industrial barstools at Dallas's kitchen counter. The whole place screams Dallas Gamble with its homey wood beams and masculine industrial touches. It's rugged, warm, and full of character all at once. Just like the man who designed and built it.

"Come here," I beckon to Ryder as I stand from my stool. "I'll cut it off."

He pads over on bare feet and watches while I locate a pair of scissors in the junk drawer and remove the offending tag. Tags are a big NOPE in Ryder's book, as are seams on socks and scratchy fabrics. I'm actually surprised Dallas let the towel tag slip by him. He's always right on top of the vile things.

"All fixed." I hand the towel back with a grin. "Now, how about those blueberry pancakes?"

"I already had cereal. Dad said we'd do pancakes tomorrow when I don't have practice."

"Oh," I respond in surprise. "Okay then." Is this part of Dallas's ploy to get me to stay for more than one night?

"Shoot! I forgot my goggles!" Ryder tosses the towel on the counter and scurries back upstairs, uncombed hair flopping with each step.

"Brush your teeth while you're up there, okay?"

When he's out of sight, I crane my neck, listening for the sound of the shower from Dallas's room down the hall. Only when I hear it do I relax back onto the stool.

I moved like a cheetah earlier, stashing myself back into my tank and snatching one of Dallas's discarded T-shirts before hauling butt out of his bedroom. His laughter followed me down the hall to the second bathroom, but I didn't dare look back.

Now he's showering, allowing me the peace to drink my coffee and stew over the wellspring of humiliation I've endured over the last day. I honestly can't decide which part to focus on first.

The confirmation that every person in town now knows exactly how horrible I am at choosing men?

Or maybe my ex acting like such a colossal idiot that my best friend feels he has no other choice than to declare himself my personal bodyguard?

How about being lucky enough to have my stupid recurring nightmare make an appearance on the *one* night my new bodyguard happens to be within earshot?

But that pity marriage proposal-slash-matchmaking plan is a real contender too.

No. It's got to be my hot best friend giving me the best night of sleep I've had in a long time while he was most likely dreaming about some beautiful, size-zero model.

Or perhaps I should just focus all my attention on the humiliation of giving said best friend a free show while flat on my back on his bedroom floor, looking like death warmed over, complete with bed hair and morning breath.

"You are a hot mess," I groan into my coffee mug.

Nelly whines from his spot on the couch, head up and ears back.

"Oh, not you," I reassure. "You're perfect. Don't ever change a thing."

Satisfied, he sighs and rests his chin back on his front paws.

I need to get to work before Dallas comes out here to "chat," but my clothes are in his bedroom—the same room where he's probably stalking around, dripping wet from his shower.

My first appointment is in an hour at a ranch just down the way, but I promised Violet at Rockers 'n Knockers that I'd stop by on my way to check on her goat. Violet is a bit of a hypochondriac, and that extends to Curly as well. She once asked me to test her billy goat for STIs 'cause she caught him looking too long at a doe.

"I was looking for that shirt."

I turn on my stool to see Dallas pulling a black T-shirt over his head. His hair is wet and mussed from the shower, and his ab muscles ripple with his movements as he saunters my way. I glance down at the Old Dominion T-shirt covering my tank top—the same tank top that's going in the trash as soon as I find a bra and some clothes. His shirt is tight across my chest, but at least it covers me up.

"Finders keepers." I shrug, spinning my mug on the counter to give me something to do with my hands.

He has the audacity to wink and say, "Looks better on you anyway."

While I mull over that one, Dallas takes his sweet time adjusting his belt and wandering into the kitchen to fix himself a cup. Only when it's full and he's made his way directly across from me to rest his elbows on the counter does he speak again.

"So, how long have you been havin' those nightmares?"

Cutting right to the chase, are we? Some things never change.

I flap one hand in the air, not meeting his eyes. "Oh that? That was nothing." I shake my head and roll my eyes for extra casual vibes. "Just sleeping in an unfamiliar place, probably." Somebody hand this woman an Oscar already! Jeez.

Dallas's eyebrows spike, his hand stilling halfway to his mouth with his coffee. "You're full of more crap than Meemaw's chickens." He takes a sip, winces at the heat, and then sets his mug on the butcher-block counter. "The only place more familiar to you than your own place is mine." When I open my mouth to remind him I've never hung out in his bedroom, he cuts me off. "And you were calling for your momma."

My throat constricts, any trace of moisture gone as tears cloud my vision. Dallas doesn't move a muscle, as if he knows the only thing keeping the tears from turning into a waterfall is his distance. I tip my head back and blink until they recede, and I can swallow again.

When I finally speak, my voice is small and scratchy. "I didn't know I did that."

Dallas nods slowly, eyes resting on his corded forearms propped on the counter.

It's absolutely no secret to Dallas—or anyone, for that matter—that I still mourn my parents. What daughter wouldn't? But nobody apart from my grandparents and my brother ever knew about the nightmares.

And now Dallas, it seems.

I clear my throat and swallow again. "I get them sometimes. Mostly the one. It's the car crash, but…not? If that makes any sense." I glance at him to see him watching me carefully now. He gives the slightest nod, encouraging me to continue. "I mean, it's my daddy, my momma, and me—just like it was. But the conversation is always different. Probably because I can't remember the real conversation." I shrug.

It's true. I blocked it all out. Even the oncoming truck with the driver who fell asleep at the wheel and killed my parents. I don't remember any of it, apart from piling in the car to drive home from Texas and then waking up in the hospital the next day with my whole body aching and a searing pain cutting across my abdomen.

"Sometimes I think maybe the dreams are my way of trying to remember. Maybe find the last few moments we were together?" I tilt my head at him.

Dallas nods again, brows drawn together. "So, they've been happening a lot recently?" he asks gently.

I shake my head. "It's been months, actually." The realization brings a hint of a smile to my lips because I've come a long way over time. There were years when the nightmares were relentless, robbing me of my sleep and sense of peace. The only saving grace sometimes was the knowledge that I could have lost my brother too, had he been in the car.

"You think the one last night has anything to do with all this Shane business?" His question is quiet, but the underlying tension is palpable.

Half of me wants to laugh and brush him off. The other half already considered this possible connection while cleaning the science experiments out of his fridge thirty minutes ago. I choose to go with the first half. "Why would Shane being an idiot make me dream about my parents?" I scoff before lifting my mug and downing the rest of my coffee.

It's time to get moving, or Curly is likely to grow a third horn or develop a gallstone.

Dallas straightens but doesn't move to intercept me when I slide off my stool and take my mug to the sink. "I don't know, doc, you tell me," is all he says.

The pounding of Ryder's feet down the stairs saves me.

"Can we stop for donuts on the way to practice?" he asks as he bounds into the kitchen.

"You already had cereal, bud. Maybe another day," Dallas replies over his mug. "Besides, I've got somewhere to be."

I give Dallas the side-eye because a) who says no to donuts? And b) he said last night that he was spending all day on a new commission in his workshop—the one twenty yards from the house.

Ryder huffs his disappointment, so I ignore Dallas and go for a distraction. "How fast can you swim one lap?" It accomplishes my goal as the kid launches into an explanation of why my question is too simple for a straight answer.

I listen while Dallas drains his mug and gathers his keys and wallet.

"Okay, Ryd. Daylight's burnin'. Let's go!" Dallas prompts before whistling for Nelly. The dog races to the front door, spinning in circles in his excitement to be included.

Relieved, I bid them goodbye and turn to the hall while the two Gambles chatter on their way out the door.

"Whatcha gonna do while I'm at practice, Dad?"

"Oh, there's somebody I need to pay a visit to. I'm pretty sure he's expecting me, if he's got any brains in his skull, so I'll be able to wrap things up well before practice is over."

I stop in my tracks at Dallas's words, but there's no use wasting my energy trying to stop him at this point. Maybe if he says what he needs to say to Shane, we can all just move on.

"Do you think this guy's got any donuts, by any chance?" I hear Ryder ask just before the door closes.

I gotta say, I like where this kid's head is at. His dad's, on the other hand? The jury is still out on that one.

CHAPTER

Five

HE FELL FROM THE UGLY TREE AND HIT EVERY STICK ON THE WAY DOWN

DALLAS

"I'm just gonna tell him to back off," I say to Nelly.

He opens one eye and closes it again, content to nap the whole way to the Hornville Oil Refinery, which is closer to the city I try to stay away from. I tried Shane's place already, and he wasn't there. He also wasn't at Shelby's, so that's something at least.

"Seriously. No fists. No shouting. Just an adult conversation about leaving Shelby alone." My hands grip the steering wheel harder, just picturing that jerk's face, but I force them to let go.

The forecourt is buzzing with workers. Half are getting off night shift while day shift is just arriving. I scan the group heading in until I see an ugly brunette who looks like he had one too many drinks last night. I hop out of the truck and holler Shane's name. It takes two more shouts before he turns in my direction. His eyes go wide for just a second before he tucks tail and almost runs toward the plant entrance.

Thankfully, I'm still in shape from working the ranch, and

I catch his elbow right before he can scan his card and escape inside. He turns to face me, tipping his nose in the air like he's got no beef with me. Smug little turd.

"Where you goin' in such a hurry, Conover?" I drawl, plastering a grin on my face. I point at his hand, the one that's wrapped in white gauze. "Hurt yourself?"

Several of his coworkers give us looks as they scan in and head to work, but none stick around to have his back. That says a lot about a man. As they flow around us, Shane lowers his voice, his dark eyes shifty and nervous.

"What are you doing here, Gamble?"

My arms fold across my chest of their own volition. I'm not one to bully or intimidate, but some situations call for it.

"I'm here to make sure you know to stay away from Shelby." I'm proud of the way my voice comes out calm yet forceful.

Shane's ugly face screws up. "I'll handle things with my girlfriend without you butting your nose in, thank you very much."

I lean in, my grin turning icy. "See, that's where you're wrong. You don't have a girlfriend any longer. Shelby made that abundantly clear when you acted like a spoiled toddler."

A few heads have turned our way again, and Shane shifts awkwardly in his dirty boots, all too aware of the attention we're receiving.

"Yo, Shaney-boy, you broke up with Shelby?" one of the guys asks as he pauses in his attempt to get around us to the door. Several other guys stop in their tracks, wanting the local gossip.

Shane's eyes shift around the faces in a panic before his face transforms into an ego-saving sneer. "I can do better, boys. You know that. I know that."

Alarm bells ring so loudly in my head I would testify in court that they actually rang out from the side of the building. But this idiot ain't done.

"Fat girls are too much trouble. Take 'em to dinner, and they eat you out of house and home, you know?"

One guy hoots and fist-bumps Shane. Rage is flowing through my body. I feel like I've grown ten feet tall and strong as an ox in a split second. The irony of this guy complaining about Shelby eating too much when she couldn't eat a dang thing during their date because he ordered food she's allergic to just sticks in my craw. Calling my best friend fat because she has curves? This fella's gonna have more than a busted hand before I leave here.

My fist connects with his face before I register what's happening. My knuckles sing, and Shane's head flies to the side. He goes down like a sack of flour, a lump of crybaby lying on the shoes of his lame friends. I point my finger in his face, fury making it tremble.

"Stay away from Shelby if you know what's good for you."

Shane, looking up at his coworkers, makes the wrong choice. Instead of backing down and being a decent human, he decides his ego and reputation are more important. His hand is busy trying to stem the flow of blood from his nose, but that doesn't stop his weasel voice from digging his own grave.

"I can't help it if she can't resist me, Gamble. We both know she'll come crawling back."

I take a menacing step forward, and one of his coworkers puts his hand on my shoulder. I shrug him off, holding my hands up as if to say I'm not going to hit the guy again, though I don't make any promises out loud. I'm sick to death of these lame boys thinking they can talk trash about my best friend right after they've treated her terribly, or she's dumped their pathetic butts. Someone needs to teach them the lessons their momma forgot to teach. And that someone is me.

"She won't be anywhere near you again because she's

engaged to *me* now. Keep my woman's name out of your mouth, you hear me?"

"Engaged to *you*, Dallas?" A woman's voice pulls my attention from Shane. Charlene Russell is standing just outside the ring of workers, her tote bag slung over her shoulder and a to-go cup of coffee in her hand. "Did I hear that right?"

My eyes slide shut for just a brief moment. I hadn't realized how many people were witnessing this little conversation between two men. But most troubling is Charlene. She took over for her momma a few years ago as the chief gossip spreader in Big Knob, even though her administrative job here at the plant pays her bills. She spreads gossip like it's a professional sport. Doesn't hurt that she's best friends with Norinne down at Knockin' Boots. Those two play the telephone game with every piece of juicy gossip that happens in our little town.

And this? The announcement that Shelby and I are engaged?

Crap, this might just be the juiciest tidbit Charlene has ever witnessed. The ladies of Big Knob have been trying to tie me down to just one woman since I copped a feel in the back of my old truck and realized girls were pretty awesome.

Well, shoot. Shelby's gonna be mad. We just hashed out that this whole thing was temporary. And private. This seems like not-so-private.

Charlene pushes the men out of the way, her grin making me want to slink back to my truck. Her short, bleached hair sticks up every which way like usual, her lipstick is the wrong shade of red for her skin type, and her eyes are lit up like a feral animal.

"You and Shelby? For real?"

You could hear a pin drop outside the oil plant, all these big men waiting for a piece of gossip like little old ladies with nothing better to do. Heck, some of them don't even live in

Big Knob or know me from Adam. I swallow hard, wondering how to play this now that Charlene and half of Big Knob are witnessing my announcement.

I grab the back of my neck and wish I could go back to half an hour ago when I dropped Ryder off at practice and make better decisions. I could have waited until Shane went home. Confronted him there. But no, I had to let my anger lead me right into this trap.

"Um, yeah. Me and Shelby," I manage to say, and even to my own ears it sounds lame.

Charlene lights up like I just told her she won the lottery. Her mouth opens wide at the same time the door to the plant slams open with a bang.

"What the heck's going on out here? Are we working sometime today?" the foreman asks. His angry growl makes my skin crawl, and I don't even work for him.

The workers all race for the entrance, Shane with them, leaving a trail of blood droplets on the concrete. Apparently, that's not unusual around here because no one bats an eye.

Charlene is the only one brave enough to hang back for a moment, her hand landing on my pec muscle with a bit of unnecessary squeezing. "I can't wait to hear how you proposed! Shelby's waited almost forty years to be proposed to, so I know it must have been spectacular!"

With a wink, she scurries inside the building while my stomach drops lower than my boots. The foreman gives me one more scowl for disrupting his morning, and then the door slams shut behind him. I'm left alone, wondering what the heck just happened and approximately how much trouble I got myself into.

Before I've even reached my truck, I realize that this is bad. Real bad. News of this sort will spread faster than my old truck can travel. Before lunchtime everyone in Big Knob will know Shelby and I are engaged. By supper, they'll be planning an engagement party.

I'll be planning my funeral.

"Crapity, crap, crap," I mutter, sliding into my truck and running both hands through my hair. Nelly scrambles to his feet and looks at me expectantly. "I messed up."

He slumps back to the seat and faces his rear end in my direction. Guess everyone's mad at me. I slap my hand against the steering wheel and try to think of damage control. I usually fly by the seat of my pants, and while that's worked for me so far, I have a feeling I've really stepped in it this time.

I haphazardly proposed to my best friend, then backpedaled and demanded she move in with me temporarily. Shelby Sweet is no ordinary woman who might just pat me on the head and laugh off my fumbled attempts to make things right. She's dreamed of her wedding since the day she was born. Has a wedding Pinterest board she updates every year. Even made a mood board she keeps in her bedroom to keep her "focused on her dream future."

Heck, the woman reads romances so unbelievable the man can go all night. I snuck one of her romances home one day and nearly laughed myself into an asthmatic event. All that to say, the woman is caught up in a level of romance that no human male—especially me, a serial dater and runner from all things commitment—could ever live up to. And in one misguided moment of chivalry, I tied her to me in the minds of every person we know.

"Oh, I really messed up," I groan, heading to the grocery store to keep Shelby from killing me with her bare hands. If there's one thing I know Shelby wants, it's romance. The second thing? Healthy food.

Despite what Shane said, Shelby gets low blood sugar. Abdominal surgery from the car accident where her parents died left her with hypoglycemia for life. I've seen her nearly pass out from not eating enough, so I've taken to keeping snacks on me just for her. So, I'll stock the house with all her favorites, grill up a juicy filet mignon tonight, and hope for the best.

It's not a great plan. It certainly doesn't solve our little issue with the whole town thinking we're getting married for real. But at least as we brainstorm a solution together, she won't be hangry.

I end up cleaning the house too, knowing Shelby likes a clean toilet and no dishes in the sink, a level of cleanliness this bachelor house doesn't often see. By the time she gets off work, the place is spotless, stocked with every snack known to man, and I've worked myself up into a tizzy with all the calls coming in on my cell phone. I ignore every single one, knowing what people are calling about.

Ryder is upstairs on the new PlayStation he got for Christmas last year. I normally only allow him half an hour on that thing, but given the shouting that's about to occur, I figure the video games are best.

The screen door slams ominously. I poke my head out of my bedroom, where I just put on clean sheets for Shelby. Nelly slinks between my legs and army crawls under the bed with a whine.

"What the hell did you just do, Dallas Beaufort Gamble?"

I wince, sucking in a deep breath and girding my loins. Literally, I put a hand over my front, just in case she's that mad. I take a protein bar out of my pocket and extend it out like a sword. And then I advance down the hallway, ready to meet my fate.

CHAPTER

Six

THE ONLY THING FASTER THAN A HORSE IS GOSSIP IN A SMALL TOWN

SHELBY

Dallas appears from the hall wearing an expression that hits somewhere between sheepish and terrified. Hanging limply from his fingers is what looks like a nut bar, and while it might make my stomach growl a little, I ignore it.

"You wanna tell me why Mrs. Godfrey just congratulated me on my *engagement* while I was in the middle of doing an ultrasound on her mare?" My pulse is still thundering in my ears, just like it has been the entire ride from the Godfrey ranch.

Dallas halts and raises an index finger. "About that…I can explain."

"This oughta be good." I cross my arms over my chest and pop my hip out.

I'm salty as all get out. The part I didn't share just now was how Mrs. Godfrey treated me like I was the fat nerd in high school who just got asked to the prom by the quarterback. As if some frickin' miracle had befallen little old me, and I should be dropping to my knees to thank God above.

I can guaran-dang-tee you nobody is treating Dallas that way.

When he steps closer, my warning glare stops him just out of my strike zone. So, he's not a *complete* idiot, at least. He extends the snack bar in slow motion, placing it on the entry table with the same care a bomb technician would use with an IED. "Shane is not only talking trash, he's not giving up—and this will help deter him while I can keep you safe."

Well, that's not good. I have to admit, Shane has me a little nervous. We'd only been dating for a few months, and it's clear now that I don't know him as well as I thought I did.

He was charming at first, always opening doors and standing from his chair when I stood. And I'm such a sucker for a guy who tips his hat at a woman. Not to mention Shane spoiled me with compliments and sweet gestures.

He acted like my doody didn't stink—until I unintentionally embarrassed him in public, that is. Now I know he's a man with deep insecurities and a temper to match. I can't believe I even felt bad enough for him to patch up his bleeding knuckles after he punched the brick wall by my head. My good sense clearly left me in that moment. Good thing I got it back when he proceeded to crack my picture frame while we were talking it out.

So, yeah, hearing that Shane doesn't intend to leave me in the past is not welcome news. I'm way too old for this crap.

"And what happens when he loses interest, and we break off this fake engagement of yours?"

I'll tell you what will happen. I'll be the recipient of several hundred pitying expressions and the name on everyone's lips as they whisper behind my back. *I mean, did she really think Dallas Gamble would settle for her in the end? Poor dear.*

"Who says we have to break it off?"

My jaw drops at Dallas's response, but he keeps yammering.

"It'll be fun living together. We spend most of our free time together anyway. This will just make it easier. And, besides, Ryd loves you. *And* we had a pact. Do I need to pull out the napkin again?"

I choke out a laugh, but this ain't funny. "Dallas, are you hearing yourself?" He may as well have said, *Well, Shelby, since we know you'll never find a man to love you, you might as well move in, take care of my kid, and save us some gas money while you're at it.*

He has the nerve to shrug those broad shoulders. "What's so horrible about marrying me?" He proceeds to shove his hands into the front pockets of his jeans.

My chin drops to my chest, and I lose a little bit of my saltiness at his hangdog expression. It always surprises me when Dallas has these moments of self-doubt. He's a successful carpenter and artisan with a great family, and everyone in town dotes on him like he's the second coming of Pedro Pascal. What more could he ask for?

I let out a long sigh and bring my gaze back to his frowning face. "Seriously, Dallas? Any woman who married you would be lucky. You're a fantastic friend, you've got a mushy heart, you're funny, and even *I* can admit you're kinda easy on the eyes too."

One corner of his mouth curves upward, and the twinkle is back in his eyes. "Aw shucks, Sweetness."

"Jeez," I groan. "I should have just let you think you were a repulsive a-hole. That ego of yours doesn't need any more stroking."

"What was that? The only word I heard was stroking."

"Shut your pie hole, Gamble."

We both laugh, the tension in the room floating away as he steps closer. I can never stay mad at him. "I can think of a lot of worse things than being married to my best friend," he murmurs.

I nod because he's not wrong. Still…

"You know I can't settle for less than the whole package, Dally." I give the hem of his shirt a tug. "I need a man to sweep me off my feet. To be out of his mind in love with me. To surprise me with flowers just because, and whisk me away on romantic getaways. I want to find love letters in unexpected places, and I want him to hold my hand when we walk down the sidewalk."

It's not hard to warm up to the subject, and Dallas can't be surprised in the least. "He'll take me apple picking with a ladder and everything and even pack us a picnic. He'll make me a playlist of songs that remind him of us and take me to a musical even though he doesn't like them, but he knows I do. And he'll always look at me like he can't believe he ever got so lucky." My smile is wistful, but only until Dallas opens his mouth.

"So, you want a cheesy lovesick eunuch. Got it."

I scowl and smack his pec. "Don't be rude. I want what my parents had." He knows this. "Their love story was cut short, but it was the most beautiful thing I've ever seen. It's worth the wait."

"Shelby, I hate to be the one to break it to you, but this guy you're looking for doesn't exist outside of a romance novel."

"He *does*. I just haven't met him yet." I fist his shirt, trying to drive my point home. "They used to dance in the kitchen to cheesy love songs, Dally. You saw it. They only ever had eyes for each other. It exists. You and I both know it does."

"No guy can live up to this standard you're setting. We've been here before." He sends me a pointed look, and I know he's referring to Marcus, another of my exes. The one I really did think I was going to marry.

Marcus and I met at a veterinary science conference when I was in my late twenties, and we immediately hit it off. He was sweet, handsome, and so attentive. We stayed up all night talking the last day of the conference, and it was the best night of my life. He called me from his car ten minutes after we parted, telling me he missed me already. I practically swooned.

The fly in the ointment was that he had a career in Virginia, and I lived here in Oklahoma. Still, we talked on the phone every night, even if it was just to say good night, and we flew back and forth whenever we could. He wrote me gorgeous handwritten love letters and sent me so many flowers I accumulated a massive vase collection. He flew out to surprise me for my birthday and whisked me away to New Orleans, where I'd never been but always wanted to go. We talked about the future and made plans for a life together. We both wanted two kids and a cozy small-town life.

Since I didn't want to abandon my elderly grandparents and Marcus had no family in Virginia, he insisted that he move to Oklahoma so we could be together. It had been a year and a half of long distance, but our life was finally going to start.

Then he had a financial setback and needed to wait a little longer before leaving his job. A year after that, he turned down an offer for a job I found him at a vet clinic in Hornville, just thirty minutes from Big Knob. He said he didn't click with the practice manager. Six months later, he renewed the lease on his apartment in Virginia, "just to be safe."

The flowers had long stopped coming and so had the love letters. The nightly conversations turned to weekly and everything just…faded away.

I admit it took a couple years of licking my wounds after Marcus, but I still didn't give up.

I swallow hard and lift my chin. "If my momma and daddy could find each other, I can find my prince charming too." What I don't say out loud is that I owe it to my parents to settle for nothing less than the perfect love they had.

Dallas watches me for a long moment and then sighs, the lines around his mouth deepening. "Okay. If that's what you really want, I'll help you. Just like I said I would last night. I'll find your Prince Charming for you."

I let go of his shirt and laugh for real this time. "Isn't that going to be a little awkward now? My fiancé interviewing potential suitors for me?"

"Leave it to me, Sweetness. I'm one smooth talker." He grins, the mischievous gleam from his eyes nearly ricocheting off the walls of his entryway.

"So I've heard." I roll my eyes when he waggles his eyebrows. "Now, how exactly will this work, hotshot?"

"Easy…" He crosses his arms and leans a shoulder against the wall. "I find the prince, tell him all about how awesome you are and how lucky I am. We all hang out together so he can see for himself. Then, when the time is right, I make a jerk move in public, you break up with me, and Prince Charming swoops in to sweep you right out of your boots. Simple as that."

"Sounds about as simple as spinal surgery on a bucking bronco."

He dips his chin to meet my gaze. "Trust me, okay?"

Instead of answering, I pat his chest, snatch the nut bar from the table, and brush past him to head for the hallway. "Thanks for this. I gotta get changed. I'm going out."

"You're seriously leaving your brand-new fiancé at home on our engagement night?!" he calls after me. "I think I'm insulted!"

"Suck it up, buttercup!" I call back. I need my girls, and I need them STAT.

DON'T FLATTER YOURSELF, COWBOY. I WAS LOOKIN' AT YOUR HORSE

SHELBY

"I heard it, of course, but I didn't believe it!" Skye looks about as shocked as a pig watching a farmer eat a BLT. "*Our* Dallas? The hound-dog-who's-sniffed-every-female-flower-garden-in-the-county Dallas? Engaged?"

We're sitting at a high-top just off the dance floor at Knockin' Boots, where the house band is warming up. It's already busy, and it's barely six o'clock.

A single glance across the table reveals an identical expression on our friend Josie Mae. Clearly, I'm not the only one thrown for a loop by this plot twist. "How many times have I heard you say Dallas is the last man on earth you'd date? When did you change your mind? How did I miss this?"

"I *knew* it!" Frankie crows from beside Josie Mae for some reason, and we all turn to frown at her. Her grin is beyond smug. The girl is delusional.

"Calm yourself, Frankie." I plonk my beer bottle on the table and shake my head at her before leaning in for privacy.

"It's not real. Your brother is just incapable of restraining himself from acting on his every ridiculous impulse."

"What a shock," Skye drawls, flipping her long, dark-blonde hair over her shoulder and bringing her cocktail straw to her lips. Since Dallas is her little brother, she's practiced at insulting him.

"What do you mean? Please make this make sense," Jo begs. She and I have been close friends since high school, probably because she dated Dallas's twin brother, Houston, so we spent a lot of time together. The three of them were my first real friends as the new girl in town at fifteen.

We all lean in, and I give my friends the short version while the band starts playing in earnest and people trickle onto the dance floor. I include Dallas's plan for getting out of this mess in the end but leave out the napkin for reasons I'm not sure of.

"Dang." Skye is the first to speak. "I didn't realize Shane was that big of a jerk. I'm actually kind of proud of my little bro for coming through like that. I can always help out too, you know." And she's not wrong. She breaks horses in for a living, she could certainly take on Shane.

"Sloppy as it may be," Jo sighs.

Frankie tilts her head and considers me. "I don't know. I think there's still something more to this. I mean, going from punching a guy to declaring an engagement seems a little extreme, even for Dallas."

I inhale through my nose, the scent of fried bar food making my stomach grumble. "I promise you, there's not. Your brother is about as attracted to me as he is to Meemaw's Silkie chickens. Besides, you know I hate Texas. I could never marry a guy named Dallas." I wink at her, making everyone laugh. I take a sip of my beer before continuing, "Obviously, this has to be our secret, so mum's the word, ladies. You know how people in town love a good scandal."

Skye mimics zipping her lips just as Norinne approaches

our table, purple hair secured in a band and giant hoop earrings dangling low. "You girls ready for another round?" She turns to me. "I figured you'd be out celebrating with Dallas, Shelby. Congrats, by the way." In contrast to a lot of people around town, she appears genuinely pleased about the news.

Norinne is a fun-loving mother-hen type who changes her hair color once a month and never forgets to ask after your kin. She and her husband, Tank, have been running Knockin' Boots since her daddy retired a dozen years back. And by retired, I mean he now spends his afternoons selling home-made moonshine out of the trunk of his Chevy and flirting with the old ladies outside the Baptist church. Pappy is living his best life.

Hoping my discomfort isn't palpable, I respond with a smile. "Thanks, Norinne. He has Ryder tonight."

"Well, lemme see the ring, girl!" she insists, leaning forward to get a peek at my hand. Well, crap.

Frankie, bless her soul, comes to my rescue. "The ring was subpar, so Skye and I told him to take it back, but he just couldn't wait to pop the question."

Skye's smile is painful at best. "Yeah. He's never bought jewelry before, so he was flying blind."

"I can't believe y'all knew he was proposing and didn't tell me!" Norinne buys it, hook, line, and sinker.

Skye repeats her lip-lock gesture, and I force a smile at Norinne, to which she flutters her eyelashes and says, "Well, do I love a good happy ending." Everyone mutters lukewarm sounds of agreement. Then we order another round and wait for Norinne to leave before we all lean in again.

Frankie harrumphs, her jet-black hair falling forward as she drops her chin. "This sucks. I was looking forward to having you as a sister-in-law, Shelbs."

I grin at her because who wouldn't get the warm fuzzies from a comment like that, but Skye is the one to respond.

"Our brother doesn't have a romantic bone in his body, Frankie. His idea of wooing a woman is buying the two-for-one special at the diner just to save a buck."

"Goodness, Skye." Josie Mae snort-laughs. But I notice nobody tries to correct Skye.

"Speaking of two-for-one specials..." Frankie trails off, and we all turn to where she's looking.

Sure enough, Dallas stands across the way, leaning against the bar like it was constructed solely for the very purpose of supporting his fine self. He's wearing a western snap-up shirt and the same jeans as earlier, his feet covered by his favorite scuffed boots. His eyes are glued on me like cat hair to a black dress.

Crap. Why did my heart just jump? I can't even begin to count the number of times he and I have met up at this exact bar. His lips curve in a knowing smile like he just read my damn mind, and the man proceeds to raise his beer bottle in a pseudo toast to me.

"Daaaaang. Somebody is *not* messing around," Jo drawls.

I turn my back to Dallas to face my friends again. I can't have them thinking his presence is affecting me in any way. Forcing a laugh, I bring my beer bottle to my lips for a fortifying gulp.

"Hey, Dallas!" Frankie chirps a few seconds later, causing me to choke on my drink. I sputter, drawing Skye's watchful eye.

"If you're here, where's Ryder?" Skye asks, giving me a moment to get myself together.

"He's with Pops."

I finally turn in my stool with what I hope is a believable smile. It falters when I realize every pair of eyes in the whole damn place is trained on us.

Sensing my panic, Dallas leans in real slow, setting his beer on the table and planting a soft kiss on my cheek. "I got this. Don't worry," he whispers in my ear. His breath tickles, causing goose bumps to rise on both of my arms.

Charlene Russell sidles up to the table, Norinne right on her heels. Those two are rarely seen apart, especially when there's new gossip to be found. Not to be rude, but doesn't Norinne have an entire bar full of patrons to wait on?

"Now that I'm off the clock, I can focus," Charlene says with a ravenous grin. Oh, yikes.

Dallas drapes a casual arm over my shoulders and greets both women. "How are you fine ladies doin' tonight?"

"I'll be better once I hear how you proposed," Charlene volleys back, her wide-eyed gaze shifting to me. "Was it everything you ever thought it would be, Shelby?" Before either one of us can respond, she barks, "Oh! The ring!" causing everyone at our table and beyond to startle in our seats. "I forgot to look at the ring!"

Unaffected, Norinne leans into her bestie with a stage whisper. "Ix-nay on the ing-ray, Char. He screwed the pooch and bought a clunker." Charlene gasps, and Dallas stiffens beside me. Oops. Well, I guess that's what you get when you spin a web of lies, Mr. Gatsby.

I pat the hand resting on my shoulder. "Hey, a guy can't be good at *everything*, right? He makes up for it elsewhere." I immediately curse myself when Charlene and Norinne's mouths curve in identical knowing grins. It does have the desired effect, though, as Dallas's frame relaxes again.

"I'm taking care of it," he improvises.

"Well?" Charlene demands, clearly moving past the ring and onto the proposal story. Her expression reminds me of Augustus Gloop from Charlie and the Chocolate Factory, although Charlene has much better hair.

"Yes, do tell," Skye adds with a smirk at Dallas as she props her chin on her hand. These Gambles are all a bunch of trouble makers. I glare at her and start to panic, but I needn't bother.

"Well, ladies, I'll tell you," Dallas begins, causing Charlene to teeter forward on her high-heeled sandals. "I thought to myself, 'What would be Shelby's dream proposal?' It took a bit, but then inspiration just struck." He snaps his fingers, and a riveted Charlene flinches but never loses focus.

"Oh, I can't wait to hear this," she croons.

"Me either," I deadpan while Josie Mae coughs loudly into the crook of her elbow.

"So, I made some calls and snuck around behind this one's back." Dallas grins at me, and I can't tamp my amusement down. He's enjoying himself way too much. I just hope Charlene and Norinne mistake my mirth for a lovesick rapt expression.

"You sneaky devil, you." I reach up and pinch his cheek as I egg him on, barely holding it together.

"And?" Charlene might actually pee her pants.

"Well, naturally, I made up some excuse to get her in my truck and then pretended I forgot I had an extra errand to run."

"Clever," Norinne throws in her two cents, but Charlene shushes her.

Dallas gazes down at me, that permanent twinkle in his eyes practically blinding me. "You should have seen Shelby's expression when we got to our destination."

When he doesn't elaborate, Charlene shouts so loud we get the attention of several nearby tables. "Where did you take her?!" When she realizes she's drawn a small crowd, she lowers her voice again. "Honestly, Dallas, you're a slower storyteller than a toothless drunk man."

I start to laugh until I realize her attention has shifted to me. "You tell it, Shelby. Where did he take you?"

My jaw locks, and I flash a panicked look at Dallas. But if I thought he'd come to my rescue, his shit-eating grin disabuses me of that notion right quick. Similar glances to Frankie, Skye, and Josie Mae yield nothing better.

In fact, Jo mirrors Skye's pose and asks, "Yeah, Shelby. Where did he take you?" I'm going to strangle her.

I realize now I have to make this believable. Where would Dallas Gamble take a woman to propose? Not that it would ever happen, but if it did…

"To the swimming hole at Beaver Hollow Falls, of course. What better place to propose than where everyone in town goes to park and make out?"

When all of their faces fall, I know I've miscalculated, so I quickly add, "But it was super romantic. He packed some of those plastic champagne flutes and a nice bottle of bubbly." My smile is brittle, I just know it.

Dallas's arm tightens around me, and he pulls me back into his chest with a chuckle. "She's just kidding, y'all."

Relieved sighs reverberate around the table and nearby crowd. Even my three so-called friends let out loud exhales. What the heck is wrong with them? They know this is all fake!

Dallas doesn't pause for long, extending his free hand to sweep through the air like he's setting a dramatic scene. Good gravy. "The sun was low in the sky as we pulled up to this empty field outside Oklahoma City. And there, in the middle of nothing, was a turquoise hot air balloon resting on the grass." I freeze because this is the furthest thing from what I expected him to say. In fact, this exact proposal scene is on one of my Pinterest boards. "Shelby's always wanted to ride in one of those. She almost started crying, didn't you, Sweetness?"

Since his smile is smug, I smile back, but I also pinch his thigh real hard. He swallows a yelp and carries on.

"So, the guy took us up, and we floated around and took in the scenery. You wouldn't believe how quiet and peaceful it is up there. Shelby was ooohing and ahhhing all over the place, not that I blame her."

I chance a glance at Charlene, and she looks like Dallas just found the key to her heart.

"And just as we passed over a gorgeous lake, I dropped to one knee and popped the question."

A round of "Awws" echoes through the bar, and again, my idiot friends follow suit, all three of them looking like they just watched the end of a super fantastic Hallmark movie. Charlene's even wiping away a tear.

"I just knew you were a romantic at heart, Dallas Gamble," Norinne gushes.

Since I've said nothing, and I don't want to sound like some ungrateful bridezilla, I add, "Yeah, it was *so* romantic, y'all. And the champagne glasses were even real!"

Apparently taking that as their cue, people start swarming me with hugs. But, once again, Dallas comes to the rescue, extending a hand and pulling me up from my stool.

It's only then I realize the band just started playing "How Country Feels" by Randy Houser, taking my smile from fake to full-blown.

"I requested it special," Dallas says loud enough for everyone to hear. Cue another round of swooning.

This is our song. Not in the romantic way couples have "their song," but in a way that's all about shared memories and a whole lot of fun times together. The clingy crowd fades away, and I let Dallas lead me to the dance floor.

"Well, aren't you the Nora Roberts of fake proposals?" I comment when we're out of earshot.

Dallas shuffles me to an open spot on the floor, hands framing my shoulders from behind. "I don't know who that is, but heck yeah."

I snort, and before long, we're both laughing and stomping and doing a well-practiced line dance as the band plays.

I smile over at Dallas to see him grinning my way too. And

I suddenly know that I can absolutely do this with him. He's my best friend, and he's always got my best interests at heart. Just like I hope I give back to him. We'll pull through this.

And who knows? Maybe we'll both find the perfect partner we've been waiting for.

Eight

SWEATING LIKE A NUN IN VEGAS

DALLAS

Everything's okay. *We're* okay.

As long as Shelby's not mad at me, I know everything's fine in the world. The woman can't fake a smile through three whole songs. She's officially not mad at me anymore, I'm sure of it. She spins around and shimmies to the final chorus of some song I'm not even really listening to. I have to physically drag my gaze away from her backside, all luscious curves in those worn Levi's. I know I need to put on a show for the town to really sell this engagement story. I know I should be gazing at her like a man who's just put a ring on her finger, but dang, she's driving me a little too crazy. I'm finding it a little too easy to stare at her with my jaw dropped to the floor.

We've just worked up a legitimate sweat when the band slows everything down into a slow dance. It's perfect for the show we have to put on, but hard on the chaotic thoughts spinning around my skull. Shelby turns to walk off the dance floor, her gaze on the table where her friends—and my sisters

—have various knowing grins on their faces. Without giving it too much thought, I reach out and snatch Shelby's hand, her oversized turquoise ring digging into my palm. The woman is obsessed with turquoise, just like her momma was.

"Dance with me, Sweetness."

I give her hand a tug, and as she's stumbling closer to me, I wrap my arm around her waist, leaning in so that my lips skate across her ear. "Engaged lovers would absolutely dance to 'Strip It Down.' Luke Bryan makes all the girls swoon, am I right?"

Shelby's body relaxes, though it takes her several long seconds to slide her hands up my arms, across my shoulders, and behind my neck. I'm hyper focused on every inch of my body that's touching hers. I mean, Shelby's always given good hugs, but this feels different. Very different. I've got her curves under my hands, and as we begin to sway to the music, I forget we're just friends.

Why don't they crank the air conditioning when they have a live band? The temperature in here is higher than a giraffe's butt.

"You okay, Dally?" Shelby purrs.

I look down to see her head tilted back, hair tickling my arm, and her eyebrow lifted in challenge. I'm quick to tell her I'm fine, but I think we both know that's not true when I look away too soon. It's discombobulating to feel so out of control. I'm usually the one to flirt like an alley cat in heat. The one to drop a line and see where it takes me. Except with Shelby, my lines won't work. And they shouldn't work! She's my best friend, for crap's sake.

She starts to shake in my arms. At first, I think she's crying, but when I look back down at her in alarm, her pretty lips are curved upward, and I realize she's laughing at me. And I don't like being laughed at when I haven't cracked a joke. Time to wrestle some control back and act like Dallas freaking Gamble. Women don't fluster me.

I dip my head and run my nose along her neck, stopping at her earlobe where I nuzzle the little flap of skin between my teeth. I feel her gasp, which makes me grin like an idiot. I let her earlobe slip from my teeth so my lips can explore her neck. She tastes like peaches and salt, a combination I didn't know I'd like so much until this exact moment.

"What're you doing, Dallas?" Shelby hisses, quiet enough I'm sure only I can hear her.

Luke's crooning away about stripping it down, and suddenly I'm thinking that sounds like a very good idea. I'd like to strip Shelby down. Get to the bottom of things between us. See if maybe being married for real might not be so bad. I think Shelby's funny as all get out. Loyal. Caring. A high achiever. Great with my son. Hot as Hades too, though I know she doesn't think so. I could do a lot worse, you know?

I pull away from her neck, not because I want to quite yet, and not because Shelby's gone stiff in my arms, but because Luke's got me thinking things aren't that complicated. Not really. When you strip away all the expectations of everyone around us, I like Shelby. I care for her with the same ferocity that I care for my family, my son. And based on the way Shelby's curves fit all snug against me, maybe there could be a little passion in our marriage between friends.

So, like with all things in life, I take action and think about it later.

My hand leaves her waist long enough to push back a lock of her hair and to cup her cheek. Her eyes go as wide as a deer seeing headlights in the middle of the night. I can feel the flutter of her pulse, the flush of her cheeks, the little inhale of air she sucks between her glossy lips.

"Grab onto my shirt," I practically grunt.

"Wh-why?" A little wrinkle forms between her eyebrows.

"'Cause I'm gonna kiss you, Sweetness, and your knees are liable to buckle."

With that cocky declaration, I lean all the way down and

capture her lips with mine. I don't go for a light peck or a whisper of a kiss, no ma'am. I claim her lips like a man starving for the one woman in this county he never gave himself permission to taste. Until now. Until everyone in this room is eyeing us. Even though I know it's all for show, I have the green light to kiss the ever-loving stuffing out of Shelby without repercussions, so I go for it.

Her gasp becomes my invitation to slide my tongue alongside hers. To tickle her mouth and taste the beer she was drinking before I stole her away to the dance floor. My arm goes tight as a bow around her waist, hauling her fully against me. I'm not sure what day it is or where we even are, but the fireworks exploding inside my head nearly take all my attention away from the details I'm trying to memorize.

Like the way Shelby goes limp in my arms, every square inch of her pliant in my grasp. Or the way her hands have fisted my shirt, probably wrinkling it so badly I'll have to borrow Meemaw's iron. Or the thundering beat that might be her heart or mine. There's not enough room between us for me to tell whose it is.

She doesn't respond at first, a problem I only notice in the back recesses of my brain. And then—dear heavens above— she does respond. Her tongue duels with mine, and we're both rabid, nearly climbing each other to get closer. To dominate. To get more.

The fireworks give way to wolf whistles and thoughts of dragging her out of here and throwing her in the back of my truck. I swear I hold the county record on how fast a man can pull jeans off a woman, but this time I'd take my time. Slow it down. Strip her down piece by piece, unveiling every creamy inch of skin I've never let myself touch.

"Jeez, get a room, would you?"

Frankie's bellow interrupts the best kiss I've ever had, and I swear to all things holy, it takes every ounce of restraint I have—not that there's much to begin with—to not snap her head off. Frankie has always pushed my buttons in a way that makes me wish she was a boy so I could tackle her and not feel badly about it.

Shelby breaks away from me, her hand going to her mouth. Her big blue eyes are blinking rapidly like she got something stuck in them. The girls grab her and push her over to their table while the band switches to another upbeat line dance. I'm left standing on the dance floor—indecently turned on—with no idea what the heck just happened. Shelby hauls herself into a barstool and puts an ice-cold beer bottle to her cheek.

I start grinning like a fool. I mean, I knew we got along, but until that explosive kiss, I didn't realize we're also compatible in other, more intimate ways. I've always known I'm all wrong for Shelby, and quite frankly, all that romance crap irritates me to no end, so it's been easy to stay away from her. There are too many non-difficult women I could be dating to waste my time trying to be the man Shelby wants. But maybe we could have some fun while we fake this engagement, you know? I'm always up for a good time.

Which to my mind means more of those kisses. I can find her a good man who'll do all the stupid gestures she's hung up on. Then we'll go back to being best friends. Heck yeah. This is a great idea.

I waltz off the dance floor and head straight for a table in the back, four men around it nursing their beers. I recognize one guy from Hornville. David, I think his name is. They look up as I approach, their conversation dying.

"Hey, David, how's it going?"

The familiar guy gives me a cool smile. "It's Davis, actually. And it's going good. How 'bout you?"

Davis, David, whatever. I only have so many brain cells. I need to reserve them to remember the ladies' names.

"Good, man. Introduce me to your friends?" I smile winningly at the three other guys, sizing them up and zeroing in on the one with a plaid shirt and fancy jeans. He's got black-rimmed glasses that he might use for reading novels or poems or crap like that. He's introduced as Judson. His handshake is firm but not too firm. He's confident, not easily intimidated. So far so good.

After we chit-chat for a bit and I find out he's single, I invite him over to meet my sisters. He follows me over to the girls' table. I make sure he stands right next to Shelby as I make the introductions. I watch the way he's polite with all of them but think maybe I catch him eyeing Shelby a bit longer than the rest. If she'd quit smirking at me, she might notice Judson is good-looking. I mean, he's not as good-looking as me, but if he can pen a sappy love letter, she can overlook it.

Before I can get too far into the possible match-up, David comes over and tells Judson they have to leave. I try not to be irritated that he and Shelby didn't get a chance to exchange numbers. I've never been a wing man for a picky girl, but it's turning out harder than I anticipated.

"See y'all around, Judson. David." I purposely get his name wrong, and he doesn't correct me this time.

"I gotta go get Ryder. You comin'?" I ask Shelby. She hesitates.

"No. This was supposed to be a girls' night. You know? Before you barged in?"

"Sorry 'bout that." I ain't actually sorry, but in my experience with women, that's always what they want to hear. "I'll see you when you get home. If y'all need a ride, just call me." I lean in to kiss her cheek, and she lets me, her skin still hot to the touch.

It's a relief to exit the bar into the cooling night air. Women are impossible to understand. They take perverse pleasure in wrapping us around their little fingers and then tormenting us. I think of all the years Pops's been grieving over Mom, and I have to shake my head to clear it of any stupid ideas. Women are fun for a while, but I have no intention of getting that wrapped up in one. Whatever that was with Shelby on the dance floor, I'll just have to blame it on the two beers I had. Maybe I'm turning into a lightweight the older I get.

My boots crunch on the dirt parking lot, sounding loud in the sudden quiet outside the bar. D'Wayne, the local man who refuses to move out of his van despite the town donating a tiny house to him, interrupts the quiet. "Woman troubles?"

He's sitting on the ground with his back to a tree, a perfect perch for watching who goes in and out of Knockin' Boots. I lift my hand in greeting. "Nah. Just pacing myself."

D'Wayne smirks. "Never thought I'd see the day Dallas Gamble paces himself with the ladies."

I shake my head. "We all gotta grow up sometime."

I reach my truck door and unlock it. D'Wayne waves his hand through the air. "That's where you're wrong, Gamble! Never grow up! All the world is made of faith and trust and pixie dust!"

Ignoring the town Peter Pan, I climb inside my truck and get the bright idea to call Houston while I drive back to the ranch. I hit his contact number and set the phone on speaker.

"What?"

I chuckle at his greeting. "Did you know there's a theory that one twin can suck up all the good personality away from the other twin in utero?"

"Shut up," Houston growls, ever the grump. "I assume you called for something more than a science lesson?"

"I'm doing fine, thanks for asking. Been thinking about you every day and just couldn't rest 'til I heard your sweet voice, brother dearest."

There's a pause. So, I up the ante.

"I just saw Josie Mae. That woman knows how to rock a pair of jeans, I'm just sayin'."

Houston's voice turns deadly. "You got five seconds before I hang up."

I use four of those seconds to laugh. Then I sober up and

get to the point of the call because that brother of mine really will hang up on me.

"I'm fake engaged to Shelby Sweet."

There's another silence. Then it's his turn to laugh, and as much as I tease him, it really is good to hear he still knows how to laugh.

"Dude. Explain yourself. And don't leave anything out."

So, I do. I explain everything, and when I'm done, he just sighs. "Well, you did the right thing by protecting her from that jerk, but dang, Dallas. You're cooked."

I guffaw. "No, I'm not."

There's humor in his voice when he responds. "You're so cooked you don't even know you're cooked. That's how cooked you are."

Then he hangs up.

And here I thought *women* were confusing.

TEN POUNDS OF CRAZY IN A FIVE-POUND SACK

SHELBY

"Did you know your sister has two new rescue swine?" I hang my bags on the back of one of Dallas's kitchen stools and raise my voice. I stopped on the way home to pick up some fresh blueberries and a couple cute blueberry dish towels. It's National Blueberry Month after all, and if I'm staying here, I've gotta bring the Shelby touch.

"Yup. Saw 'em rolling around in the mud when I was mucking stalls," he calls back from upstairs. Must be supervising Ryder's shower. I look at my watch and see it's already seven.

Dallas's house sits on ranch property, close enough to the main house that it's convenient but far enough away that nobody is going to disturb his privacy. But it means you drive past the barns and outbuildings on the way here.

I toe off my sandals. My work boots never leave the back of my truck, seeing as I'm not a person who enjoys horse poop in my living space. "Did she tell you their names?" I pad to the bottom of the stairs, noticing that the mess I cleaned up in the living room before work is already back.

It's been a few days since the scene at Knockin' Boots, and our engagement story has made the rounds all over town. As has the way we apparently attacked each other on the dance floor. But if I thought things would be awkward after that, Dallas's behavior hasn't changed one bit, so I'm following his lead and pretending it never happened.

Secretly, though, that impromptu make-out session has been using up way too much of my brain capacity. Of course, I knew Dallas was both experienced and naturally sexy, but holy hormones! When his tongue pushed past my shocked lips, several long-dormant places in my body lit on fire—and even a few I didn't know had nerve endings. The soles of my feet in my favorite boots even tingled while my toes curled up tight. I've never been kissed like that in my entire life. There was nothing choreographed or calculated. It was just pure animal instinct.

"Do I want to know?" Dallas calls back from upstairs. "She's incapable of using a normal name like Porky."

I grin. "I promise you do."

"Okay, lay it on me."

"Tammy Swinenette and Snoop Hogg!" I snicker as big and little Gamble appear on the staircase, Ryder in Spiderman pjs and Dallas in another of his T-shirts paired with jeans and bare feet.

"Pigs are really good swimmers. Did you know that?" Ryder asks as he skips the last step and jumps onto the wood floor.

"Too bad we don't have a pool to test that theory," Dallas says.

Ryder pivots as only an eight-year-old boy can. "We could put them on the trampoline."

"Sorry. I have to work that day." I turn and head for the fridge, my stomach grumbling as I open the door. "Oh my gosh. Is that salsa from Eduardo's?" I spin around to face Dallas again. He's leaning on the raised countertop, eyebrows lifted.

"Yeah. I had to run to Hornville today, so I picked some up." I could kiss the man. Oh, wait, I already did.

As if I have to remind myself.

"Shelby, are you gonna live here from now on?"

My head jerks at Ryder's question. "Umm…" Why wasn't I ready for this?

Thankfully, Dallas comes to the rescue. "Come pick which movie we're gonna watch tonight, kiddo."

I take advantage and push the distraction. "You looking forward to school starting next month, Little G?"

"Nah. I wish it would be summer break forever." He watches as Dallas scrolls through the movie options on the TV.

"But you get to see all your friends."

Ryder only shrugs. The kid kills me. He's so smart and funny and loving, but being on the autism spectrum presents a lot of challenges that most of his peers don't even have to consider.

"We should plan a fun adventure before summer's over," I declare.

He spins from the TV, eyes bright now. "Like what?"

"I don't know. Maybe a camping trip? Or we could go to the big city and visit the aquarium." Considering he swims like a fish, it might be compulsory at this point.

"Can we, Dad?"

Dallas nudges his son's shoulder. "Maybe. We'll see what the calendar looks like."

I head to the bedroom to change and then busy myself preparing movie snacks, gathering everything on a tray I unearth from a high cabinet. As soon as Ryder sees the giant bowl of popcorn, he props himself on his favorite bean bag chair and digs in. I, on the other hand, plan to focus on the chips and salsa. "So, what are we watching?"

"Jumanji," Ryder informs me. "I like the part where Bethany has to learn how to pee like a boy."

"Well okay then." I settle my butt onto the couch next to Dallas and prepare to be dazzled.

"What's wrong with your foot?" Dallas asks thirty minutes later as the Rock sends a smoldering gaze to the camera.

I glance over at him and then down at my hands, where they're rubbing my right foot. "Nothing," I whisper. "I just pulled a muscle or something. One of Gavin Heeley's fillies has a head wound, and the little drama queen didn't feel like cooperating."

Without a word, Dallas palms my calf and pulls my foot onto his lap where he proceeds to knead it with his strong fingers and thumbs. I'm pretty sure I groan out loud.

Honestly, if this is what it's like being married to Dallas, I could get used to it.

By the time the credits roll, Ryder is fast asleep in his giant bean bag chair, and I have half a mind to join him. Dallas rises from the couch, stretching his arms above his head and revealing a slice of tanned and toned abdomen which I studiously ignore.

"Oh, hey, I almost forgot." His voice is scratchy as he shuffles to the entryway, and I wait for him to return and explain himself. When he reappears, a small black projectile nearly hits me in the face. Good thing my reflexes are honed from years of working with huge animals who could kill me with one misstep.

"What is this?" I pick up the small box from the couch cushion where it landed, and it looks like a jewelry box.

"Open it up and see."

My hands begin to tremble for some stupid reason. The lid opens with a click, and I have no idea why, but I bark out a laugh before slapping a hand over my mouth and checking that I didn't wake Ryder.

"And people ask me why I've never gotten married," Dallas drawls, complete with an eye roll at my antics.

"No! I'm sorry, it's just…" I have no idea how to finish that sentence because inside the box lies the most quintessentially *Shelby* ring I've ever laid eyes on. There's a row of three stones—one large one in the center banked by two smaller ones—in an intricate filigree setting that looks like flowered vines curling around the centerpiece. It's exquisite and absolutely *the* ring I would choose for myself.

"You didn't have to do this," I finish lamely. I mean, I guess it's good to have a ring because people keep staring at my bare finger. But I just figured we'd go with something out of a Cracker Jack box, if at all. "It's not…real, is it?" There is no way he's spending true engagement ring kind of money on something so temporary. "'Cause I'm not sure if jewelers accept returns." Please let it be fake.

I can't make out his expression, partly because he's in shadow. "No."

"Oh, thank goodness." I laugh with relief, quieter this time. I have to say it's a beautiful ring, even if it is costume jewelry. I wonder where he found it.

I close the box and bring it with me as I clear the snacks and take them to the kitchen. "So, what are people saying to *you* about all this?"

Dallas joins me, grabbing the popcorn bowl and emptying the unpopped kernels into the trash. "Oh, you know." He adopts a super redneck-ey tone. "'Dang, Dallas, I never thought I'd see the day you settled down.' That kinda thing." I take the bowl from him to wash it, and he grabs a dish towel. "Although D'Wayne said he'd shoot me dead if I broke your heart. I'm pretty sure he meant it too."

"Aww. I've always had a soft spot for him." Dallas takes the wet bowl and starts to dry it while I move on to the rest.

"I guess nobody will be too surprised when we break up then. Your reputation as a bachelor is set in stone in these parts."

He reaches up to put the bowl back in a high cabinet while I duck under his arm to get to the fridge. This is a choreographed routine we've had down pat after years of movie nights and last-minute suppers. "Why would I want to invite heartbreak like that?"

"You mean falling in love with someone and throwing caution to the wind?"

He hands me the mostly empty salsa container. "Yeah. Seems crazy to me. You've watched Pops all these years. The man is still in pieces over my momma, and it's been eighteen years. No thanks."

I straighten and turn from the open refrigerator door. "I guess my parents were lucky in a way. Nobody had to go first and leave the other behind."

"Not to mention divorce rates," Dallas barrels on. "Half the town is full of bitter divorcees. I remember when Derek and Jenny were so gone over each other he even skipped our guys' trip to Vegas because she got the flu. Now the only thing they can agree on is how much they despise one another." He looks like he either wants to spit or puke.

"Maybe." I shrug and close the door before leaning back against it. "I don't know. None of that stops me from holding out hope. But it's good to know yourself and what you do and don't want for your life."

Dallas perks up at my words. "Speaking of, I ran into a guy in Hornville I used to know a while back. A friend of a friend kind of thing. We got to chatting, and I think he might be perfect for you. He was wearing fancy-pants clothes and was on his way to donate blood, if that says anything."

"Oh yeah? What's his name?"

"Elias Keller."

"Okay." I nod. "I can work with that. "What does he do?"

"Don't know. But we'll find out on Thursday when we meet him for dinner at Pound Town. Figured keeping it low-key with burgers would be a good move."

The reality of the situation settles in, and I put a hand over my stomach. "I can't decide if what I'm feeling right now is anticipation, terror, or indigestion."

"Better put a trash can next to the bed just in case."

———

"Stop fidgeting."

"I'm not." I absolutely am. I'm twisting my new ring on my finger like I'm trying to draw milk from it.

"You are," Dallas insists.

"What if this guy is a serial killer?"

It's Thursday evening, and we're seated beside one another in a window booth at Pound Town, Big Knob's burger joint. Buck Silver, the seventy-five-year-old owner, is obsessed with Christmas and keeps the place decorated year-round. You'd think it would be obnoxious, but it's a town favorite.

I woke up the morning after movie night to find the ring box and two antacids laid out on the bedside table—though I thankfully didn't need the latter—as well as a note from Dallas that he was taking Ryder back to his mom's. They share custody during the summer in a casual arrangement that seems to work well for everyone.

It's been a week since I moved in, and Dallas keeps insisting on taking the couch. I offered to clean out his spare room and put a blow-up mattress in there for myself, but he's having none of it. The sooner I move back to my place, the better. Besides, I hate feeling like Shane is in any way controlling my life. But, to Dallas's point, if I move out now, rumors of our split will blaze across town within the hour. People are becoming seriously invested.

I spent way too long in bed that morning staring at the engagement ring—correction...*fake* engagement ring—that I almost missed my first appointment of the day. When I got back to Dallas's after work, he plonked the box on the kitchen table and gave me the stink eye. I took that as my cue that he wanted me to wear the thing.

"A serial killer who donates blood and wears dress shoes?" Dallas asks. He's wearing one of his signature band T-shirts and a backward baseball cap that looks way better than it should on him.

I shrug. And fidget. Dallas reaches over and covers my wringing hands with one of his large, calloused ones.

"How is it you've had a dozen boyfriends but never been on a date before?"

That earns him a glare. "Of course I have. Just never with my fake fiancé in tow."

"Dallas," a deep voice greets my bestie, and I look up to see a very handsome man who looks to be in his early forties, with neatly styled dark hair and bone structure that tells me he's likely a descendant of Zeus. Gotta love those Greeks.

When his eyes shift to me, his smile turns even warmer, as does my belly. Why have I never asked Dallas to find me dates before?

"Elias, meet Shelby Sweet, my fiancée." I do my best not to start at his words, and we all shake hands as Elias ducks to avoid a huge swath of tinsel garland and settles into the bench seat across from us.

"It's a pleasure to meet you, Shelby," Elias says as he carefully unfolds a reindeer napkin and lays it across his lap like a perfect gentleman.

"You too." I smile.

"Interesting place you've got here." Elias gestures to the surroundings that could double as a North Pole storage unit on January 1st.

"A popular spot for families who like to get a head start

on Christmas card photos," Dallas quips. "But the burgers are phenomenal."

I nod in agreement. "Dallas tells me you two know each other from the old days. I'm surprised we've never met before."

Dallas nudges me. "Well, if you hadn't gone off to school for all those years, maybe you would have, *Dr.* Sweet."

"We've got a couple of mutual friends, that's all," Elias shares. "So, you're a doctor?" He leans in with interest, and I notice he has a dimple. Be still my heart.

"Yes." His warmth makes it easier to still my hands. "I'm a veterinarian."

His responding smile is nothing short of dazzling. "I'm jealous. You get to hang out with dogs." Good lord, he's an animal person.

"Not so much, I'm afraid. I'm actually a large animal vet, so I mostly hang out with livestock. Still cute, just bigger." I take a sip of my water while enjoying his hearty chuckle. This guy definitely has potential. Good job, bestie!

"Wow."

The waitress, a local high school student, stops by to take our order. Her Santa hat headband is flashing green and red. I consider getting a salad but then decide I don't feel like it and order an avocado turkey burger instead.

"And what do you do, Elias?" I ask once she leaves.

"I'm a college professor, but I'm on sabbatical at the moment while I'm writing a book."

"Now it's my turn to 'wow.' What do you teach?"

"Poetry."

My eyes flash to Dallas, and it takes everything I have to not choke on my drink. "Where have you been hiding Elias all this time, Dallas?"

His jaw looks a little tight when he responds, "Oh, I don't know."

Elias and I go back to chatting, enjoying ourselves

throughout the meal. Dallas is awfully silent, but I figure he's just trying to give me time to get to know Elias to decide if he's our prince charming candidate.

Because the sooner we find the prince, the sooner this fake engagement can be over with, and our lives can go back to normal. And there's nothing Dallas wants more than that. I'm sure of it.

CHAPTER

Ten

THAT PLACE IS BEING HELD TOGETHER BY TERMITES HOLDING HANDS

DALLAS

What the actual hell is happening here? Shelby's cheeks are flushed. Elias has shifted further across the bench seat to be directly across from Shelby, not me. These two can't seem to remember I'm even sitting at this table. Rude, if you ask me. Which they won't because they're too busy flirting. Doesn't Elias see the big ring on her finger?

You know, I liked this guy. Thought he might be perfect for Shelby, but I'm seeing his true colors now, and they're ugly.

"Hate to break this up, but Shelby has an early day tomorrow, and my honey bear needs her sleep." I slide out of the booth and hold out my hand to Shelby. If I hear one more Christmas carol from the speaker above my head, I might scream.

She blinks up at me in surprise. "Don't we need to pay first?"

My polite grin turns into a grimace. "I already did." *Which you'd know if you were paying me any attention at all.*

"Thanks, man. That's awfully nice of you." Elias, the fiancé-stealing jerk, shakes my outstretched hand like we're buds. Pals.

Well, he can pound sand. No way am I setting him up with Shelby.

I release his hand as soon as possible and hold it out again to Shelby. She takes it, sliding out of the booth while giving me weird looks. I wrap my arm around her waist the second she's standing, hauling her against my side. She lets out a surprised squeak. I gesture for Elias to take the lead. Not gonna let that crook walk behind us and have the privilege of staring my fiancée's backside. No sir, no ma'am.

The goodbyes are rushed, and I'm sure Shelby's gonna let me have it during the truck ride home for being rude, but I don't give a crap. I get her settled and come around the front of the truck, rolling my eyes when I see Elias getting into a small hybrid car I wouldn't be caught dead in.

I barely get my door shut before Shelby lights into me. "What is your problem, Gamble? That was a perfectly nice man, and you had to go all caveman on us. Me Dallas. She mine." Her voice is dripping with sarcasm and a terrible accent.

"That's a Tarzan phrase, not caveman."

She practically levitates off the seat. "Missing the point here, Dallas! He was hot. A professor of poetry?? He's my dream man, and you had to be rude to him!"

I scoff, turning the wheel toward home. "He's not your dream man."

"Says who?"

I turn toward her, now just as furious. "Says me. Your best friend. The one who knows you best. Did you not see his lame car? Or the way he lifted his pinky when he drank his beer? Men don't do that."

Shelby's mouth pops open. "Are you actually serious right now?"

I stop at the four-way intersection, looking both ways before taking off again. "Dead serious. Besides, you have my ring on your finger, and that pig was flirting with you. The last thing you want is to get messed up with a man who doesn't understand boundaries. That's how affairs happen."

Shelby snaps her mouth closed and crosses her arms over her chest. Ha! She knows I'm right. I let her stew on that while I drive. It's only when we're pulling up the driveway to my house that she speaks again.

"I would like to point out that while he was definitely flirting, there's no difference between what he was doing and what you've been doing your entire life. If you have a problem with him, you have a problem with your own behavior."

With that bombshell dropped, Shelby slides out of my truck and starts walking to the porch like she's won the argument. I run after her, anger and what feels like a creeping sensation of humiliation, fueling me to lash out. I snag her elbow just in front of my screen door.

"What the heck is that supposed to mean?" I demand over the chirping of crickets surrounding us.

Shelby lifts her little nose in the air and huffs like I'm the biggest idiot in the world. Normally, I would agree with her, but I'm not sure how the tables got turned here, and it's making me want to dig in my heels.

"You know what I mean, and if you've got any sense between those ears, you'll think on it tonight." Shelby pulls her arm away from me, and I let her go. The screen door almost clips me in the face when she doesn't hold it for me as she passes through.

I growl and follow her inside. She toes off her boots by the entryway table and spins to face me.

"One last thing. Don't ever call me honey bear again."

Honestly, with her cheeks heated and her lips puckered

like that, she kind of looks like a pissed off bear. I just manage to control the chuckle. "I think honey bears are cute."

"Dallas," she growls, stomping her foot.

And that's cute too. But I'm no dummy, and I keep that to myself. I'll just have to call her honey bear in my head. She can't police my thoughts.

And telling me to think on her comments about my flirting? Well, that sounds a lot like introspection, and I don't like to do that much. Life's too short to think on all the ways you're failing. Better to just stumble through this life making people smile. I may have faults, but I've singlehandedly made every woman in this county smile like a schoolgirl. Even ol' Mrs. Perkins. I think when I get to those pearly gates, that'll be enough to grant my entrance.

Shelby heads to my room while I strip down to my briefs and make a beeline for the couch. If she's going to be staying here long term, I'll need to come up with a better sleeping situation. My back can't take much more of this insufferable couch.

My phone pings with a series of texts. I pick it up and wish I didn't.

Houston: You know what they say, you should always sleep with your fiancée before the wedding to check out your sexual compatibility.

Houston: Or will you be practicing celibacy during your marriage with Shelby?

Houston: Come on. Answer me. I've been contemplating this all week. I have to know.

Houston: Do they make a reverse Viagra? Something to kill the mood? 'Cause you're gonna need it, boy.

———

I'm woken up before the sun is up the next morning, my phone vibrating off the damn coffee table. I manage to feel around the floor and pick it up, squinting with one eye to see Ridge's name on the screen.

"Hey." My voice is rough, but I'm wide awake. Ridge wouldn't be calling this early unless something is wrong.

"Shelby with you?" Wind muffles Ridge's voice, so I know he's outside.

"Yeah. I mean, no. Well, yes." *Jeez, Dallas, your brother doesn't need to know our sleeping arrangements.* "What's wrong?"

"Got some calves not breathing right. Pops and I separated them from the herd first thing this morning, but we need help to figure out what's wrong and to check the rest of the herd before it infects all of 'em."

"You sure they're not right?" Ridge isn't exactly the most optimistic person in the world. He's been known to be a bit of a hypochondriac when it comes to the herd.

He grunts. "The thermometer I stuck where the sun don't shine tells me this is serious."

I grimace, scrubbing a hand over my face. I never did take to ranching like my big brother and my parents, but I help out because it's the family business. Besides, the ranch can't really sustain all of us financially anyway. My woodworking projects bring in a steady paycheck, more so than ranching full-time would. Also, I tend to leave all rectal procedures to Ridge and licensed vets, namely Shelby.

"I'll go wake her up and be right over," I promise, ending the call and heading straight to my bedroom.

Shelby's curled on her side, sleeping peacefully. I rip the blankets away and nearly swallow my tongue seeing her in those stupid pajamas that leave very little to the imagination. She wakes instantly, already fighting mad.

"What are you doing?" She sits up and tries to snatch the covers back, but I hold them in front of me instead, just now realizing I forgot to put jeans on first.

"Ridge called about the herd. We have a problem."

That's all it takes to have her shifting into business mode. She leaps out of bed and points to the door. "Get out so I can get dressed."

"Yes, ma'am." I let go of the covers and head to get dressed myself but stop at the doorway to glance over my shoulder for one last look at those pajamas. Shelby's standing there next to my dresser, frozen in place with her hands gripping a pair of jeans. Her teeth have her plump bottom lip in their grasp.

Well, looky there. Shelby Sweet is staring at me as I walked away.

My grin is instant. And smug. "Like what you see, Sweetness?"

Her gaze flies to mine, eyes widening. She spins away with an audible huff. "Get out, Gamble!"

The grin only intensifies. "Yes, ma'am."

I close the door behind me. There's a bit of pep to my step as I find my clothes from last night and pull them on. Always did like a pretty lady's eyes on me.

By the time I get my boots on and find my wallet, Shelby's ready to go. We hurry to her Blazer without talking about the arrangements. I know her vehicle's loaded with all the equipment she needs for a vet visit, but I take the keys from her hand.

"Hey!"

"We can argue later about the fine line between old-fashioned gentlemanly gestures and overstepping toxic masculinity. For now, get your butt in the truck, and let's save my family's ranch, huh?"

She huffs, but does what I say, slamming her door just a little harder than necessary. "I can drive just fine, you know."

I crank the engine and back out of the driveway. "Just 'cause you're capable doesn't mean you should. What kind of man would I be if I let a woman drive me around?"

Shelby looks left and right out the windshield as I creep

down the dirt road that connects my house to the big house, careful to take it slow in the pitch black. "Well for one thing, you'd be a man who reaches his ranch much quicker. Would you step on it, grandpa?"

I put my elbow on the doorframe and take my time. "When safety is first, you last."

I can hear her eyes rolling in her head, but she doesn't argue with me further. We reach the big house a few minutes later, the headlights showing Pops waiting for us. Shelby hops out first and runs to him with her heavy medical bag in her hands. Pops updates us on what's going on.

"Pretty sure it's bovine respiratory disease. The two we put in the side paddock have fevers and labored breathing."

Shelby nods, focused on the job. "Shoot. I'll confirm the diagnosis. I've got antibiotics on hand, so we'll get them fixed up as quick as possible. You boys need to check the rest of them. Any sign of labored breathing or even runny noses means they need to be isolated until I can look them over."

Pops nods. "Will do."

Ridge is headed our way on horse, flanked by two more saddled horses for Pops and me. He's got his jaw clenched hard, which means the situation ain't good.

"How did they come down with it?" I ask the question I know we'll all be asking once we confirm this hasn't spread to the rest of the herd. Pops and Ridge are always so careful that something like this doesn't happen. We stay up on vaccinations and follow all protocol when introducing calves to the herd.

Ridge provides the answer, venom in his tone. "Calf got loose from the Kincaids' the other day when we had that lightning storm. Spent the morning with our herd before I got her out. Been warning them for months that their fence was weak on the south side. Fools didn't do a thing about it."

With a nod, Shelby heads for the paddock. She's got a job to do and probably doesn't want to get mixed up in another

Gamble versus Kincaid argument. We've hated that family for three generations, and one of their calves infecting our herd is only going to ramp up the feud. Entire herds can be wiped out by BRD, and if that's what happens here, you can bet your bottom dollar we'll be taking this feud to a courtroom.

"Those bastards have stolen horses, cattle, and Great Grandma's famous blackberry pie recipe that they're profiting from to this very day! Don't let 'em steal our ranch!" Meemaw yells from the front porch with a chicken in her arms. Dang. She must have decided to wear her hearing aids today. And what is she talking about with this blackberry pie nonsense?

Pops and I mount the horses, give Meemaw a wave, and with a click from our mouths, we're off. We roam around in the dark with the help of three high-powered flashlights, checking over every cow, steer, heifer, and calf until we find five more who show symptoms. It takes us until mid-morning to complete the inspections and get those five over to Shelby for her diagnosis. I'm hungry and tired by the time we dismount. More of the cattle might come down with symptoms, so we'll have to do rounds twice a day for the next week at least to stay on top of things.

Seven sick calves won't ruin our business, but if more fall sick, it could very well be the end of Big Ridge Ranch. It's not like we turn a high profit anyway. The time for lucrative family ranches ended at least a generation ago. Commercial ranches with tens of thousands of head are where the money's at.

We find Skye in the paddock helping Shelby with the calves. Noticeably missing is Tiff, Ridge's wife. That woman couldn't hit the water if she fell out of the boat. Needless to say, none of us have taken a liking to her much, and lately it seems like she and Ridge fight more than they share some kind of enduring love.

Ridge instantly goes to one of his calves, squatting down

to scratch its cute head and whisper something in its ear. The poor thing looks and sounds miserable.

"Grab another syringe for me, would you?" Shelby asks of Skye, nothing but cool efficiency in her tone while she loads another calf into the squeeze chute.

She takes the vial from Skye and injects the calf in the neck while crooning to it to keep it calm. She finishes, unloads the syringe gun, snaps off her gloves, and faces Ridge. Now's not the time to say it, but I'm proud of her. Seeing her work is a thing of beauty. Calm under pressure, highly effective, and knowledgeable as hell.

"We vaccinated all the newest calves for this just last week," Ridge grumbles.

"Fourteen days is peak immunity. Just didn't have enough time." She sighs. "All seven of them have it. I'd bet my truck on it, but I took samples for the lab to confirm."

Shelby lets the statement linger there. Skye looks at me. I look at Pops. Pops looks at Ridge.

"Crap," Ridge spits out, standing up and moving away from his precious calf. He pulls the cowboy hat off his head and runs his fingers through his hair before plopping the hat back on. "There'll be more."

Shelby winces. "I'm afraid you might be right."

"Surely we can do something to prevent the rest of the calves from coming down with it, right?" Skye asks.

Shelby nods. "Definitely. Get the mothers on over here to calm the little ones and keep them nursing. Let's keep the calves in a low-stress environment. Any storms, move as many of them into the barn as you can. And I'll work on getting some higher-end colostrum. Give them as much as they'll take."

"I'll text Houston and see if he can spare some time to come back and help us this week," I offer.

Ridge huffs like an angry bull. "Save your breath. Houston will never put family before the rodeo." Ridge's voice is as harsh as one of those lightning storms. "I'll go talk to the Kincaids."

"Now, don't run off with a hot head, son," Pops drawls.

Ridge's look could kill. "They need to be taught a lesson. 'Bout time they start ranching the right way and taking care of their calves." With that ominous threat, he stalks out of the paddock and back to his horse.

Skye and Shelby return to the calves. Pops says he'll go inside and make us all a late breakfast since we're going to be here a while. As for me, I pull out my phone and text Houston.

Me: Enough with the jokes. We have a serious problem with the ranch. We need your help. Call me ASAP.

CHAPTER
Eleven

IF YOU FIND YOURSELF IN A HOLE, STOP DIGGING

SHELBY

"Your fiancée is more stubborn than Skye's one-eared mule!" Pops shouts to Dallas as the latter heads our way from the paddock.

No way am I letting any of the Gambles pay for my time this morning. "I could say the same about you, old man," I volley back as I stash my bag in the back of my truck. I love my Blazer. She's big, she's quirky, she's Cookie-Monster blue, and I don't care what Dallas says. I'm driving us back.

"Who you calling old man? I'm sixty-five. I'm a spring frickin' chicken."

I can't say much in response since even I can admit Pops is a bit of a silver fox. No wonder his kids are so ridiculously attractive.

Meemaw squawks from the porch, "What's that about my chickens? You better not be messing with Isadora. She's got a show next week and I can't have her looking tired and raggedy. She's a shoo-in for the Feather Legged Bantams category!"

"Nobody's bothering those evil things, Meemaw!" Dallas brushes dust from his jeans as he joins us by the truck. "Pops just has his panties in a twist because Shelby won't charge him for today!"

"I told you that you can pay for the colostrum, didn't I?" I pin Pops with my best schoolmarm look. BRD is no joke. It can wipe out an entire family business in no time flat. The last thing the Gambles need right now is a bill from me. To lose even a few head means a cut to their bottom line. While cattle aren't the ranch's only form of income, every bit counts.

"If y'all are getting hitched, you may want to talk to your better half about getting paid what she's owed. You can't survive on love alone."

Dallas laughs as I close the door and lower my voice. "For Pete's sake, Pops. You know we're not really engaged." Far as I can tell, nobody outside the family is on to us, and my pride wants to keep it that way.

"Don't let Meemaw hear you. She's already planning the reception. Expect feathers and weed." Pops sends me a wicked grin that's far too similar to his son's.

"Sounds like a good time." Dallas winks, and the two men exchange identical laughs.

I cross my arms and nudge Dallas with my hip. "Did Dallas tell you he's promised to find me the perfect man?"

"Well, shucks, Shelby." Pops removes his hat and presses it against his chest. "I'm afraid my heart was claimed fifty years ago."

I can't help it. I pull the man into a hug. "Well, it's no mystery where Dallas got his ego—or his sense of humor." Pops cackles and hugs me back with one arm, returning his hat to its rightful place with the other. "Have Ridge call me when he gets back. I'll be wanting to stop by the Kincaid's after my rounds today."

"Will do. Thank you, darlin'."

"Anytime. I'll be back this afternoon."

I climb into the driver's seat before Dallas has a chance to protest. Just as I'm pulling the door shut, Pops gets in one last comment, the old troublemaker.

"You know, Shelby, you could do a lot worse than my boy here. Just sayin'."

Like I haven't thought of that before. But Pops is a realist. He's also a trouble maker.

"I will literally fight you for first dibs on your shower," I say as soon as I've turned the truck around. "That shower-head is almost worth marrying."

"Exactly what have you and my showerhead been up to, Ms. Sweet?" Dallas drawls from the passenger seat. When I respond with an eye roll, he continues, "Don't think it escaped my attention that you're driving this time."

"Look at you using your eyes." I carefully steer the truck over the gravel and dirt toward the east side of the property where Dallas's house sits.

Although I gave him a hard time about driving like a grandpa earlier, the truth is I drive like a senior citizen myself. Always have. Too many ways things can go wrong.

Then, for some stupid reason—maybe to make up for my sarcasm—I make a confession he doesn't need to hear. "One thing that always drove me nuts about Shane was his reckless speeding in that souped-up truck of his." He always brushed me off when I'd ask him to slow down, assuring me he was an excellent driver.

"I'd ask you to confirm that his eyesore of a vehicle is compensating for something, but I honestly don't need the mental image." Dallas fakes a shudder as I pull to a stop in his driveway.

That has me laughing out loud, but Dallas's next words shut me right up.

"Shane clearly never realized how precious his cargo was." And with that, he opens his door and hops out, boots hitting the drive with a crunch. "I'll take the upstairs bath-room and leave you alone with my showerhead."

———

"Well, Brad, don't let the door hit ya where the good Lord split ya." Dallas wears a self-satisfied smirk as he watches my second potential Prince Charming of the month flee the scene.

He seemed like a nice guy, not that I was given very long to acquaint myself. Dallas doesn't appear to have a firm grasp on the concept of matchmaking if his current strategy of grunting and being rude to all potential suitors is any indication.

I cross my arms over my chest and consider his smug face from my seat across from him. This time, it was just coffee and pie at Stuffin' the Muffin, but Brad didn't last even halfway through his first cup. "I don't know whether to laugh or punch you in the face."

Dallas casually sips his coffee like he hasn't a care in the world. "Have you always been this violent, or are you upset you're turning forty next week? I promise it's not that bad."

"That's because when men age, they grow a few gray hairs that make them even more attractive. We women, on the other hand, grow full mustaches and need industrial-strength bras to keep our boobs off our kneecaps. Luckily, I'm not there yet, but I can feel my hormones starting to conspire against me." When he looks at me like a cornered antelope, I abandon the topic. "Stop trying to change the subject." My elbow hits the table, and I ignore my chai latte. "What was wrong with Brad?"

Dallas appears downright flabbergasted at my question and eyes me like I'm two sandwiches short of a picnic. "Thank God I'm here because your character judgment is hopeless."

"The man is a firefighter. He's a civil servant!"

"That may be so, but he spent so much time looking at your body he forgot where he was. I'm shocked he didn't burn himself by dribbling scalding coffee down his chin."

The world doesn't have enough eye rolls to respond to that adequately. "Newsflash, Dallas. I'm a girl. I'm used to it." When my eyes drop down my body, his follow. "As your best friend, I might be essentially asexual to you, but I'm not that easy for most mere mortals to ignore." Hey, if I'm gonna be heavier than I want, at least I got nice curves to go with it. My grandma always said God never closes a door without opening a window, God rest her soul.

I lift my gaze back to my friend, but his lingers on my chest.

"If anyone has the right to look at you, it's your fiancé," he responds with enough vehemence it has my brows spiking.

"Ah, the irony." Honestly, how did I get myself into this situation in the first place? Oh, right. My taste in men.

Dallas drops the attitude and leans into the table, setting his coffee down. "Wait, what do you mean, I think you're asexual?"

I don't hesitate. "Junior year, Mr. Merchant's chemistry class. And I quote, 'You're probably the only girl in school I wouldn't dare cross that line with, Shelby.'" Teenage me will never forget that one.

"I meant it as a compliment," he protests. "And, besides, I only said that because you said I was the last guy on earth you'd ever hook up with."

I did say that. Of course I did. "For good reason."

Okay, being Dallas, he can't help but notice I'm a woman. But it doesn't mean anything, and it never has.

He doesn't respond, and I let the silence extend for a few moments until he finally relaxes back in his chair and reclaims his coffee. "Yeah, well, considering we're still best friends, we turned out to be pretty smart for a couple of dumb high school kids, I guess."

Billie Mars, one of the staff, appears beside our table, her hair pulled back in a high ponytail and tight top. "Where'd that hot guy get off to? I was hoping you'd introduce me." She twirls her pony with her finger like a teenager.

"He had to go to confession," Dallas deadpans.

I shoot him a quick glare and get busy derailing this line of conversation. "How's your daddy doing, Billie?"

"Real well." She nods. "Thanks for asking." Her father had a heart attack last month, so I'm glad to hear he's on the mend. "He's back at work and everything."

"Probably doesn't hurt having a sweet daughter like you keeping an eye on him. I know a pretty face always makes me feel better." Dallas offers a wide smile, his mood clearly shifting, Brad the firefighter all but forgotten.

She giggles and shoves his shoulder. Thank goodness a customer rings the bell at the counter, or she might climb in his lap next. Talk about awkward.

Dallas sips his coffee, oblivious as usual. "Seriously?"

"What?" He's the picture of innocence. No wonder his momma always let him get away with murder.

I gesture exasperatedly to the front counter. "She's probably going in the back to write her number on the back of our bill." I ignore Dallas's responding smirk. "You just can't help yourself. It's like I said the other night."

"I'm a flirty person. What do you want me to say? Everybody knows I don't mean anything by it. It's not like it's harming anyone."

"I could say the same about Elias—or Brad for that matter, even though he hardly had a moment to flirt before you scared him away."

"He was too busy imagining you topless."

"Hey, Shelby." Emilia Davies, a client of mine and a loan specialist at Big Knob's bank, waves as she nears our table. "Dallas," she acknowledges my fiancé with a little less warmth.

Happy for the distraction, I smile her way. "Hey, Emilia. Any word on Peaches?" Her mare is about to foal any day now.

"About ready to split in two, I reckon." A pretty, poised redhead in her early forties, Emilia has always been known for both her friendliness and candidness.

Dallas reaches over from his seat to pull out Brad's abandoned chair. "Can I ask you a question, Emilia?" When she nods and drops into the offered chair, Dallas continues, "We went out a few times, didn't we?"

She coughs out a half-laugh. "I might be a little offended you posed that as a question. Although I suppose it *was* a decade ago."

Dallas nods, all business now. What is he up to? "But we had a good time, right?"

Emilia shoots me a hesitant glance. "Are you sure this is a line of questioning you want to pursue with your fiancée sitting right across from you, Dallas?"

"Oh, don't worry about me." I brush off her concerns. "If I wanted to avoid all of the women in Dallas's illustrious dating history, I'd have to move to Portugal." I cross my legs and settle in. "I'd actually like to see where this is going."

Emilia pauses to assess my expression. Satisfied I'm being straight with her, she finally addresses Dallas's question. "Yes, Dallas, we had a good time. Brief, but good."

"See, Shelby?!" Dallas snaps straight in his chair, a hand thrown in my direction. "You act like I left a trail of devastation in my wake."

I open my mouth to respond, but Emilia beats me to it. "Oh, I was devastated. Absolutely." She turns to me, as if Dallas isn't even part of the conversation anymore. "I don't mind admitting that now that I'm happily married to Ben." I smile because her husband of five years is a lovely man who I'm certain writes her thoughtful love letters and surprises her at her office on her birthday with a dozen roses. "Things definitely worked out like they were supposed to in the end, but I listened to my fair share of Alanis Morissette while wishing your fiancé would suffer a painful death."

What did I just say about Emilia's candidness? I have to bite both lips between my teeth to keep from laughing.

Dallas's coffee mug hits the table with a loud clank, drawing our attention his way. "I'm gonna choose to ignore that last part." But his brows draw tight at his next question. "Did I really break your heart?"

Emilia sighs and apparently decides to throw him a bone. "I thought so at the time. Just like all the others did. But, rest assured, I'm all healed up."

"I don't know what to say, Emilia." His resemblance to a kicked puppy stirs all sorts of things in my chest. I should feel some sort of relief or even victory that Emilia literally just proved my point for me, but I can't muster much of anything but affection for the doofus sitting across from me. Until his next words, that is.

"You're a heck of a gal and quite the looker. I've always thought so," is what my best friend chooses to say.

Aaaand with that, Emilia stands to go. "I'm sure my husband would agree with you. Although I have no plans of sharing this bit of news with him since he might not take kindly to another man saying so." She squares her shoulders like the confident woman she is and nods. "Take care, you two. And congratulations. Good luck, Shelby."

I stay seated, slowly shaking my head at Dallas for longer than strictly necessary.

"I don't know what to say." He drops his head onto his forearms, where they rest limply on the tabletop.

As his best friend, I can't let him suffer for too long. "Aw, cheer up, Dally. At least you don't *actually* have a fiancée."

He lifts his head just enough to meet my eyes. "But *they* all think I do. Jesus, does everyone in town think I'm a monster?"

"No. Just me." I grin. "But you're *my* monster." And there goes his head again.

"I think I need a family intervention from Houston and Ridge," he mutters into his lap. "Those grumpy dudes couldn't flirt their way out of an open door. Maybe they can teach me how to suck at it."

I lean forward to pat him on the head. "Please don't. The world needs Dallas Gamble's signature charm and wit. Just maybe be more aware now when there could be hearts involved, yeah?"

"Yeah." He finally straightens, a little less desperation in his expression, although those parentheses between his eyes might be permanent now. "You know, maybe being engaged will be good for me. It will break me out of bad habits."

"Maybe it will be a good reset for both of us," I say. "And look at it this way, you can still flirt all you want, you'll just do it with men and on my behalf."

This gets a small grin out of him. "Somehow that doesn't sound as appealing. But you're right."

"Care to say that again?"

"No."

We finish our coffee and put our dishes in the bus bin on our way out. The summer humidity always does a number on my curls, and today is no exception. I fight with the afternoon breeze as it whips my hair around my face while we wander down the sidewalk toward my office and apartment. I need to pick up some more things if I'm staying with Dallas longer.

The results from the lab came back, telling us what we already knew. The calves all have BRD, so it's all hands-on deck over at the Gamble place.

"Hey, animal girl!" D'Wayne shouts from across the street where he's set up camp today. His signature orange stocking cap sits atop his wild gray hair, despite the heat. "Tell your sherpa to bring me a slice of Meemaw's blackberry pie next time."

I snicker to myself and wave. "Will do, D'Wayne!" He loves calling Dallas my sherpa because, more often than not, he's carrying something for me when we pass D'Wayne on the street. Dallas waves too, even though D'Wayne was talking to me. I've been "animal girl" to him ever since I found his cat after a tornado about twenty years back. Part of me thinks he has trouble remembering names, so he often calls people by strange nicknames.

Dallas and I continue down the sidewalk, and after a beat, he asks, "You know what I said about turning forty earlier? I might have lied."

"How so? Are your boobs sagging? Is your body falling apart?" Not from where I'm standing, that's for sure. I don't mention that part, though.

"Bite your tongue. It's just…I'm not usually one to step back and take stock too often, but I've been doing a little more of that lately. And not just today."

"Oh yeah? How so?" This is the side of Dallas nobody but me gets to see, and I always love it when I get a glimpse.

"I don't know. Maybe I'm having a midlife crisis or something. I mean, things with Ryder are good—or as good as they can be. It's easy to second-guess your parenting."

I nod, swatting at a sweat bee that's circling my head. "But you're a fantastic dad." I mean, this is the guy who installed an indoor swing and bought the best trampoline on the market a millisecond after learning they could help Ryder's sensory issues. "That kid is lucky."

"Thanks for that." Dallas slows his pace when he realizes I'm practically speed walking to keep up. "But sometimes I think about the example I'm setting for him. I pretty much do my own thing and put my own whims ahead of other priorities. I should be helping with the ranch more. Maybe helping Hallie with Ryd more. Heck, maybe taking a chance on a real relationship for once." He shakes his head as if trying to knock something loose. "I don't know. I'm probably talking nonsense."

No. I'm not letting him dismiss his own uncertainties and emotions. So, I link my arm in his and give it a tug. "Sounds like you've got a lot to think over. And you know you've always got me to bounce things off of. Just say the word."

He grins down at me, a warmth in his eyes that fills up something that was half-empty in my chest. "I probably don't say it enough, but I'm really lucky to have you in my life, Shelby Sweet."

Right back atcha, big guy. Right back atcha.

CHAPTER

Twelve

HOT AS A TWO-DOLLAR PISTOL

DALLAS

Nelly's tenth whining fit in as many minutes makes me turn off my sander and flip up my goggles. "I know, buddy. I wish I was skinny dipping in the lake right now too, but duty calls."

He blinks his doleful eyes and slumps back down to the hardwood floor I laid myself when I built my shop. He's killing me with that innocent face, but I have to get this project done for my client. I'm already a week late delivering the custom dining room table built from the client's own oak tree that fell in his backyard. There's a burnt streak running through it from the lightning that struck it. It's actually one of the coolest pieces I've done. I should be proud of my work, but all I feel right now is exhaustion. Between riding around the ranch and checking calves, my own woodworking, my son, and pretending to be Shelby's fiancé, I'm beat. Something's gotta give.

I pull out my phone and call Houston again. It's noon. He should be up by now, even if he rode last night. Despite my irritation at him deserting the ranch and only rarely coming home for visits, I'm proud of the dude. He's made a name for himself on the rodeo circuit, managing to win a few events on the Rockies circuit and avoid major injury. Rodeo is a bit like gambling, though. He can't seem to quit until he's won an overall, which is where the big money's at.

"You're, like, obsessed with me," Houston deadpans by way of greeting.

"Yeah, well, I'm up to my elbows in the backside of an animal more times than I'd like, so I figured I'd share that experience."

"If that's your way of trying to get me to come home, you're doing it wrong."

I lean back against the table I'm building, swiping the sawdust from the scruff I haven't had time to shave. "Seriously. I'm not cut out for full-time ranch work. Especially with my woodworking taking off recently."

"And you think I am?" Houston scoffs. "I've got back-to-back rodeos lined up, man. I can't just pull out of one when they're using my name for advertising to get butts on bleachers."

"Not even when it's a family emergency? They don't make exceptions for that?" I ask with a bit more heat in my tone. I'm tired of that being his excuse every time we try to get him to come home.

Family before all else.

That's the credo the Gamble family has always lived by. And Houston is turning his back on it. On us.

"You being careful with Shelby?" Houston changes the subject like he always does when he knows I'm mad at him.

"I'm always careful with Shelby," I grouse. I stand back up and run my hand along the bottom edge of the table. There's a tiny knot there I need to sand down.

"No, I mean *real* careful. That girl had a thing for you a

long time ago. Don't go play-acting your way into messing with her heart."

I scoff, nearly choking on my own spit. "She did not!"

Houston's chuckle is annoying. "She did. Oh, she was real subtle about it, but I specifically remember catching her staring longingly at you when we were seniors. Be careless with the randos' hearts, but don't do that to Shelby. She's my friend too, you know."

My knees give way, and I sit my butt down on the old rickety chair I keep in the shop. The wheels fly across the floor, crunching over sawdust. Nelly barks and chases after me, his tail going crazy. "If that's true, why didn't you ever say something?"

Houston yawns loudly in my ear, pissing me off even more. "What would have been the point? I knew you didn't feel that way about her and telling you would have only embarrassed her. Again, Shelby's my friend too. I didn't want you breaking her heart."

There's a commotion on his end of the phone. "Man, I gotta go. Someone's always gettin' in a fight." With a click, he's gone.

I shake my head and stare at my dark phone screen. Just like Houston to drop a bomb and then abruptly leave. What does he mean, Shelby had a thing for me? Never, not once, did she and I cross that friend line. We mutually agreed right from the start to only be friends. Partly because Houston is right. I wouldn't have been able to give her what she wants, so why ruin a good friendship?

He must be wrong. That's the only option here that makes sense.

Lifting my right hip, I pull out my wallet and stare at the napkin, both our signatures faded over the years but still legible.

"There's no way," I tell Nelly. He licks my arm, then starts sneezing out the sawdust, making a racket. "There's no way

Shelby had a thing for me. Not then, not now, not ever. And that's that."

I tuck the napkin back in my wallet and get busy finishing this project. When I've got it completed to my satisfaction, I text the client to schedule a pick-up time and head for my truck, intent on getting to Ridge and seeing what kind of help he needs over there.

When I get to the big house, Shelby's truck is in the driveway. Nelly came along but abandons me to chase after Meemaw's chickens. I head for the paddock, wanting to see if this morning's round netted any more sick calves.

Ridge is nowhere to be found. Pops is pacing while on his cell phone, looking like he's ready to try his luck in a fistfight. Shelby's down on the ground in the corner of the paddock with a calf I don't think was here yesterday. Wade Barlow, the young farmer who rents part of our land, is hovering just a bit too closely to Shelby, his gaze taking in her backside as she's crouched down.

I clear my throat, and his eyes shoot to mine. He lifts his hand to wave at me, stupid grin on his face, like we're pals. Okay, fine, normally we are pals, but not today. I glower at him and decide we need better rules on who can come into the paddock.

"Got some wheat to harvest, Barlow?"

Shelby glances up at the sound of my voice, but her hands stay busy, working on the calf. I step up to the group, putting my body between Shelby and Wade's eyeballs. He won't be staring at my fiancée on my watch.

"Finished up yesterday," he proudly proclaims.

A man in overalls and a worn-out straw hat shouldn't have that much confidence. I appreciate the rental income he provides the family, and I definitely appreciate farmers in general. I just don't appreciate him sticking to Shelby like white on rice.

"Awesome. Now get out."

His smile slips from his face. "Oh, so it's one of those days, huh?"

Shelby snorts below us but doesn't say anything. Frankie, who just came through the gate and heard only the last part of this conversation, hollers.

"Hey there, Wade! How many ground squirrels did you kill this harvesting season?" Oh, dang. Looks like Frankie hasn't forgiven him for flirting with her wife before Wade knew who she was.

Wade pulls off his hat and pretends to be contrite. "I'm just a peaceful farmer. I don't slaughter animals." Then he mumbles so quietly only Shelby and I hear him. "Unlike you ranchers."

It's a long-standing joke between us, one we'll never quit arguing about. Thankfully, none of us takes any of it seriously. With both of us glaring at him, Wade tips his head, flips us the bird, and scoots out of the paddock. Shelby stands up, wiping her hands on her thighs.

"This poor thing is miserable. We lost two calves yesterday, and Ridge brought in four more with symptoms this morning."

We all look over at Pops, who's now growling into the phone. "Who's he talking to?"

Shelby makes a face. "I think it's the bank."

Dread lines my stomach with lead. I know the land and the big house are paid off, but property taxes and ongoing expenses of running a ranch this size required Pops and Meemaw to take out a loan a few years ago. When everything goes right, we can make those payments and still make a living. But when calves start dying off, things get dicey.

This place is Momma's family legacy, and I know Pops feels a lot of responsibility for making things work. In fact, Momma always wanted us to expand the ranch, but we just haven't been able to. Pops and Ridge fight over who's to blame for that.

"I've got three more to look over before I head out," Shelby says, quietly moving away to the other calves. I don't blame her. I wouldn't want to stick around in uncomfortable silence either if I didn't have to.

Frankie looks back at me, determination in those brown eyes. "Skye, Meemaw, and I have some ideas to help us out. Don't you worry."

I make a face. "Uh yeah, I do worry. Whatever Meemaw says, cock fights are illegal, okay? And no, we ain't turning this land into a pot farm."

Frankie grins. "Make a lot more money that way."

"No, Frankie."

"Alright, alright. Calm down." Frankie looks behind her where Shelby's helping another calf, then wiggles her eyebrows and drops her voice when her eyes come back to me. "Want to tell me why you were about to put your hands around Wade's red neck?"

I lean in, whispering as quietly as I can. "He was staring at Shelby's butt!"

Frankie giggles. "So? She's got a great butt."

I avoid commenting on that. "He still shouldn't be looking at it."

Frankie tilts her head to the side, studying me, and a warning bell rings in my head. I've made a misstep somewhere, but I'm not sure where or how or why.

"You ever wonder why you're so protective of Shelby?"

I shrug. "No. She's my best friend. Of course I'm protective."

Frankie nods but doesn't lose that cocky grin. "Is it possible you have feelings for her that go beyond friendship?"

To that idea, I scoff. Loudly. "I have feelings beyond friendship for every woman."

"But not Shelby," Frankie confirms.

"Correct." My brain tries to bring up what Houston told me this morning, but I tell it to shut up.

"Have you considered why?"

"Huh?" Now she's lost me. Woman logic is circular and windy and littered with leaps into fairytale land.

Frankie leans in, entirely too excited. "Like maybe if you ever let yourself go there with her, you'd fall head over boots in love with the woman?"

I stare at her, refusing to even acknowledge that notion. "Does Morgan know you've lost your mind?" I lean away and step around her. "If you'll excuse me, I need to hose off before my sawdust causes more respiratory damage to these calves."

Frankie's laugh echoes after me. Dang, sisters are annoying.

On the side of the faded red barn, I breathe in the warm air, stretching my back and wondering if Ryder and I can sneak away this weekend to the lake. Summer sure is hot around here, but it doesn't last long enough for my liking. We need to enjoy it while we can. Shelby can read her latest romance novel on a picnic blanket, and he and I can practice his backstroke while getting a reprieve from the heat. That idea sounds like the perfect summer weekend plan.

I grab the hose off the side of the barn and crank the spigot. Letting the first bit feed the dry ground, I strip off my shirt and belt, hanging them over the fence post. When the cooler water flows, I lift the hose over my head and let it rain down over me, washing off the sawdust and sweat. Damn, that feels amazing. The cool water reminds me of all the times us kids would run through the sprinklers in the summer.

I have to scrub my hand over my skin to dislodge off all the wood shavings, but I get the job done. It's only as I twist to shut off the spigot that I find Shelby standing outside the paddock, frozen in place, staring at me.

My skin heats all over again, and it has nothing to do with

the hot summer sun. I slowly slip my hand down my chest, flinging off some water. "Want me to turn it on again so you get a longer show?" I holler, teasing her. I don't even think about it. Flirting is just a reflex at this point.

Shelby snaps back to attention. "No, thanks. I don't want to get nauseous!" Then she sticks her tongue out at me.

"Real mature!" I holler back.

She spins and struts back into the paddock with the syringe in hand, giving me a glimpse of the backside that had Wade mesmerized. Can't really blame the guy.

Then Frankie's accusation and Houston's warning play on repeat in my brain, and I get dressed, putting Shelby firmly back in the friend box I've always kept her in. Things are way less confusing that way.

CHAPTER
Thirteen

HANGIN' IN THERE LIKE HAIR IN A BISCUIT

SHELBY

Do cowboys make calendars like firefights do? If they don't, they should. Holy mother of pectorals!

Day to day, it's easy to forget how hot Dallas is. I mean, there are so many other things about him to distract from the packaging. Like how he sings so off tune that Nelly can't help but join in the howling, and how truly terrible his dad jokes are, and how he insists on first eating all the crust off his sandwiches and is subsequently shocked every time when the rest of it falls apart in his hands.

Or how he gets giddy as a schoolgirl at the start of a new woodworking project, and he rides a horse like he was born on one. And he tells the best stories about anything at all, but mostly about his family. And how he listens in a way you know he's not just thinking of what he wants to say next.

But every once in a while—and especially in these last weeks I've been living with him—I am acutely reminded of exactly how breathtaking the man is. Case in point, this cowboy shower scene that's playing out behind me right this freaking minute.

One second, I was scraping cow patties off my boot, and the next I looked up to see my best friend with his head thrown back under the hose spray, water gliding over his muscular upper body and plastering his jeans to his thick thighs. All he needed was a Bluetooth speaker blasting "Pony" by Ginuwine, and he could sell tickets.

Of course, when he caught me staring with my tongue hanging out, I came to my senses. Thank goodness. Lusting after my bestie is not allowed. Even if we already shared the best kiss of my life. Nope.

"What's the matter? You look a little flushed," Skye says, appearing at my side out of nowhere.

"What? Who? Me? No." Jeez. I sound so guilty I'm embarrassing myself.

Thankfully, she lets me off the hook. This is one very good reason why we're friends. Frankie will get all up in your business like a chihuahua sniffing for bacon on your breath, but Skye understands that sometimes a girl just needs to keep stuff to herself.

"Pops looked upset. Is it the calves? How many now?"

I exhale loudly, taking in the scene around us. Nine mommas and their calves stand swishing their tails or napping in the paddock to the west of the barn. A water trough has been hauled over for extra hydration, one of the farm dogs drinking from it like it's his personal water dish. "We're up to nine diagnosed and still living as of last count. Haven't lost any more since we talked yesterday, though, so there's that."

"If Ridge hadn't already ripped the Kincaids a new one over their fence and crappy animal management, I'd be on Lulu's back right now delivering a big ol' talking to the likes of which they've never seen. Who is running things over there anyway?" Skye is fit to be tied, not that I blame her.

"I stopped by to offer my services, but Boyd declined, of course. They've got a vet in OKC they bring out."

"No surprise there. Those rich jerks wouldn't dare use a local vet, no matter you could run circles around any stick-up-their-butt big city doctor. Besides, they only care about their mineral rights, not the poor animals they pretend to farm."

Since I can't argue with her there, I get back to the matter at hand. "Hey, just thought you should know Pops was on the phone with the bank. Don't know what was said, but I'm pretty sure the conversation explains the look on his face."

"Crap." Skye's manicured brows scrunch together, and she glances toward the house where Pops must have disappeared. "Okay, thanks, Shelbs. We'll talk later."

I nod and head for my truck. There's an arthritic alpaca named Weasel waiting for me on the other side of town, and the last thing I need is to hang around here waiting for more cowboys in showers.

"Hey! Where you goin'?" Speak of the devil.

I spin to see Dallas, thankfully wearing a T-shirt now, even though his jeans are still stuck to him like a second skin.

I clear my throat and square my shoulders. "Gotta get to my next client."

He runs a hand through his wet hair as he gets closer, and now we're in the middle of a shampoo commercial. I need to get out of here. "Let's grab drinks tonight at Knockin' Boots. Whaddya say?"

And maybe because he's shooting me that lopsided grin, or maybe because I can't resist country music and a beer, or maybe because he's my best friend in the world, I nod. "Sounds like a plan."

Not five minutes after I pull onto Big Knob Road, my phone rings on the dash. I smile before hitting accept and pressing the speaker button.

"Hey, little brother. What's up?" My brother, Archie, lives

in Tulsa, a good three and a half hours east of Big Knob, where he works as a lawyer.

"I should be the one asking *you* that." His voice has a frustrated edge to it. Uh oh. "Dallas? Really?"

I decide to play dumb to buy myself half a second. "You know I hate Texas, Arch. So, no, I have no plans to visit Dallas anytime soon." I turn the steering wheel to take a back road and skip downtown.

"As much as my younger self always claimed, you've never been stupid, and you're not now. Tell me why Charlene just texted me that you and Dallas are getting married?"

Why can't Charlene—and everyone else in this town, for that matter—mind her own business? Sure, I consider pretending I don't know what he's talking about. What is he going to do, drive here to call my bluff? But things always have a way of coming to light when it comes to Archie and me, so, of course, I give in.

"It's complicated."

"So is *my* love life. Explain."

I sigh and shake my head at the rows of waving wheat stalks catching the summer breeze as I pass. "We're not really engaged. We're just pretending."

"How old are you? Ten?"

"Very funny. It's for a good reason. Well, kind of." When he doesn't miraculously change the subject, I'm forced to continue. "You remember Shane?"

"I remember you telling me about him. I also remember thinking to myself, I hope he isn't anything like Richie. Or Marco. Or that bounty hunter guy—what was his name?"

Must we recap my entire dating life? "Olaf. And he wasn't a bounty hunter; he was a bail bondsman." Olaf actually wasn't bad. I just kind of got bored with him, if I'm being honest.

"Fine. My bad. So, what about Shane?"

"Well, turns out your hoping didn't work. Thanks, though."

"Damn, sis. I'm sorry. Maybe you should look into becoming a nun. I hear convent life has evolved a lot in the last couple centuries."

Archie might be the most practical person I know. He's the guy with a 401(k), a condo in a well-established corner of Tulsa, and a life insurance policy—even though he's single.

"Unless the pope decides to let nuns marry and have kids, that's not gonna work for me." My truck tires throw up red dust as the road turns to dirt, and I inhale the earthy scent through my open window.

"Okay, so how does Shane being an idiot require you to propose marriage to Dallas?"

"Who says I was the one to propose?!" I sputter.

I'm shocked Archie doesn't pass out from choking so hard on his laughter.

"Rude," I'm compelled to add.

Still chuckling, he says, "Sorry, Shelbs, but you sewed yourself the first of *many* wedding dresses when you were twelve, and Dallas Gamble was voted most likely to die single from a venereal disease in high school. Just using my basic deduction skills here."

"Well, Sherlock, I'll have you know that neither of us proposed. Dallas just sort of…announced it. In public. In front of Shane."

"Oh crap." He's not laughing now, is he?

"Oh crap is right," I barrel on. "And now the whole town thinks we're engaged because Dallas was trying to do this stupid noble thing and protect me!"

"Protect you?" Crap. "What does that mean?"

Double crap. "Um, nothing. How's work?"

"Nothing, my butt. If you don't tell me, you know Gamble will be my next call, so you may as well spit it out."

Archie may be my little brother, but his protective streak is big and burly. And so is his affection for me.

So, I tell him about Shane being aggressive and rude and slightly stalkerish. And even though I do my best to tone it down, it takes all the way to the Fultons' farm and poor Weasel to talk him out of storming out here on his trusty steed (a practical, midsized SUV) to avenge me.

"Let me know when you set a date," he finally says when I tell him I need to go.

I pull my keys from the ignition and pause. "Have you even been listening this whole time?" Sometimes I wonder if I'm the central character in my own psychedelic nightmare.

His response? "Yeah." And then he hangs up.

———

"Shelby'll have a lager. Just the bottle, no glass. And an order of hummus with the pita things toasted and extra carrots."

Norinne eyes me over her reading glasses before turning to Dallas. "I've been taking her order for going on twenty years, Dallas. I know what the woman drinks."

Dallas lets her comment slide right off his back, smiling at both of us and leaning back in his side of the booth. "Just making sure my woman gets what she needs."

Norinne grins and finishes jotting on her order pad. "I don't know what you did to him, Shelby, but next time I'm in need of a miracle, I'm calling you up." I'm not entirely certain how to take that, but I smile back anyway. Norinne is good people.

I survey the bar, and it's the same scene as always. Couples taking up booths along the walls lined with old photographs of Big Knob from the 1890s when Andrew Johnson (not the former US president) founded our little town. Chatty groups of townsfolk are throwing a few back while they play darts and gossip.

We're not drawing quite as much attention tonight, as people in town have gotten used to the idea of us being together. For the first week or so, we were a science experiment everyone kept marveling at under a microscope. Glad that's no longer the case.

I wonder if Dallas is right, and we can really pull this off. Our friendship needs to go back to what it was before I lose my mind. I mean, why have I been getting all hot and bothered just because we're living together?

I chance another glance at Dallas to find him watching me with a wrinkled brow. I hope he can't read my mind.

A few weeks ago, Dallas could have smiled and flung his arm around my shoulders, and I would have tipped my head back and told him he was a goober. Now I get nervous butterflies in my belly.

When Ryder is staying with us, it's more like the old days. We play games and watch stupid shows, and I try my best to make them both eat salad. But when he's gone, the tension in the air is harder to ignore. I'm sure I'll get over it. Lord knows, I have to.

I blame it on that kiss. And here we are, back at the scene of the crime.

"We can go if you want." Dallas's words bring me upright.

"No! Sorry. Did *you* want to leave?" This is dumb. I'm letting my worries become such a distraction that I'm horrible company.

"Not unless you do?" He looks uncertain.

What is happening here? Since when are we so polite and deferential with one another? This has got to stop right now.

My smile is sincere now, and my focus is firmly on Dallas. "I was just up in my head. It's nothing." I shake my head. "Did the client love the table?"

Dallas's grin is back. "Of course he did." He laughs at my eye roll. "He did say it was worth the drive from OKC to pick it up, so I'll take that as a win. And now I can pay the electric bill this month."

He's kidding—his creations actually go for increasingly high amounts these days—but I'm pleased for him. He gets to do what he loves for a living, and not a lot of people can say that. It does remind me of something, though.

"Hey, you still haven't let me pay for anything at your place." Despite my bringing this up numerous times, I've gotten nowhere with it. When I finally suggested I move back to my place, it didn't go over any better.

"Last I checked, you were still paying for your own place. No need for you to pay twice."

One of the other waitresses drops our drinks off, and I lean in to keep our conversation private. The band hasn't started yet, so it's best to keep it down. "At least sleep in the dang bed, Dallas. You're walking around like an ogre who just escaped a dungeon, all hunched over from that couch." Okay, that's a lie, but I have seen him rubbing his back lately, even though he fibs and says it's nothing.

"You're not sleeping on the couch." His tone is firm.

"Then we can share the bed. It's a king. There's room for *three* people in that thing." Now, why did I just suggest that?

Dallas appears to have the same second thoughts. "I'm not sure that's the best idea. You don't seem to own any pajamas that aren't X-rated."

"I'll buy some."

"Please don't." He winks, and I just know I'm blushing.

"Here's your hummus, hon." Norinne sets the platter on the table between us and dashes off.

Dallas grabs his beer, slides out of the booth, and crosses to my side. When I look up at him with a raised eyebrow, he motions for me to scoot over. So, I do, but I do it laughing to myself.

"Are your hands so tired from sanding that you need me to feed you?" I ask as he settles in.

Instead of answering, he snakes one arm around my shoulders and cups my jaw with the other hand.

Just as I open my mouth to ask what he's doing, I spot Shane watching us from the far side of the bar. He has a beer in one hand, the other shoved into his jeans pocket. And from the expression on his face, I can tell there's no way in hell Dallas will be letting me move out anytime soon.

It's with that thought in my head that I throw all common sense out the window and close the distance to meet Dallas's lips with my own.

Eh, my apartment isn't really that great anyway.

The second our lips touch, fire races down my spine and swirls low in my belly. I'm right back on that dance floor, immediately lost in Dallas. If my kiss surprised him, it doesn't show. His fingers delve into my curls and grip the back of my head, pulling me closer. He skims the tip of his tongue across my bottom lip and slides it inside when I let out a quiet whimper.

If we were standing, I know for a fact my knees would buckle right now, just like I know Dallas would catch me before I fell. I bring my hand up to curve around the side of his neck, pressing the pads of my fingers into his warm skin. His whiskers tickle my chin as he angles for better access, making me burrow closer.

Amber and cardamom, mixed with a woodsy note, fill my nose as I draw in a breath to remain conscious. I shiver when Dallas deepens the kiss and pulls firmly on my hair to angle me again. I fist his shirt and swallow his groan, starting to lose control.

It's only when I shift to get a knee under me and climb onto his lap that Dallas pulls back, breath labored and eyes drunk with lust.

"Whoa there, tiger," he half-growls and half-laughs.

I blink a few times, and reality begins filtering back in. We're in public. At a bar. And I'm practically mounting my best friend in front of people I grew up with. In fact, there's Pastor Dan. I manage a weak wave his way and make a note to avoid him for the next fifty years.

Several people cover their mouths to hide their mirth, and I bury my flaming face in Dallas's shoulder as his body shakes with laughter. But not before noting that Shane has disappeared.

CONFUSED AS A GOAT ON ASTROTURF

DALLAS

It's day seven of waking up so frustrated I'm not sure I slept at all. I'm pretty sure that's not healthy. Middle-aged guys can't handle this sort of temptation without an ensuing heart attack. Yeah, Shelby's taken to wearing oversized sweats and T-shirts to bed, and I've been joining her, both of us religiously sticking to our own side of the bed. But just the idea of her being so close all night is driving me out of my mind.

I blame the kissing. Dang, the woman can kiss. She's feisty in conversation but then goes all soft and warm and malleable in my arms. Honestly, I've become a little obsessed with her mouth. I find myself staring at her lips when we're talking, daydreaming about ways I can get her in public and therefore have a reason to kiss her.

Heck, sometimes I wake up in the middle of the night and just stare at her sleeping like some kind of creep, wishing I could pull her into my arms and wake her up with a kiss that turns hotter.

Instead of doing any of that, I slide out of bed, and will my thoughts to behave. I told Ridge I'd ride out with him at daybreak to look over the herd. Nelly lifts his head from his dog bed. I swear he's shaking his head at me. I shake my head at him, and he whines as he lowers his head back to his paws.

He's taken to ditching me in favor of shadowing Shelby. Even my own dog prefers her company. Believe me, he deserves the stern look.

My worn jeans feel like concrete as I try to stuff myself into them. I don't think I can be married to Shelby and remain celibate. It's impossible. One glance at her licking her lips after she eats supper at my table and I'm ready to throw caution to the wind and damn the consequences.

I am all too aware that I sound like a teenage boy who can't control himself. At the ripe old age of forty, you'd think I'd have a handle on my raging hormones, but it's like this fake engagement with Shelby has created some sort of midlife hormonal renaissance.

Ridge isn't the only surly one this morning as he and I ride out on Whiskey and Echo, Ridge's preferred no-nonsense horse. We're quiet, enjoying the scenery while a sense of dread puts a damper on the morning. The humidity is cranked high already this morning. Even the insects are taking the day off to keep cool. I'm hopeful we won't find any more sick calves. With the ones we've lost already, we'll take a pretty significant financial hit this year, but it won't devastate the ranch. At least according to Pops. I don't want to think about what will happen if we find more.

"Who pissed in your Cheerios?" Ridge finally asks after we've been riding for over half an hour.

I look over in surprise. Ridge isn't a talkative guy on a good day. I figured he'd appreciate my sour mood and the quiet ride even more.

"I could ask you the same."

Ridge grunts. "Tiffany Grace is going to her parents in South Carolina for a visit."

I deserve a gold buckle for holding back the eye roll. There's a time and place for talking crap about Ridge's wife, and to his face is not one of them. "Seems like an odd time to leave when we need all-hands-on-deck."

He doesn't answer for a bit. When he does, his tone makes it clear he doesn't want to talk about it. He never does. Those two have been having problems for the entirety of their marriage. There's no love lost between the rest of us and Tiff. We keep nudging Ridge in the direction of divorce, but he's stubborn as a mule. Guess he wants to wallow in his unhappiness for the rest of his life. Sounds like torture to me.

"Can I ask you a question?" It's out before I have a chance to rethink what I'm about to ask.

Ridge grunts, which I take as a yes. He has a lot of grunts, and after forty years of knowing the guy, I pride myself on knowing the difference between his various grunts.

"How'd you know you were in love with…your wife?" I stumble over my words, refusing on principle to call her Tiffany Grace. The woman's got her nose so high in the air she can smell a storm coming from across the Gulf.

Ridge's jaw clenches even harder than usual, but as we come over the ridge and see a cluster of the cattle we've been looking for, he answers me. "Not sure I'm the authority on this topic, but when she had me so crazy in the head I couldn't live without her, I put a ring on it."

I grimace, spitting out a laugh. "So, being messed up in the head is how you know?"

"Yup," Ridge mutters, then clicks his mouth and takes off toward the herd, leaving me behind to contemplate what I'm pretty sure is bad advice. Because, according to Ridge's definition, I'm in love with Shelby.

And ain't that a kick in the pants?

"Crap," I say to the breeze. "Maybe I should have asked Pops."

But Pops would get all twinkly in the eye and inquisitive. Then he'd tell Frankie about our conversation, and she'd be all over me, asking about my feelings and wanting to talk it out. I'd rather she save her breath for breathing.

I eventually catch up to Ridge and the herd. We sort through the young ones and check on their condition. When neither of us finds any sick calves, we ride on, the boulder on both our shoulders a little lighter.

"You know, I think my issue is I have too much blood in my brain."

"Huh?" Ridge looks over at me like I've officially lost it.

"No, no. Hear me out. I think I've figured it all out." I toss back my head and laugh at the puffy clouds dotting the great big sky, high off the sheer genius of my idea. "I've been pretending to be engaged to Shelby, which means I haven't been flirting or dating anyone else. I wouldn't embarrass Shelby by stepping out on her. So, all that blood is usually further south, and it's messing with my thinking."

I look at Ridge expectantly, waiting for the confirmation that I'm brilliant. I mean, come on. This has to be what's going on. It's certainly more plausible than being in love with Shelby, right?

But I don't get an "atta boy." I get an aggressive head shake like I'm an idiot. Ridge slows his horse, then turns to his bulky upper body in the saddle, wrists crossed on the pommel. "Here's what you're gonna do, little brother. You're gonna romance the heck out of her and see if there's any sparks. You see fireworks and lose your head, you'll know."

"Isn't that just physical compatibility? I've felt that way countless times for various women."

Ridge grins at me, and it's nice to know he still has the muscle capacity for it. "Nah. There's a difference. Do what I said, and if it feels like every other woman, then you know it's not love."

I roll that around in my brain. "You know what? You're kind of smart."

Ridge clicks at his horse again, calling over his shoulder as they take off, "Don't you forget it."

———

The front door slams shut just after seven. I rush out of the kitchen and have to press my fist to my mouth. Shelby's bent over, pulling off her clean boots at the entryway, looking gorgeous in skin-tight Levi's, a work shirt, and her hair a mass of curls around her shoulders.

"Sorry I'm late!" she calls, not realizing I'm behind her.

Dropping my fist, I force myself to focus. I have a plan in place for tonight. I gotta figure things out before it gets awkward between us.

"Welcome home." I walk closer, and as she straightens, I hold my hand out to her. She takes it, looking at me with questions in her eyes. "I've got a bubble bath all set up. You've got just enough time to enjoy that before the spaghetti and French bread are done."

"What's all this?" Shelby asks, cheeks flushed and expression hesitant. Like spaghetti is something to be excited about. Sadly, it's about the only thing I can make from scratch that doesn't taste like shit. Ryder gets spaghetti twice a week when he's with me, poor guy.

I shrug. "You said yesterday you haven't been sleeping well. Figured I'd show you the domesticated side of Dallas Gamble."

Shelby laughs but lets me lead her to the bathroom where the steam from the bath has fogged up the mirror. She gasps at the mountain of bubbles. "Did you use the whole bottle?"

I glance over her shoulder. Huh. Yeah, those are kind of

high, now that she mentions it. She might not even be able to see above them once she sinks into the tub. "Ryder doesn't really do bubbles. I wasn't sure how much to put in." I scratch the back of my neck. "So, you *don't* use the whole bottle?"

Her tinkling laugh is my answer. She stares at me. I stare at her, mesmerized by her lips stretched into the prettiest smile I've seen. And then her smile drops.

"Well, get out now, Dally!"

I startle, backing out the door. "Sorry. Yeah, enjoy. I'll go get supper ready."

She shuts the door in my face, and I run a hand over my five o'clock shadow. *Jeez. Get your crap together, Gamble.* I'm feeling more and more like the idiot Ridge thinks I am. I stand there until I hear a splash, and then my brain conjures a scene that has me darting away from the bathroom to the kitchen to distract myself.

I'm just stirring the spaghetti in the big pot one last time when Shelby appears in sweatpants and a tank top, hair piled high on top of her head, a few loose strands hanging in her face. I notice her big toe has a chip in the red polish. I make a mental note to paint her toes tonight while we watch a show before bed. She doesn't paint her fingernails because of her work, so she makes a special effort to keep her toes polished. Always has.

"Ready to eat?" I ask, turning back to throw food in a bowl for Nelly so he'll let us eat in peace.

The oven timer goes off. Shelby grabs the oven mitt before I can, and then she's bending over again. My gaze goes straight to her curvy backside. Not even a pair of sweats can hide her beauty.

Suddenly, I'm not hungry for food at all. I had a plan for tonight, but now I'm throwing that out the window. I need to put Ridge's idea to the test. Shelby sets the bread on the stovetop and pulls off the mitt. When she spins around, I grab her by the hips and move her into the center of the room, away from the hot surfaces.

"Alexa, play 'We Danced' by Brad Paisley."

Shelby gasps, startled by how close I've gotten or by the song choice, I'm not sure. The music starts to play, and I pull her into a slow dance. She drops her forehead to my chest.

"Dallas," she murmurs, voice thick.

I pull her closer, spinning her slowly around the room. "I should have been dancing with you more often. They would have wanted that." Referring, of course, to her parents and the song they played that day I met them. They died in the car crash just a week later.

Shelby sucks in a shaky breath, but lets me lead her around the kitchen, the words sinking in and turning this from a casual friend supper to something far deeper. I think about what Ridge said. *If it's like every other woman, then it's not love.*

Shelby has never felt like any other woman. She's entirely separate from every encounter I've ever had with a female. She's already head and shoulders above any of those experiences, and we haven't even done more than kiss.

As the second half of the song plays out, I back her up and pin her against the countertop. She lifts her head from my chest. Her watery eyes open wide, and her tongue darts out to lick her bottom lip. My fingers squeeze her hips and then they're traveling, sliding under her tank top and smoothing across her waist. Damn, her skin is so soft. Quick puffs of air hit my chest, and I realize she's breathing hard. I haven't even touched any of the good parts, and Shelby's out of breath.

"Can I kiss you?" I ask, like I'm a preteen needing confirmation he can kiss a girl for the first time.

What is wrong with me? I've kissed her multiple times already. But this…well, this feels different. There's no one here to see us. No fake engagement story we need to keep up. No pretenses. No stories. No reason other than I might not be able to function if I don't get my lips on hers in the next two seconds.

F

"Dallas?" Shelby whispers, her head now tilted back in offering. Oh lordie, she's already going soft, and I haven't even taken her into my arms yet.

"Yeah, honey?"

She reaches between us and fists my T-shirt, pulling me violently closer. "Kiss me already!"

My grin is quickly lost as I wrap my arms around her waist, hike her up onto the counter, step between her knees, and kiss the stuffing out of my best friend. My tongue plunders her mouth before I even get my hands up to her face, needing to be closer like I need to breathe. My fingers dive into her hair and snag on the sloppy bun. She moans into my mouth, and goose bumps line my skin. She whimpers, shaking like a leaf.

Her hands slide under my shirt and scrape up my back, nails digging into my skin. I nip at her bottom lip, the one that's been taunting me for weeks, then plunge back inside her mouth. She's mewling in the back of her throat, the knowledge of her desperation for the same thing I want making me absolutely wild with need. I can't think straight. I just…need.

"What song would you like me to play now?" Alexa blares from the speaker right next to us.

Shelby jumps, and our lips part ways. We're both breathing hard, and Shelby's bun is hanging precariously on the side of her head. Her lips are red, and her clothes are disheveled. I take her in, thinking she's never looked hotter.

She pats my chest and pushes me back. "Come on, cowboy. Food's getting cold, and you know I get hangry at the drop of a hat."

I have to shake my head to clear the lust that has me feeling like tossing her over my shoulder and running to my bed. Shelby hops off the counter like that wasn't the hottest make-out session since I learned how to take off a girl's bra. I clear my throat. There's no hope for it. I will never get that kiss out of my head.

Shelby turns with two loaded plates, handing me one, then reaching up and pulling out the hair tie so her long locks fall down her back. She heads for the table like this is just a normal occurrence before supper.

How can she not understand that everything's changed?

We didn't pass the test. According to Ridge, I'm head over boots in love with my best friend.

And I ain't mad about it.

CHAPTER
Fifteen

WHEN IN DOUBT, LET YOUR HORSE DO THE THINKING

SHELBY

Turns out our high school drama teacher was dead wrong—and maybe a little mean. She told me I was better suited for the costume crew than the stage, implying I couldn't act my way out of a paper bag. But I proved her wrong just now when I tore myself out of Dallas's arms and pretended he hadn't just rocked my entire world.

My knees are literally shaking as I carry my plate to the supper table and proceed to chatter incessantly about Skye's new sheep while Dallas grunts and shoves spaghetti in his face. By the time we're done eating, I've hit my acting limit, so I shoo him away, insisting that since he cooked, it's only fair I clean.

But honestly, I just need him out of my space. He grunts some more and disappears to his workshop, allowing me to have my nervous breakdown in private. I'm so discombobulated, I don't even check out his Levis as he leaves.

"What was that?" I implore Nelly, who sits patiently at my feet waiting for me to drop some spaghetti on the floor. He only tilts his head and lets out a small whine as I transfer the dishes to the sink.

"I mean, there's nobody here but us. What was he thinking? What was *I* thinking?" I absolutely encouraged Dallas and participated with vigor. A lot of vigor. So much vigor, I can't seem to catch my breath.

When Nelly still doesn't answer, I do it for him. "I'll tell you what it was. Your daddy is just a hot blooded male, and that's all there is to it. It means nothing to him. It's a reflex. And since we've been forced together so much recently, it was bound to happen, right? To Dallas, a kiss is the same as a handshake. It changes nothing."

Sensing this might take a while, Nelly sinks to the floor and rests his chin on his paws.

"He's just not thinking. I'm not built like him, though. A kiss *means* something to me." I switch on the tap and start attacking the first plate like it stole my husband. "I've never been the type to just indiscriminately sleep with any guy who comes along." I fling my hand out, throwing bubbles into the air and not caring.

The second plate gets the same treatment as the first, followed by the bread plate and spaghetti pot as I mumble to myself. When I'm done, I smack the tap off and turn to Nelly with both wet hands propped on my hips.

"But why not? My fortieth birthday is the day after tomorrow! I'm not a teenager or some innocent twenty-something!" Nelly lifts only his eyes, giving me a pathetic puppy look, so I plop my butt on the floor, crossing my legs so I can deliver some good pets and scratches.

Naturally, my voice changes, since talking to an animal at such close range demands a tone reserved specifically for babies and pets. Anyone who doesn't use that tone is highly suspect, in my opinion. "I am a grown woman with grown needs, Nelly. I can decide for myself if it means something or not. Sometimes it's healthy to let it be what it is and not fight it, right?"

Nelly sighs and presses his head into my hand. "Yeah, you're right. I can let a kiss—or even more—be just for fun." I boop his nose. "Not that I'll let it go that far with your daddy, so don't worry."

My phone vibrates on the counter, so I hop to my feet to grab it. Josie Mae's name lights up the screen.

"Hey, what's up?" I ask.

"You free for a beer?

"Uh oh. Not even a hello. Must be bad." When her only response is a mirthless laugh, I ask, "Knockin' Boots in thirty?" That'll give me enough time for a quick shower. Besides, it's in the best interests of my sanity to avoid Dallas for the rest of the night.

"Meet you there. And prepare to get a ride home. We're drinkin' tonight."

"So, he's at Jeremy's?" I ask Jo forty minutes later. The crowd is sparse tonight, and the music from the overhead speakers is set on low.

When I got here, she was already halfway through her first vodka cranberry and ready to unload. Turns out she and her oldest kid, Tad, got into it and he ran off to daddy. I love the kid, but he's got a lot of growing up to do.

"Yup. And Sophie is already making plans to take over his room and redecorate. She says she needs it for her clothes and makeup."

This makes me laugh. Sophie is such a quintessential girls' girl, just like her mom. But I know Jo needs my support, so I don't hesitate to chime in. "I think it's perfectly reasonable to ask your twenty-two-year-old kid to pay rent if he wants to still live at home and eat your food." I sip my beer and nod at my friend in solidarity.

"Thank you!" She throws both hands out, narrowly missing

her now-empty glass on the tabletop. "When I was twenty-two, I had a job, a four-year-old, and another on the way while I was finishing my degree online. Tad has a YouTube channel and an addiction to cheese puffs, and not a whole lot else. It's time."

"Agreed. If Jeremy wants to let him live at his place for free, though, I'm afraid you really can't do much about it."

"Jeremy is essentially a forty-year-old child himself, so I'm sure they'll bond over being butt hurt by the big bad witch."

"I prefer to think of you as the good witch," Norinne says as she approaches and sets two fresh drinks on the table. I take a good swig from my current bottle. I need to catch up.

"Black really isn't my color." Josie Mae scrunches her nose at Norinne. "And neither is green, come to think of it."

"I'm sorry, Jo," I say once Norinne leaves. "Tad'll be back, but I know you're going to miss him, even if he drives you crazy sometimes."

"I know. What can I say? I love the snot out of that kid." She takes a pull on her straw and shrugs. "I really only want to do what's best for him."

"And that's what makes you a great parent."

Jo straightens in her chair and starts playing with her straw. "Speaking of great parents, how is Dallas?" I should have known this was coming.

I don't respond at first, preferring to suck down a little more liquid courage. "Is it ever weird for you to see Dallas around town?" I finally ask.

"How so?"

"I mean, surely there's been a time or two when you've spotted him and thought for a second he was Houston, right?" They are identical twins, after all. Although it's easy for those who know them to tell them apart.

"I guess." She shrugs and lifts her glass for another sip.

"And that's not weird?"

"Shelby." She eyes me squarely. "Houston and I dated in *high school*. That was a different lifetime."

"I know. I'm being stupid." I shake my head. "Maybe I'm feeling nostalgic."

"You know what I think?" The question is obviously rhetorical, so I drink my beer and don't have to wait long to find out. "I think kissing Dallas has knocked something loose in your head."

"Ha! Maybe."

Her glass is now curled up in her hand like she's cuddling it to herself. "Ooh, do tell."

"I don't know. He's such a flirt."

"That's nothing new."

"But it is with me. Well, sort of." I pause, listening to Thomas Rhett crooning from the sound system. "He's always been flirty with anyone who has two X chromosomes, me included. But he's been more...intense since we got engaged."

"Fake engaged," Josie Mae corrects me.

"Yes, of course."

"Just checking."

"Don't be ridiculous." I wave her off. "But now he's being all touchy-feely, even when nobody is around."

She tilts her head, her sheet of midnight hair cascading down her arm while she chases her wayward straw with her tongue. "Interesting."

"No, it's really not. This is *Dallas*. He has the restraint of a fourteen-year-old boy."

"And what about you? Does Shelby have a mind of *her* own?" Jo giggles. She's always been a lightweight.

I ignore her, and because I'm now feeling a little tipsy too, I spit out the truth. "I don't know what I think. I've never really given my whole heart to someone, you know? But at this point, I'm wondering why dating a dirtbag like Shane is perfectly acceptable but being with someone who's a decent human being isn't. It's just physical. I don't know. The last thing I want to do is ruin our friendship."

Her response baffles me. "Dallas and Hallie are great friends."

"What?"

"No." She lays her palm on the wooden table between us. "I just mean Dallas and Hallie used to date, but it doesn't affect their friendship *now*. They're just pals. Well, and parents, of course."

Huh. "That's true. I guess I never thought about it. But you're right. There's never any awkwardness between them. Not even with Bowen, and he's well aware his wife slept with Dallas."

"It's called being adults." Jo nods sagely. "Maybe they can sit Tad down and show him how to be an adult."

"That may be the worst idea I've ever heard."

"Eh, I was just spitballing." She shrugs again and goes in for another sip of cranberry vodka but then pauses. "Spitballing…that's such a weird term, isn't it? I mean, it's actually really disgusting when you think about it." Her lip curls. "Chewing up paper and blowing it through a straw. Getting your saliva everywhere. What *is* that? And what does it have to do with brainstorming?" She gasps. "Brainstorming! Another weird word! Is there a hurricane in your brain? What is this madness?!"

And I don't know if it's the beer or the actual topic, but now she has me going. "And what about the word disgruntled. I mean, really? Have you ever been *gruntled*?"

Josie Mae raises an index finger in all seriousness. "I have *not*."

"You ladies want another round?" Norinne asks.

My response is immediate. "Oh, absolutely."

————

"Oh, Daaaaally," I sing-song quietly as I toe off my sandals, not really calling for him but also *kind of*? Norinne's husband,

Tank, just dropped me off after delivering Josie Mae to her house. Sophie is spending the night at a friend's, so Jo will sleep it off before she has to mom again.

The house is quiet, but Dallas left the hall light on for me. He's such a nice guy. And a great roommate.

"Feelings schmeelings," I murmur to myself as I tiptoe from the entryway to the hall.

The bedroom door opens with a gentle creak, the light from the hall illuminating a bare-chested Dallas sprawled on his back on the bed. I look over at Nelly, who's eyeing me like I've disturbed his slumber. I put my finger to my lips and shush him.

Dallas doesn't stir as I step closer and watch his chest rise and fall in a slow rhythm. I wonder if the light smattering of hair would tickle against my bare skin. I really should find out. If only for science.

When I close the space to stand over him, I let my eyes trace the strong line of his stubbled jaw and the hollows under his cheekbones until I reach the lines radiating from his eyes. Laugh lines look good on the man. Even the stray strands of silver that have started to color his golden-tipped locks look incredible on him.

I can't help the sigh that escapes my lungs.

Unfortunately, it's loud enough to cause Dallas's golden eyes to blink open—right before he rockets up to a seated position, hands fisting the sheets in a death grip.

"What are you doing?!" he practically screeches. Nelly huffs from his bed on the floor.

My eyes have flown wide. "Nothing!"

"Are you…" His mouth closes and then opens again as his chest heaves. "Watching me sleep?"

"No! I just got home!"

His hair is a ruffled mess. "So, you're…checking to make sure I'm alive?"

"No!" I insist again.

"Then what are you doing?"

Well, since he asked, I suppose I should just lay it on him. "Getting ready to slide into bed with you."

He sputters and coughs, so I do the only thing I can and awkwardly pat him on the back until it stops.

"Am I still asleep?" he inexplicably asks once he's recovered his voice.

"I don't think so." I did have a few beers, but I'm pretty confident in my answer. "Do you...not want me to?" I haven't really thought far enough ahead to plan what I'll do if he's not on the same page.

Dallas watches me for a few beats before asking, "How many beers did you have?"

"How many beers did *you* have?" I can go tit for tat.

"Shelby." His voice has a growl to it that makes my lower belly quiver.

"Dallas, it was just beer. I'm not drunk." I imitate his growl. "Yes or no? It's a simple question."

"Shelby," he repeats, this time sounding almost pleading.

"You didn't answer the question." I lean over him, but not touching him. "Yes. Or. No?"

He lets out a strangled, "Yes," and before he can say anything else, I pounce on him. He catches me with an *oof* and continues with, "but..."

I cut him off and straddle his lap. "No buts. Just you and me doing what we want to do."

"Shelby." Again, it's like a plea.

I pause. "Do you want me to stop?"

I swear his eyes roll back in his head as he tilts his face up to me. "No."

Nelly gets up with a whine and leaves the room.

HELD TOGETHER BY HAIRSPRAY AND A PRAYER

SHELBY

The first question I ask myself when I crack my eyes open is *how bad would it be to call off work?* Dallas stirs, moving the bed.

"What time is it?" I ask, my voice little more than a croak as I stretch.

"Six thirty." His answer comes not from behind me but above, causing me to whip my head around and find him propped up on an elbow, staring down at me.

"Were you watching me sleep?"

"What if I am?"

I scrunch my nose. "I'm sure I have bedhead, and my makeup is smeared everywhere. I probably look like a raccoon."

"Correction. You have *sexy* hair. And you look like a sexy raccoon."

I bury my face in my pillow, laughing at his nonsense. In no time flat, he swipes the pillow out from under me, pinning me on my back with the weight of his body. I'm trapped with no option to retreat as he looms over me.

"Mornin', honey." His eyes are as soft as his voice as they dance over my face. I want to wipe away the mascara smudges, but I can't move my arms. I'm feeling way too exposed.

"What time are you getting Little G today?" I ask, hoping to draw his focus from examining my features and boring a hole into my soul with those eyes. Why is he looking at me like that?

Instead of answering, he responds, "You should take the day off and stay in bed."

"The thought did occur to me, but I don't think your calves or any of the other livestock in the county care that I'm sleep deprived."

He ignores my attempt at humor. "I'll take the day off too. We'll tell everyone we're sick." He leans down to drop a kiss on my lips, but I manage to wrestle one hand free and slap it over his mouth before he makes contact.

His brows snap together, and he mumbles into my palm, *"Wha re ouu oin?"*

"I have morning breath."

He pulls my hand away and pins it down again with embarrassingly little effort. "I don't care."

"Well, I do." Using all my strength, I roll out from under him and lunge to my feet. This is getting way too intimate for my own good. Time to reset those boundaries. "I gotta hop in the shower anyway. Full day ahead."

"Shelby." His tone is low and holds a hint of warning.

"Dallas, whatever is running through that head of yours, you don't have to worry," I assure him as I grab some clean clothes from the dresser. "Like I said last night. We're two compatible adults perfectly capable of separating feelings from actions." I lean back over the bed and boop him on the nose to reinforce my point. "Don't worry."

Then I haul butt to the shower because it really wouldn't take much for him to lure me back into bed.

After I get my work done and take a much-needed nap, I'll have to see where his head is at. Because now that we've gone there, there's no reason we can't keep a good thing going—as long as we both keep our heads while we're at it.

———

"I heard Meemaw and Phyllis scheming about a dance they want to do for everyone. Just thought you'd appreciate the warning," Norinne tells me from her spot in front of one of the bathroom sinks.

"Good Lord above." I exit the stall and join her at the sinks, where I frown at my reflection.

We're all gathered at Knockin' Boots for my fortieth birthday party. The girls went all out and decorated a corner of the bar in my favorite color, complete with a matching cake and a signature cocktail they named Turquoise Titillation, for some reason. It's a fantastic party, despite the one thing that has me frowning.

Norinne pauses with her lipstick tube poised a few inches from her face. Her hair is a deep blue today, and it complements her coloring better than the purple did. "What's the matter, hun? It's your birthday. You should be smiling ear to ear, or we're not doing our job as party hosts."

I send her a tepid smile. "Oh, it's nothing. The party is great, thanks. I just got my period, which is particularly annoying because I just had it two weeks ago." I switch on the tap to wash my hands.

"Well, that's not exactly the gift a girl wants for her birthday, is it?" She swipes a coat of fire-engine red stain on her bottom lip. "I feel you, though. Before I hit perimenopause, you could set a watch by my cycle. Twenty-eight days on the dot." She repeats the stain on her top lip.

"You're too young for that," I protest. "Aren't you only a few years older than me?" When she only shrugs and rubs her lips together, I continue talking. "I've always been regular, but lately it's been all over the place."

She pauses again and responds with a weighty, "Oh." Well, that doesn't sound good.

"What *oh*?" I stare at her in the mirror, wet hands dripping into the sink.

"Well…you're forty." She says it like she's apologizing.

"So?"

Norinne stashes her lipstick in her apron pocket and turns to me, so I do the same, ignoring the water now soaking into my top. "Let me ask you this. Have you started noticing any other changes? Like trouble sleeping? Waking up all sweaty in the middle of the night for no reason? Feeling particularly moody? Maybe more hair in the shower drain? Anything like that?"

"Kind of?" My response comes out more as a question because I'm suddenly terrified of what she's implying. The nightmares have always marred my sleep, but my sleep quality has gotten poorer in recent months, despite the absence of the nightmares. And the hair! I've been telling myself that maybe my head was shedding like double-coated animals do for the summer. And I have definitely been more emotional this year. Oh no.

"I hate to break it to you, Shelby, but you might be starting perimenopause."

Sensing that denial is the best course, I protest, "But I'm barely out of my thirties!"

Norinne pulls a couple paper towels from the dispenser and hands them over. "I was forty-one when it started for me. Now I'm almost done."

"But… but…" My head is spinning in both directions at once as I absently tear the towels to shreds. "I haven't even had any babies!"

I can only imagine the look on my face because it immediately propels Norinne into action. She pulls me into a hug so tight I'm nearly asphyxiated and then whirls me around to the door, only to shove me through it.

"Char! Emergency special! STAT!"

"On it!" comes Charlene's voice from somewhere as I'm frog-marched to an empty high-top table and helped onto a stool.

"Now, you listen here, Shelby Sweet." Norinne levels me with serious eyes and pries the damp, shredded paper from my death grip. "No need to panic. You've still got time." She pats my hand and tries on a halfhearted smile. "That said, you and Dallas are gonna want to get moving on this, you hear? Better safe than sorry. The good news is that making babies is no hardship, especially with that one, I reckon." She grins at me for real this time.

Charlene drops a glass of amber liquid between us, and Norinne slides it in front of me. "Now, drink up and enjoy your party. You can think about babies tomorrow."

I do as I'm told, the liquid fire burning as it goes down and making me cough. "What *was* that?"

Charlene waves me off. "Oh, nothing. Just a bit of Pappy's apple moonshine."

Oh boy. Pappy doesn't mess around.

"Go have fun." Norinne takes the empty glass and shoos me off the stool. "I'll distract Meemaw and Phyllis for you."

Skye waves me over from the party corner, and I head in her direction, feeling distinctly less steady than I did before my run-in with Norinne.

"You okay in there?" Dallas asks through his bathroom door.

"No."

"You drink too much, birthday girl?"

I assess my reflection before answering. "No." I just spent the last five minutes mumbling to myself while leaning forward to inspect my hairline. "Maybe." My part is definitely wider than it was a year ago. I'm sure of it. "Probably."

Stupid Pappy. Stupid Turquoise Titillation. Forty is too old to make poor drinking choices, even if it is my birthday.

"Open up, Shelby. I've got a glass of water for you."

I woman up and push away from the sink. When I open the door, Dallas stands there looking like James freaking Dean all grown up and aged to perfection in his jeans and T-shirt. He extends the glass to me, and I take it. "Thanks."

"You feelin' ill?"

I swallow a sip of water and set the glass on the bedside table. "No." My butt drops to the edge of the bed. "Well, not like you mean."

"What's the matter then?" Dallas comes closer and sits down next to me, real concern in his eyes.

I open my mouth to say *nothing*, but the truth comes out instead. "I'm *old*." Then, like the total baby I'm being, I flop onto my back and cover my eyes with my arm. A wave of dizziness hits me, but I stay where I am. It'll pass.

Dallas's choking laughter echoes off his bedroom walls. "You're not old. You're eight months younger than me, and I'm not old, so that makes it impossible for you to be."

"You're a man," I bellow with the grace of a rhinoceros.

"And?"

"Your organs aren't shriveling up into infertile raisins with no purpose left in life but to sit there and mock you!"

"Uhh." I can't see his face, but I imagine he's wincing—and probably lost.

I toss my arm aside and pull myself upright, blinking a few times as I steady myself. "My ovaries are choking out, Dallas! Not to mention I'm going bald and not sleeping right, and I'm moody as crap!" This does nothing to temper his mirth. "It's not funny."

"You're not going bald. You have gorgeous hair."

Aw, that's nice. "Yeah? Well, not for long. Pretty soon I'll be like Norinne with a dead rat on my head!"

"What are you talking about?"

"Okay, so it's not a dead rat. It's actually quite nice, but did you know Norinne wears wigs?! Don't tell her I told you, by the way."

His eyes widen. "So, none of that hair is hers?"

"No! She says she's got every color of the rainbow and just switches them out when she feels like it. She's been wearing them for the last three years because she's losing her hair due to perimenopause!" I reach for the glass again, suddenly parched. Why does drinking so much make you so thirsty?

"Peri-what?"

"Menopause."

"But that happens to *older* women."

"That's what *I* said!" Dallas shifts his shoulder just in time to miss the water splashing from my glass as I toss my hand out. "Turns out I *am* old!"

"Wait, so you have this too?" Now you're gettin' it, Dally.

"Apparently! Oh gosh, Dallas, I don't know how I'm gonna weather this without losing my mind. Oh! Speaking of, I just found out tonight that I have unrelenting brain fog to look forward to. And hot flashes that make you sweat through your clothes even in the dead of winter." Just the thought of hot flashes has me draining the glass in one go.

"I'm sure Norinne was exaggerating."

"She absolutely was not. I looked it up on the drive home."

Dallas's chin pulls back on a loud gasp. "We need to *do* something about this!"

"I know!" We both consider the side effects for a silent moment. "But you know the worst part?" Oh no, I can feel the sting in my nose telling me tears are on their way. Stupid hormones!

Dallas turns, his knee bent on the bed so he can face me. "Hey, it's okay. Whatever it is, we can fix it."

"No, we can't." The tears spill over, wetting my cheeks and dripping onto my ruffled top.

He takes the empty glass from me and tosses it on the bed before engulfing both of my hands in his larger ones. "You forget who you're talking to? I'm Dallas Gamble. I fix stuff for a living."

"Not this." I swallow past the lump in my throat, not bothering to wipe my tears. It feels too good having Dallas hold my hands. "I won't be able to have babies. Stupid shriveled ovaries."

"Last I checked, Norinne barely graduated high school. I doubt she secretly got her medical license since then. The woman can sling a good drink, but a qualified medical professional, she's not."

"It's true, Dallas. If I wait any longer, I won't be able to get pregnant. My egg shop is having a going-out-of-business sale."

"Okay, then let's get you pregnant." He shrugs, indicating to me that he's the only living adult male on the planet who still believes in the stork.

Practicality has never been his strong suit, so I spell it out. "Even if one of the guys you're flirting with ends up being my Mister Right, I can't just beg him to get me pregnant on the first date. It takes time. More than I have, I'm afraid."

But he only shakes his head. "You're not listening, Shelby. I meant *I'll* get you pregnant."

I feel my eyes pop wide. "What? Why would you want to do that?"

"Why not? I love being a dad."

Oh Lord, he's too sweet for words. But this can't happen. "You're a great dad, Dallas, and I know we've crossed a few lines in our friendship already, but that's way too big of an ask." And way too much risk to my heart, I silently add. I'm pretty sure seeing Dallas cradle a baby we made together would shatter the restraint I've been able to hold onto for the last twenty-five years when it comes to him.

Maybe I'll get a sperm donor. I've always been sensible with my money, so I've got a healthy nest egg, no pun intended.

"You didn't ask," he corrects me, still calm as a capybara. "I offered."

"And God knows, I love you for it, bestie." I finally pull my hands from his, but only to lean over and hug him.

"Right back atcha, Sweetness. I'd do anything for you."

He smells like cardamom and clean sweat, and with his arms holding me close, I can't help but think how lucky I am to have him in my life, even if babies don't end up working out for me. I should probably follow Norinne's advice and think about babies tomorrow. "How about we get a midnight snack and fall asleep to an audiobook?"

He releases me and pulls back, holding out his hand. "Probably a good idea. I don't think you have the focus tonight for what I had planned." When I take his hand, he winks. "We'll rain check for tomorrow when you're not so titillated by turquoise."

He helps me up, and I rummage through my bag for my phone before scrolling to my audio app. "Okay, your choice," I say. "The latest Karen Smirnoff thriller or *The Billionaire CEO's Secret Amnesia Bride*? I think they both sound good."

CHAPTER
Seventeen

SHARP AS A MASHED POTATO

DALLAS

"Drink your tea," the duke commanded, his breeches surely so tight they were putting him in quite the mood.

She took a sip, only to nearly gag as fire raced down her throat. "Wh-what is this?" she rasped.

"Whiskey. Perhaps now you will not faint for a fourth time."

She glanced at her teacup, then took another tentative sip. She found she rather liked the taste of whiskey now that she was properly braced for it. Perhaps this was the missing ingredient from all the boring tea she'd been forced to drink during the season. She giggled out loud, then clapped a gloved hand over her mouth.

"Dad?" Ryder's voice echoes across my workshop, startling me. I hit pause on the audiobook I'm listening to while I stain the matching coffee tables I'm just about finished with. The morning sun is streaming through the windows and making my work look that much better. I could do without the heavy smell of chemicals coming from the varnish though. "What are you listening to?"

"It's an audiobook called *The Duke and His Devilish Desires.*

I don't really have time to sit down and read, so I figured this would do."

Ryder comes over to inspect the tables. Nelly lifts from where he's been napping to greet my son. "Do what?"

Sighing, I carefully place my brush across the top of the stain can. "I'm trying to understand women."

Watching Shelby cry the night of her birthday made something in me break. I meant it when I offered to give her children, but I don't think she understands how I feel about her. She probably thinks I'm still that guy who flirts with every female. I've got to come up with a way for her to take me and my feelings seriously before we waste any more time. Her poor ovaries don't have much left before self-destruction, according to the articles I've been reading about perimenopause. Frightening stuff.

I also saw the title of the romance novel Shelby started reading yesterday and instantly downloaded the audio version. I figure if I can understand what she loves about these fictional heroes, I can simply copy what they do. Surely, she'll fall in love with me if I make a grand gesture like her fictional friends. I pat myself on the back in my head. Look at me go, already using Shelby's language. Now I just have to figure out what grand gesture to make.

Ryder wrinkles his nose. "It's not really that hard. Mom says women want to be listened to. Which seems a bit basic. Doesn't everyone want to be listened to?"

I clap a hand on his shoulder and wonder if now's the time for another birds and bees lecture. Probably not. I haven't figured out anything further about women worth imparting.

"I think listening might be just the first step."

He gags and spins in a circle, mimicking another flip turn. Nelly darts around him, tail wagging. "There's *steps*? Like, how many? Two? Four? A hundred? How many, Dad?"

Oh boy. There he goes, down a rabbit hole lined with

questions on a subject I know nothing about. Time to try redirection. "Hey, did I ever tell you about the day I met Shelby?"

Ryder stops moving, and Nelly sits like a good boy. "Weren't you my age?"

I ruffle his hair. "Just a bit older. Teenagers." And then I tell him the story, embellishing along the way because why not make the story even funnier? When I get to the end, I have a lightbulb moment. "Hey, buddy. Want to help me out with something?"

———

"I need a favor," I say the next day as I stop by the ranch to help out.

Ridge is in a mood, stomping around and scaring all the sick animals. Nelly even took one look at the guy and headed off in the opposite direction. Ridge lifts his head to scowl at me. Hey, at least he didn't take a swing at me.

"I'm doing this grand gesture thing for Shelby when she gets here to check on the calves. Pops and Frankie are in on it. I'd appreciate it if you just let it happen. Don't spread your sunshine."

"What do you mean by that?" he growls. I don't miss the way his hands ball up into fists. Dang, he's not taking Tiff's absence very well at all.

"The grand gesture thing or the sunshine thing?" I clarify.

"All of it."

"I'm recreating the day we met. It's some romantic crap that Shelby loves, so I'd appreciate it if you'd keep your bad mood far away from my grand gesture."

His top lip curls up. "No problem." And then he stalks away.

"You know, you should get your hormones checked. You

might be in perimenopause!" I call after him, remembering what I read about mood swings.

He raises his right arm in the air and flips me off. A few moments later, I hear the front door to the house slam shut.

I shake my head at his foul mood and pull out a walkie-talkie from the set that I gave both Pops and Ryder. I'll have to deal with Ridge later. Stepping out of the paddock, I only have to wait a few minutes until I see Shelby's blue heap of metal turn into the drive. I press the button on the side of the walkie-talkie.

"Standby, good men. The eagle is almost in the nest."

The thing squawks in my hand before Ryder's excited voice rings out. "Wait. An eagle? Can I come see?"

Pops saves me from his own walkie-talkie in the house. "The eagle is Shelby, son."

It squawks again. "Why didn't you just say Shelby?"

I grin, wishing Ryder was right by my side instead of back behind the barn so I could rough him up in a bear hug. Gosh, I love his brain. Shelby's car finally comes to a halt, a dust cloud fanning out behind her. I press the side button again. "Okay, Ryd. Let her loose!"

Shelby steps out of the truck and slams the door shut. I hide the walkie-talkie in my back pocket. "What are you doing here? I thought you were delivering the end tables?"

I walk toward her, grinning like a fool. Damn, she's pretty. Tight blue jeans, a cotton work shirt, and coppery hair tied up on top of her head. Something about a smart, capable woman really revs my engine. Especially now that I know what it takes to get her to drop her toughness and whisper my name like sweet nothings.

"Hey, Sweetness. Imagine seeing you here."

She tilts her head like she's trying to figure me out. And then her gaze skates over my left shoulder. I hear hooves digging into the dirt. Shelby points, and I turn to see our old milking cow, Clara, leaving the barn like she's breaking out of prison. I whistle, and Clara's eyes widen.

"Well, crap. One got loose," I say loudly.

Shelby spares me a single bewildered look, and then she takes off after Clara, already crooning at her with that voice that makes animals and men alike melt at her feet. Clara slows, then turns in Shelby's direction, wanting to bask in her attention. I follow, my plan unfolding perfectly. I wait to play my part until Shelby gets her hands on Clara's head to give her a good scratch.

"Did you steal my cow?" I ask, real innocent like. If I had to choose a new career, I'd have to say acting would be a good one for me.

Shelby looks at me like I've suffered a stroke. "I'm sorry, what?"

I point to her, pushing back a full-on grin. "Did you steal my cow?" I lean in and whisper as loudly as I can. "Now you're supposed to deny it. Remember?"

Shelby's fist plants itself on her hip. "Have you lost your mind?"

"I have not! This cow was just running down the street!" I declare. Okay, fine. We're switching roles. I can run with that.

Shelby's mouth flops open, then snaps shut.

I soldier on. "Well, I thank you for catching her for me." I hold out my hand. "Dallas Gamble."

Shelby lets go of the cow and takes my hand with all the reluctance she showed me the first time we met. "I don't know what you think you're doing. Mind filling me in?"

I flash her my flirtiest smile. When her cheeks take on a pink glow, I know I still got it, even after all these years. My stage whisper is unnecessary because no one else is around to overhear us getting off script. "I'm recreating the day we met, Sweetness. It's what you call a grand gesture."

Shelby guffaws. "I know what a grand gesture is, Dally."

"Then play along!" I let go of her hand to redirect our

attention to the cow that we need to put in the trailer I already placed in the driveway, but Clara's gone. "Oh, crap."

Shelby's gasp rings out as we both turn to see her chewing up Pops's flowerbed in front of the house. I run over there as fast as I can, knowing Pops will kill me if Clara ruins the flowers. He's been tending these flowerbeds in Momma's absence for years now.

The walkie-talkie screeches from my back pocket. "I've gotta pee. Can I leave the barn now?"

I pull out my device and press the side button. "Yes, Ryder. Go to the bathroom. I'll get Clara."

The moment of distraction is all Clara needs, though. She's abandoned the flowerbed to sniff the brood of Silkies that have come around the side of the house, intent on seeing what's going on out here. One flies in the air with a wild flap of her wings, not appreciating a large cow nose sniffing her backside. Another pecks at poor Clara's ear. She retaliates by stomping her hooves, which makes all the chickens dance and squawk.

"What are you doing to my precious chickens?" Meemaw hollers from the front porch. Oh, great. She was snoozing in her chair with the television droning on just a few minutes ago.

The walkie-talkie screeches again. "Is that my cue to start the music?" Pops asks from the kitchen.

"Stay away from my babies, you beast!" Meemaw screeches.

Clara doesn't like the screaming, though. She head-bops a chicken, sending it flying back several feet. Meemaw gasps. "I'm gettin' the shotgun!"

Jeez.

Shelby reaches my side as Ryder streaks past on a mission to find the bathroom. She hands me a rope. "I'll talk to her. You get this around her neck." She's fighting back laughter, and as embarrassing as this is, I don't blame her.

Shelby sweet-talks Clara away from the hens long enough for me to rope her and start leading her back to the barn. Thankfully, we make our escape before Meemaw can get the shells in the shotgun. Shelby comes with me to the barn, tossing me sidelong glances as I grumble under my breath. I may kick a few rocks while I'm at it too.

She waits to speak until I get Clara in her stall and feed her some carrots as a reward, even though she didn't follow directions at all. I pull my cowboy hat off my head and circle it around in my hands. When I lift my head, Shelby is smiling at me from ear to ear.

"Recreating the day we met?" she asks softly.

I wince. "That could have gone better."

Her smile is contagious, though, because I feel myself smiling back before long. Shelby launches herself at me unexpectedly, her arms squeezing the ever-loving hell out of my neck. I wrap my arms around her waist and hold her tight. At least she doesn't hate me for botching the grand gesture.

"Thank you," she whispers in my ear.

"For messing that up spectacularly?" I whisper back.

She shakes with laughter, and I join in. By the time she pulls away, we're both laughing so hard we have tears in our eyes. I sling my arm around her shoulders and walk her to the paddock so she can get going on checking out the calves.

So much for a grand gesture to make her fall in love with me. I better read a few more romance novels before I try again.

Eighteen

BUTTER ME AND CALL ME A BISCUIT

SHELBY

One of the many traits that makes Dallas so likable is his willingness to do just about anything. The man is always up for a good time, but he's also the first to volunteer when somebody needs a favor or a boost.

Anytime he hears the opener, "You know what we should do?" he's already out of his chair and ready to go. Road trips, tractor races, arm wrestling, skinny dipping, roping contests, dares, random favors, you name it.

I'll never forget our senior year spring play when the male lead got mono and there was nobody to fill in. The whole cast was devastated until Dallas waltzed in and volunteered for the gig. Despite him forgetting lines or reading them off his hand, his charm won over the audience, and the whole cast got a standing ovation.

Then there was the weekend he and Houston drove out to Missouri, where I was stressing out in vet school, and they kidnapped me for a Kenny Chesney concert. It turned out to be one of the best weekends of my life, one we still talk about.

And the time he fixed Jeannie Rochety's leaky roof while she was in the hospital having surgery, and nobody could figure out who did it. To this day, I'm the only one who knows.

So, it shouldn't surprise me that Dallas would get a wild hair and reenact our first meeting as some kind of grand gesture. Especially knowing how upset I was on Friday night with the perimenopause bombshell. It's exactly the thing a great best friend would do to cheer me up, and I don't know that I'll ever forget the sight of Clara and those chickens going at it. Thank goodness Meemaw's favorite, Isadora, wasn't involved or we all might have been shot.

"Hey, Shelby, you got a minute?" Skye calls from the barn.

I peel off my gloves and drop them by my gear. I'm pretty much done here, and my next client isn't until this afternoon. Plenty of time to help Skye and grab some lunch in town. I've got no clue where Dallas snuck off to, but I see Ryder shadowing Pops as he feeds the horses.

"What's that noise?" Ryder asks, his features pinched as his head cocks to the side. We all stop to listen, and sure enough, there's a low-frequency rumbling sound.

"Damn oil well." Pops scowls. "The Kincaids ain't keeping up with maintenance. Those pumpjacks probably haven't been serviced in months. I'll have a word."

"It's super annoying," Ryder complains. "Can't we tell them to shut it off?"

"Afraid it's not that simple. Come on now and help me feed Lulu."

Ryder frowns but does as he's told.

"What's up?" I ask Skye. She's standing at the barn door with their pretty Appaloosa named Tango.

"Probably nothing. I was exercising Tango yesterday, and it felt like she might have been favoring her front left."

"Lemme take a look." Skye holds Tango's rope while I test her joints and examine her hooves and shoes. "I don't see anything. She's letting me maneuver her around without being jumpy. Shoes look good. Walk her around and let me see."

Skye leads her in a few circles as I watch, but she looks fit as a fiddle. I check my watch and make a decision.

"Go on and saddle her up. I'm gonna grab something, and then I'll take her for a ride just to make sure."

"You sure you have time for that?"

"No problem." It's been a while since I've gone for a good ride, despite it being one of my favorite things to do. "I'll enjoy it."

Satisfied with my answer, Skye takes Tango back into the barn, and I head to Dallas's truck that's still parked by the house. He must be helping Ridge with something on horseback because both Whiskey and Echo are gone.

I swing open the passenger door and go right for the glove box where Dallas keeps a stash of protein bars. It'll have to do since it looks like I'm not getting lunch today. I shove one in my jeans pocket, but just as I go to close the glove box, something catches my eye.

"What the…"

Closer inspection reveals a white box with a label that reads Ovulation Test Kit, along with numerous pamphlets about fertility. Where in Sam Hill did he get this? Did he really buy this for me?

"Dallas, you big softie." I smile, imagining him walking into the pharmacy in Hornville and asking what his perimenopausal friend might need to help her get pregnant. I shouldn't have said anything to him. I haven't even made an appointment with my gynecologist to confirm my decrepit state, and here he is taking action. He's probably out right now finding me a man who has baby fever.

"She's all set!" Skye hollers, and I close both the glove box and the truck door before heading over.

I give Tango a few pets and tell her what we're going to

do, then mount her. We take a few paces, and it's clear she's ready to ride, so I give her the reins, and we take off in a canter heading west.

The rolling plains open up before us as we crest the first hill, tall grass swaying in the afternoon breeze, with the odd cluster of trees dotting the fence lines. The sky is an enormous sheet of blue, nearly cloudless, the only decoration being a group of birds circling to our left.

Tango's hooves beat out a steady rhythm on the compact dirt, changing pace as she breaks into a gallop. I let out a *whoop*, my nose filling with earthy red dust and a hint of sweet hay. The breeze is glorious against my skin as we speed through the grass and across a dry creek bed until we near the river.

"There's not a thing wrong with you, is there?" I ask as I slow her down, and we approach the riverbank.

"You caught me." Dallas's voice nearly startles me out of the saddle.

"Give a girl a warning, Gamble." I laugh and dismount, holding Tango's reins as we wander in the direction of his voice.

We finally round a huge oak tree, and there he is, shirtless and waist-deep in the river. From the pile of clothes on the grass, I don't have to wonder what he's wearing on his bottom half.

"It feels great. You should come in." He runs both hands through his thick, wet hair, droplets flying in every direction. He looks like a model for an adventure advertisement.

I secure Tango's reins to a tree branch and start toeing off my boots. It is August in Oklahoma, after all. "I figured you were helping Ridge, but here you are playing hooky."

"More like hiding from the humiliation of my failed grand gesture." He scrunches his nose, making him look just like his son.

"Oh, I wouldn't say that." My socks are next, and then my

jeans. "Where did you learn about grand gestures anyway, cowboy?"

He swirls his hands through the water surrounding him and shrugs. "Some woman on a podcast was talking about them being her favorite part of a romance book, so I figured you might like it. Had to ask Siri for specifics, though."

"I did like it." I hate that he went to the effort and worried he messed everything up.

"Even though I messed it up?"

"Hey, you made me laugh, so that's gotta count for something." Off goes my shirt, leaving me in just a tank top and underwear. I can't believe how casually I can undress in front of him now. Used to be, I'd wear a cover-up around him, or at the very least a modest one-piece bathing suit. But he's made me feel so beautiful lately, it's easy.

"Wasn't really what I was going for."

"Well, if you were trying to cheer me up, you did the trick."

He makes a noncommittal noise. I wade in up to my knees and pause, letting my body get used to the crisp water temperature. "Can I ask you a question?"

"Shoot." He's still staring, but at least he's recovered his ability to speak.

"Why do you have an ovulation test kit in your glovebox?"

His brows spike. "You snoopin' through my things, Sweetness?"

"I needed a protein bar."

He nods and pauses. "Can I ask *you* something?"

"Shoot."

"Why do *you* think I have an ovulation test kit in my glovebox?"

I'm up to my waist now and can't help smiling at him. I want to jump into his arms and stay floating in this water with him forever. "Because you're sweet, and you want to help me have a baby."

"Correct on both counts." He winks, snaking out an arm and snatching me. I yelp, and he pulls me into his chest.

A drop of water falls from the tip of my nose. "Well, I have unequivocal proof I'm not pregnant at the moment since I'm on my period."

"Ah." He nods sagely. "Shark week."

I break free and splash water at him. He throws his arms up to block it while laughing his butt off.

"You're an idiot," I inform him.

"You're not the first one to tell me that." He pulls me in again, and I let him. We proceed to splash through the water together, enjoying the chance to cool off.

He looks down at me, his expression one I can't figure out. It's happiness, but there's a note of something else. Something too closely resembling adoration to make much sense in the context.

I open my mouth to say something snarky and probably smug, but reality comes crashing back in before I can. "Shoot! I'm gonna be late!" I totally forgot about my appointment.

Dallas's eyebrows spike, and he shakes himself out of his stupor before leading me safely to the bank. "Totally worth it," Dallas says as he watches me climb out of the water.

"Totally worth it," I agree. I grin back as I attempt the impossible task of getting dressed with wet skin. I wiggle and stumble and yank and curse, both of us laughing until Dallas finally takes mercy on me and helps.

As I ride away, I can't help but take one last glance at him as he dives back under the water. Tango and I need to double-time it back to the barn. If Skye can unsaddle Tango and brush her down for me, I can just make it to my next client. Phyllis hates tardiness as much as I do.

But even from fifty yards out from the barn, I can tell something is wrong. Ryder's wail hits my ears, and I dig my heels into Tango's flanks to gallop the rest of the way. Her hooves throw up dirt when we come to a stop by the barn. Ryder is on the ground, his fingers clawing into the dirt as he screams and bangs his head against the hard dirt. Pops stands above him, distraught and panicked, his hat in his hands and his head shaking side to side.

"I don't know what to do!" he shouts my way. I dismount, and there's no one to take Tango's reins, so I have to simply throw them over a fence post. I race over and drop to my knees, one hand to Ryder's head and the other to his back. He immediately bucks me off like the baddest-ass bronc on the rodeo circuit.

"What happened?" I ask Pops as I pull my work shirt over my head and shove it between Ryder's forehead and the dirt. Luckily, he lets it be.

"I don't know!" Pops worries his hat brim, shifting foot to foot and looking older than he did just an hour ago. "He got agitated when we were talking about school starting, and then I had to tell him tonight's plans changed, and he wouldn't be staying here after all. Then he just…lost it."

"Ryder?" I try touching his back again and get the same bronco response. "Honey, can you hear me?" Still nothing.

"Do we need to call 9-1-1?" Pops asks in desperation.

"No," I reassure him. "I don't think so." With all the racket from Ryder's wailing, I can't hear much else, so I ask Pops, "Is that noise still coming from the Kincaids' place?"

Pops closes one eye like it might help him think. "Pretty sure it is, but I can't hear it over Ryder just now."

Crap. We should have anticipated this earlier when he mentioned how annoying the sound was. Something like that can overwhelm his nervous system in no time flat, especially combined with changing plans and probably even the thought of school starting.

"Stay here with him. Come on down here and talk to him

so he knows you're here. Use a soothing voice. I'll be right back."

Without waiting for an answer, I race to Dallas's truck and throw open the bed. One of his tool bags sits near the tailgate, and I tear it open, throwing its contents left and right until I find what I'm looking for. I'm back by Pops's side with a pair of noise-canceling earmuffs in seconds.

Ryder has thankfully stopped banging his head, but he's still trembling and wailing. I mentally cross my fingers and lay my hand on his head. "Ryder, sweetie. Can you hear me?" This time, he pauses and hiccups once before loud racking sobs take over. My heart breaks in two, and I gently roll him to his side. He lets me.

"I'm going to put your dad's big earmuffs on you, okay? They'll block out all the noise and give you some quiet, alright?" When he doesn't answer, I go ahead and slide them on. I count it as a victory when he doesn't claw them off. Not wanting to go too quickly, I let him lie there for a few more minutes while rubbing his back until the sobs slow, and his little body stills.

"Pops, call Dallas and tell him I'm taking Ryder home." Pops nods as I scoop Ryder in my arms and walk him to my truck. Without a word, Pops grabs the keys from my hand and opens the passenger door for me. I don't argue, instead sliding in with my charge in my arms, cradled close. I murmur soothing words as we make our way down the dirt road to Dallas's, even though Ryder can't hear me through the earmuffs. When we get out of the truck, I'm beyond relieved to find that the oil well noises are inaudible from here.

"I'll have your truck back in a bit. I'm going to find Dallas myself," Pops says after opening the front door for us. I nod and carry Ryder in, not stopping until I reach his favorite bean bag chair in the living room. I deposit him there and run upstairs, two steps at a time, to get his weighted blanket.

When I get back down, I wrap his limp body up and settle him in my arms again while I sink into the rocking chair in the corner.

He falls asleep within minutes, his breath coming in tiny puffs from his rosebud lips. His skin and clothes are covered in dust and dirt, and there are pink scratches across his forehead. The earmuffs have been knocked askew as well, but all of that can wait. I hold him, rocking back and forth while he sleeps, and I call on all the gods for some peace for my little man.

I don't hear Dallas when he comes in twenty minutes later because my prayers were answered a little too well, and I'm dead to the world.

Nineteen

DON'T SQUAT WITH YOUR SPURS ON

DALLAS

"Seems like it's been going better, huh?" Hallie asks as I place our son's duffel bag in the back seat of her SUV. Her husband, Bowen, shakes my hand and hustles their two kids across the church parking lot to give us time to chat.

I shut the door and face her. I called her straight away after Ryder's episode earlier in the week.

"Yeah, I've been doing what you always say to do. Giving him a bit more structure and minimizing his sensory triggers." I shrug, feeling guilty about Ryder's meltdown, but grateful for the women around me who knew how to handle him. "I was trying to give him a summer where he could just be a kid, you know? Roam around the ranch and see where life takes him. I guess I got a little lax."

Hallie puts her hand on my arm. "It happens to me too, you know. I'm just glad he trusts Shelby so much." She turns and starts walking to church. I follow. "It's looking awfully real for two people faking it."

The abrupt change of topic takes me by surprise. Then again, Hallie and I try to always be open and honest with each other. "I think I might be an idiot for thinking I could ever fake it with Shelby."

Hallie gives me a knowing smile. It's the truth. When I think about finding my boy curled up in her arms, the two of them asleep like there's nowhere else in the world they'd rather be, if I hadn't been in love with Shelby by then, that would have done it.

"She's something else," I say quietly.

"Must be to catch the heart of Dallas Gamble." Hallie's tone is dry, but there's no heat behind it.

She and I are good. Always have been. We agreed we weren't right for each other, but we made one mighty fine kid together. I'm grateful for her and Bowen. The three of us have made a pretty steady parenting team for Ryder. The addition of Shelby has only made things better.

Now I just have to convince Shelby to give this marriage thing with me a try for real.

"You want to get married in the church?" Hallie asks as we reach the steps.

I rub the back of my neck. "Uh, we haven't really discussed it yet."

"Better hurry. The calendar fills up quick!" Norinne pipes in as she approaches, shamelessly listening in to our conversation. If her lipstick gets any brighter, we'll all have to start wearing sunglasses.

"I always knew you two would get married." Mrs. Perkins shuffles by, sucking her dentures. "Well, I actually thought Dallas might die of an STD before he reached middle age, but seeing as you didn't, I knew you'd marry that girl."

"Jeez," I mutter under my breath while Hallie cackles.

"Praise the Lord!" Mrs. Perkins hollers, then climbs the stairs at a snail's pace.

Norinne leans in close while we all wait for Mrs. Perkins to clear the stairs. "Don't look now, but Boyd Kincaid's behind us. Heard Ridge went over there and ripped him a new one again the other day. Almost came to blows." Norinne fans her face. "I'd've paid good money to see that brother of yours in a tussle."

Hallie can't stop laughing. I give her the stink eye, but that just makes her laugh harder. "I'll be sure to tell Ryder to steer clear of the Kincaid's property for a bit."

"For a bit?" Norinne shouts, then lowers her voice when she remembers we're surrounded by townsfolk who'd love to get a bit of gossip before the service starts. "The Gambles and Kincaids have been feuding for generations! I, for one, have picked the Gambles' side, just so you know." She pats my arm like I should thank her for her loyalty in a neighbor dispute that started before I was born. No one in my generation even knows exactly what happened. There are stories that seem highly inflated and perhaps even entirely fabricated, but still the feud remains.

Thankfully, Mrs. Perkins has entered the church, leaving the path clear for us to do the same. I see Shelby sitting in a pew with Ryder next to her, talking her ear off.

"Excuse me," I mutter, leaving them all to find the one woman I never seem to get sick of.

Ryder smiles when he sees me. I hope that never changes, though I have a feeling the teenage years might test me. He loves attending church and seeing his friends before and after. The way the format is the same every time is a consistency he can thrive on. As for me, the church service gives me an excuse to hold Shelby's hand, stroke my thumb across her skin, and whisper in her ear.

When we're dismissed, Ryder gives us a quick hug, then turns to run off to find his siblings. "Don't go far! Meemaw is making your special dinner!"

"I won't, Dad!" He doesn't even look back, but I know

he'll follow directions. This is the routine he needs. Hallie and I agreed to go back to our set schedule, like we do during the school year. I'll be dropping him off at his mom's after dinner so he can get settled in for the first day of school tomorrow.

I turn to Shelby and wrap my arms around her waist, pulling her close so I can drop a chaste kiss on her lips. Her cheeks go pink at the attention.

"Did I mention you look like the hottest thing since fried chicken?" My gaze drops down her body to take in the blue flowered dress that shows off her curvy waist and flared hips. "Dresses on you aren't fair to the other women in town. Every male eye is on you, Sweetness."

She blushes harder. "Dally."

"What? You know it's true. Your curves are legendary." I drop my head, so my lips are right by her ear.

Shelby pinches the back of my arm, making me squeal like one of Skye's swine. It's effective at making me let go of her, though. "For shame, Gamble. You're in church!"

I thread my fingers through hers—mostly to make sure she doesn't pinch me again—and tug her toward the aisle. "Never stopped me before."

I swear I can hear her roll her eyes as she follows behind me. We nod hello and stop briefly a few times to chat with people we know. When we finally make it outside, Ryder's hugging his mom and stepdad by their car. He comes running over to me and Shelby and climbs into the back seat of my truck.

"Think she made cornbread?" he asks, focused on food, which makes sense. He's become an empty pit of hunger lately.

I help Shelby up into the truck, leaning over to put her seatbelt on for her. "Of course, Meemaw did, buddy. She knows it's your favorite." Shelby slaps my hands away playfully when I linger a little too long. I shoot her a wink and shut her door, before rounding the hood and climbing inside to head to the big house.

"Dad, can I search for a video on your phone?" We haven't even left the church parking lot, and his brain is going a million miles a minute.

"Sure, bud. What for?" I dig my phone out of my back pocket and hand it to him. He has the YouTube app working before I can blink. He knows how to work my phone better than me.

One of the guys I recognize from my trip to the Hornville Oil Refinery, steps right in front of my truck, oblivious to his impending death because he's too busy texting on his phone. I slam on my brakes, and my phone goes flying out of Ryder's hands to the floor of the truck. Shelby says an expletive under her breath, the same one I say out loud as I roll my window down.

"Watch where you're walking!"

The guy lifts his head, glares at me like I'm the one who did something wrong and keeps texting as he heads to his truck. Shelby snorts in the seat next to me.

"I'm taking my seat belt off!" Ryder announces, clearly needing to grab the phone. I wait until he's back in his seat and buckled, much to the annoyance of the person behind me.

Once we're on the road and on the way to the ranch, Shelby twists in her seat to see what Ryder's researching.

"I want to see how cornbread is made because I don't like corn on the cob, but I love cornbread. Which makes no sense. They're both corn."

Shelby grins. "I'm pretty sure it has to do with the addition of sugar."

Ryder's already lost in the phone. "I'll let you know."

Shelby turns back around, and I reach for her hand, holding it there on her thigh.

"I hope that guy back there isn't on your list of possible

suitors. He probably wouldn't have looked up from his phone long enough to see who he was talking to."

Jealousy, hot and heavy, fills my chest. "Absolutely not. You ain't dating a guy whose idea of flirting is to message you in an app." I shake my head. "Men these days…"

"Speaking of men…" Shelby says, a wry twist to her lips.

I squeeze her hand. "Do not ask me about other men right now, Shelby Sweet."

She holds up her other hand in peace as her mouth drops open. "I wasn't!"

I side-eye her. "Good. It's the Lord's Day, you know. Get your brain out of the gutter."

She tosses her head back and howls with laughter like I knew she would.

She's still smiling when we pull down the long driveway to the big house. The potholes have expanded in just the last week alone. Shelby has to let go of my hand to hold the handle in the truck for dear life. Ryder pretends he's getting thrown back and forth, Raggedy Ann style, laughing his head off.

Pops comes out on the porch to greet us, already changed out of his Sunday best and into a pair of worn Levi's and a crisp white undershirt. He and Meemaw went to the crack-of-dawn service so they could work on Sunday dinner. Ryder hops out and goes running for him. I grab his noise-canceling headphones and take them with us in case the noise from the Kincaids' starts to get to him again. Not gonna have a redo of the other day. The screen door slaps shut behind us, and the scent of fried food hits.

"Meemaw's been frying up our favorites," Pops says, finally setting Ryder on the ground. "She made you cornbread."

Ryder nods. "I wonder how much baking soda she used. There's two schools of thought on the best ratio."

Pops ruffles his grandson's hair, amused. "And she made Sooner steaks for you, boy."

I grin, mouth already salivating. "What did she make Shelby?"

"Oh, I don't need—" Shelby tries to interrupt.

"Did someone say Shelby?" Meemaw calls out, entering the living room. Her red apron has chickens all over it with the words Fluent in Fowl Language across the middle. "I didn't forget you, girl. In remembrance of your ex-boyfriend, I made calf fries."

Shelby chokes, and I have to pat her on the back when she keeps coughing. Pops is trying to hold back the laughter, and Ryder is just confused. I'll have to make sure he doesn't look up calf fries on my phone. He might be scarred for life.

"Thanks, Meemaw," Shelby finally rasps, though I doubt she'll let fried bull nuts past her lips, even for Meemaw.

Meemaw shakes her hips to the music in her own head, and that's when I know she's already dipped into the devil weed. Dinner oughta be interesting then.

"Did I hear someone say calf fries?" Ridge grumbles, joining the group.

I clap him on the back. "Missed you at church, brother."

He merely grunts in response. I lift an eyebrow in Pops's direction. He gives me a slight shake of the head. Guess Ridge is still upset about Tiff being gone.

The screen door bangs open again, and a gaggle of women arrives.

"The party's here!" Frankie calls out.

"I brought the margaritas!" Morgan follows up with.

Skye lets out a whoop that hurts my ears. I take the head-phones out of my back pocket and put them on myself. Shelby elbows me in the ribs.

I made a serious miscalculation. If I'm trying to woo Shelby into falling in love with me, exposing her any further to my crazy family is not the best route.

Leaning down, I whisper in her ear. "Can we just skip dinner and go home? Get naked in the bedroom again?"

Shelby's face flames bright red. She snatches the headphones off my head. "That wasn't exactly a whisper."

I look around the room, seeing various amused expressions on my family's faces as they stare at us. *Well, crap.*

"It's the Lord's Day, dummy!" Meemaw hollers from the kitchen.

SHELBY

"What would queen diva Dolly Parton do in your shoes?" I ask my reflection as I finish washing my face. It's rarely a bad idea to invoke Dolly's name, but it's damn hard to get a firm answer.

It's the evening of the Sunday dinner where Dallas announced to his entire family—and probably some nearby neighbors—that we're together like a real couple. Luckily, I escaped too much interrogation, mostly thanks to Ryder's presence and his incessant inquiries into why Dallas wanted to get naked. Everyone silently agreed the answer was skinny dipping, so I fully expect to find Ryder trying to go to swim practice naked in the near future.

I did, however, get plenty of knowing looks, so I expect my phone to blow up before long.

Ping!

And speak of the devil, there it goes now.

Skye: You know I try not to pry, but are you sure you know what you're doing?

Ping!

Frankie: I knew it! *hug emoji* *wink emoji*

Ping!

Morgan: Please feel free to tell my wife to mind her business

Ping!

Ridge: Does my brother's butt need to be kicked? I'm more than happy to do it.

I drop the phone face down on the countertop with a long sigh and finish patting my face dry.

The days since Ryder's big meltdown have flown by. The heat is causing issues for livestock countywide, so my schedule has been brutal. I've gotten home late most nights with only enough energy to shower and fall into bed.

Dallas has been equally busy keeping things steady for Ryder, helping out at the ranch, and fitting in his wood-working in the wee hours. Today is the first day we've had off to catch our breaths, and with Ryder starting school this week and the temps expected to start dropping soon, I imagine we'll have free time to make even more poor decisions together.

Thus, the Dolly question.

Ping!

In this case, I imagine Dolly would keep flirting with the hot guy and try not to think too hard about it. But I've been an overthinker since the womb, and it's getting harder and harder to justify what's been going on. There's an expiration date to this little bubble Dallas and I are living in, and it's fast approaching. If I have to lie to one more person and say we're "still looking at our calendars" to set a wedding date, I might go stark raving mad!

Ping!

And that's not even considering Ryder. He finally asked point-blank if we're getting married like his mom and step-dad. We basically said that, as best friends, living together and marriage aren't really that different, and that we'd make a decision on it later. He accepted that answer, but the kid is way too perceptive to keep believing it for long. Questions are coming, and I don't want to lie to him. I'm sure Dallas doesn't want to either. It's just asking for trouble.

But with no Prince Charming in the wings, this breakup plan of Dallas's isn't looking good. Not to mention, I seem to have lost interest in finding anybody suitable. Nobody can really compare to Dallas when it comes down to it. He makes me happy. Sigh.

Ping!

Dang it, people!

I hang up the towel and flip my phone over again to see what fresh hell awaits.

Frankie: Personally, I don't think you should change your last name. Sweet is too perfect

Skye: Just tell me to mind my own business. I only want you to be happy.

Pops: My door is always open if you need me, darlin'

"Y'all, you're killing me," I say as I adjust my pajama top.

But I'm not dumb enough to ignore the number one rule about people. When someone tells you who they are, you need to *listen*. And Dallas has made no mistake over the years about saying and showing who he is. He's always up for a good time, but he is *not* the settling-down type. Period.

And I'm not the type he'd want to settle with even if he were! I swear, one look at how perfect he and Hallie looked side by side at church was reminder enough that Dallas's type is the furthest thing from me. I've never been—nor will I ever be—thin, perky, proper, *or* poised. I lean more toward voluptuous, cheeky, sarcastic, and tired.

Ping!

The writing is on the wall. We'll go back to being "just friends" soon, and, in addition to being deprived of the best nights of my life, I'll be on deck as the favorite topic of gossip once again—this time for not being able to hold onto the town stud.

Perhaps I should reconsider Archie's advice and look into convent life. Except nuns aren't allowed to have babies, so forget that. No, I need to visit a sperm bank and probably move to Italy.

Ping!

Yet here I am getting ready for bed and dotting perfume behind my ears. "You'd better stop if you know what's good for you, girl." Oh no, is talking to yourself another sign of perimenopause? I stare myself down in the mirror one last time. "You know what? You're right, Dolly. Screw it!"

Then I leave my pinging phone where it is and take my tired self into the bedroom, intent on sinking into this thing with Dallas yet again. Even if it could be for the last time. I find him lying on his back, head of messy golden-brown hair resting on a pillow and one hand thrown over his eyes. His firm chest is bare, the white top sheet pulled up to his waist.

"Truth or dare?" I ask.

His arm falls to the side, and he blinks at me in the doorway, his mouth curving in a smile as he takes in my pajamas. The silky top dips down in a low V that perfectly showcases the ladies and falls just north of my waist. It's paired with short tap pants in the same vivid blue with tulip vents at either side.

"Sorry, I couldn't hear you over the dirty thoughts running through my brain."

My lips tip in a self-satisfied grin, and I prop one hand on my hip. "Truth or dare, Dallas?"

He chuckles and pushes himself to a seated position, back resting against the headboard. "I'm pretty sure the last time we played Truth or dare, we were still in high school."

I take a few steps closer, reaching back into my memory. "And if I recall correctly, you ended up in the river. No surprise there." What I don't mention is how we almost kissed.

"A man ain't a man if he doesn't follow through on a dare. Even when it's cold as a witch's tit." He fakes a shudder.

I come closer and drop my butt to the bed. "Come to think of it, have you *ever* chosen truth?"

"Now, why would I do that when a dare is so much more fun and unpredictable?" He's like a big kid. No wonder he and Ryder get on so well.

"So, can I assume you're choosing dare this time too?" There are more than a few things I could dare him to do right now.

But he surprises me by saying, "Maybe it's time I go with the truth."

I still, climbing onto the bed, not quite sure what to think of that. I was fully expecting the dare. Maybe this is a sign. Maybe I should use this opportunity to come straight out and ask him what's in his head and what we're going to do about us. Ask him if this game we're playing is as dangerous as I'm beginning to fear it is.

Instead, I chicken out and crawl closer until our faces are only a foot apart. "Okay, Dally, tell me the truth then. Do you like my new pjs?"

His answer is to lunge forward and tackle me to the bed. I outright giggle as he bites my neck.

"Is that answer enough, you little smarty pants?" he rasps against my throat before nipping at me again. I thread my fingers through his hair.

He lifts his head, propping his weight on his elbows as he looks down at me with lazy eyes. I scan his face, taking in the laugh lines fanning from his eyes and the rough stubble dotted here and there with silver. Dang, he's handsome. My fingernails graze the stubble.

His gaze flicks back and forth between my eyes, and his lips part. I can tell he's about to say something weighty, but I can't hear it. Not right now. I'm not ready for reality to crash in just yet. So, I lift my head and press my lips to his.

Being a red-blooded man, he's easy to distract and is soon lost in the kiss just as deeply as I am. Long minutes later, I open my eyes as he backs away from my lips to breathe.

He's clearly unbothered as he says, "Your turn, Sweetness. Truth or dare?"

We could play this game all night. And we do.

CHAPTER
Twenty-One

NEVER MISS A GOOD CHANCE TO SHUT UP

DALLAS

I finished the historical romance audiobook and started in on another one, *Nailing and Caulking the Fixer-Upper*. This one is right up my alley and also from this century. Maybe the reason my grand gesture failed is because I was basing it off of Victorian England, and this is the American South. Let's hope I'm on the right path this time because everything has been going so well with Shelby. I can't see a future without her in it.

And not as my best friend.

As my everything.

It's the opening day for the annual Knockers County Fair in Hornville. We'll take Ryder to it this weekend when he's back from his mom's. Shelby and I have been going to this thing together since we were fifteen.

Ridge refused to come because Tiff is still gone, though he doesn't normally come even when she is in town. He's at his best friend, Korbin's, house, checking out a new horse. Skye hitched a ride with us, decked out in a saloon girl outfit that had Pops cringing. Fathers never like to see their baby girls in bustiers and feathers, but Pops was smart enough not to say a word and start World War III. Frankie and Morgan came in their own vehicle and are waiting for us outside the turnstiles to enter the fair.

"Are we ready to eat all the fried foods 'til we puke?" Frankie hollers, drawing chuckles from several people around us. Morgan claps, egging on her wife, which is highly inadvisable. As someone who grew up with Frankie, I know she doesn't need any encouragement to be ridiculous. She thrives on eye rolls.

"I think I'll stick to the chicken on a stick," Shelby responds.

"Slap some deep-fried butter on it first," Frankie adds. "And follow it with a deep-fried Twinkie."

"I want to see if I can push my way up to the front of the stage," Skye says, changing the subject and taking her ticket out of the front of her corset. "That lead singer of the opening band is gorgeous!"

"Girl, with that outfit, you can take over the world," Morgan agrees, linking her arm through Frankie's and handing their tickets to the poor teen manning the turnstile. He's got his gaze fixed on my sister's cleavage. I clear my throat, and he snaps out of it, his face going bright red when he takes Skye's ticket.

"I really wish Houston would come home. The estrogen-testosterone balance is off," I mutter to Shelby, handing two tickets to the teen and waiting for Shelby to go through the turnstile before following her.

She turns back to wait for me and slides her hand into mine like it's the most natural thing in the world. "Any word that he might?"

I swallow down the frustration with my twin. Tonight's

supposed to be about fun, not worrying about the ranch or picking fights with my family. "Not yet."

Shelby must sense my reluctance to talk about it because she lets the subject drop. "What's first? Rides, food, or music?"

I lift our conjoined hands and spin her around like we're on a dance floor. She grins, falling into my chest. I dip my head and press a kiss to her lips that's not totally decent out in public. Thank goodness for cowboy hats that provide a little screening.

"I have a session at the photography booth reserved for us," I manage to say when we come up for air. My family must have wandered off to find their own fun, as evidenced by the lack of squawking from my sisters.

"You do?" Shelby looks up at me, eyes wide. She's so pretty today with her painted-on jeans and black blouse with a fringe that swings whenever she moves. Turquoise jewelry covers her fingers, throat, and wrists.

"Sure do, honey." I tug her down the first row of tents, knowing exactly where I'm headed. I already stopped by this morning to set the scene. Amazing what a vendor will let you do when you slip them a few twenties and shoot the breeze for a bit.

When we get to the photography booth, I twirl Shelby around again, just to see that fringe spread out and hear her giggle. When she's stable on her feet, I step behind her and put my hands over her eyes.

"What are you doing, Dallas Gamble?" she asks pertly, hands going to her hips. She doesn't pull away though, so I know she's all bark and no bite.

"Step into the tent, Sweetness," I whisper in her ear. I feel her shiver against me before she follows my directions. I wait until she's square in the center of the tent and the photographer has given me a wink and stepped out the back, leaving us alone.

I pull my hands away from her eyes. "Shelby and Dallas. Throughout the years."

Shelby's mouth drops open as her head swivels right and left. Covering every single wall is a pinned picture of her and me, both at this fair and every other event we've gone to together. Every available surface has a candle, the dancing flames lighting up the tent like a fancy restaurant.

The photo I had blown up into a poster size is from the night we made our pact and posed in this very booth. In the photo, Shelby's staring up at me in a western dress that did amazing things to her figure. I'm standing in a long leather coat, one hand on a rifle, the other wrapped around Shelby's waist. We both look much younger. The picture is in sepia, drained of color, but sparking with an energy between us that I tried to ignore back then. It's clear as day to me now.

Shelby and I have always had chemistry. More than that, we've always loved each other. Just took me a few decades to figure out I'm *in* love with her too.

"Dally," Shelby breathes, taking it all in. When she finally turns to me, there are tears in her eyes. "I remember that year."

We both turn to look at the poster of us. "You remember us getting drunk as skunks after the fair?"

Shelby laughs. "I do."

I can't hide how much hearing her say those words affects me. I want to hear them from her mouth in a different kind of setting. Where she's in white, and I'm promising to love her forever.

I step forward and take her hand, voice raspy with emotion I'm not sure she's ready to hear about yet. "Let's get into costume and add another photo to our history."

Shelby gives me the kind of smile I tuck away in my memory banks. There's a softness in her eyes as she gazes up at me that matches how I feel about her. I've finally done something right. Which is why I have to ruin the moment by slapping her on her gorgeous butt. She yelps and swats my chest playfully.

"Go on, get dressed, woman." I add a little extra twang to my voice just to get into character.

While Shelby steps behind the trifold partition to change into the dress I already placed there for her, I slide into the long leather jacket, pull a heavy-duty gunslinger belt around my waist, and loop a turquoise bolo tie through my collar.

"Umm…" Shelby's voice comes from behind the partition.

"Something wrong, honey?" I ask, knowing full well what she's thinking. Most of the material of that barmaid dress is in the long skirt, not the top. The lace will just barely cover her top. This is why I paid the photographer handsomely to keep everyone else away so our photoshoot would be private.

"So…" Shelby comes out from behind the partition, looking so stunningly beautiful I choke on my own spit and have to cough my way to having a voice again. "Where's the rest of it?"

"Dang, Sweetness." I walk over to her, gazing down at all those curves on display just for me. "You are the pertiest woman I've ever seen."

Shelby blushes but tries to brush off the compliment. I grab her hands, pull her over to the backdrop, and have a seat on the barstool. She plops down on my lap due to the momentum, just like I wanted her to. I band my arms around her waist and tell myself I won't stare at her like a teenage boy. At forty years old, I must have a small bit of self-control by now, right?

I whistle, and the photographer comes back inside the booth. "All ready for your photos?" The guy is old, the same photographer from when we were kids, except now he's missing a few teeth and most of his hair. Somehow, he still has the bellbottom pants though.

"I can't believe you did this," Shelby whispers, looking over at me.

I squeeze her waist, wanting so badly to kiss her right now. "Have to document every year with my best friend."

She smiles softly, and I get lost in her eyes. I think about twenty years from now, still tricking her into falling into my lap. The teasing. The support. The love that's never failed, even after all these years.

Gosh, I've been an idiot not to see this woman right in front of me.

"Just like that, you lovebirds," the photographer rasps.

We both jolt, clearly having forgotten where we are. He gives us directions for a few more ridiculous poses. We're done in fifteen minutes, assured he got some great shots of us together. Shelby trips over the bearskin rug on her way to change out of the barmaid costume. I drop the rifle to steady her.

"Oh, sweet mother of moondust," the photographer dead-pans from behind us.

We both look over in time to see that the rifle has knocked over one of the candles. A great whooshing noise fills the tent, and suddenly the entire bearskin is up in flames. Shelby gasps, and I lunge into action, trying to kick the bearskin out of the tent before the whole structure catches fire. I don't manage it, though. The flap of material at the entry catches a bit of the flame. Sadly, the tent material is clearly synthetic and lights on fire like I sprayed lighter fluid on it.

"Get out!" I shout over my shoulder.

Shelby and the photographer run out the back while I stamp my feet on the rug as quickly as I can to put it out. Several guys run up and toss their drinks on the tent, slowing down the progression of the fire. People are either screaming and running away with their frightened children or running toward us with their own drinks in hand. The next few minutes unfold in slow motion, cups and buckets and ice being thrown in every direction.

Shelby presses into my side, panic clearly written all over her face.

"I'm okay, Sweetness. You okay?"

She nods, but I can feel her trembling.

The fire is put out thanks to my fellow Big Knobbers, but not before we draw quite a crowd. Billows of black smoke fill the air, and I'm pretty sure I'll be paying for that photographer to get a new tent before the evening is over. Worse than all of that, though, is the jeering face I see right at the front of the crowd.

Shane. Shelby's ex-boyfriend.

Firefighters run past us, making sure the fire's totally out. Shelby's still trembling, latched on to me like she's scared out of her mind. *Crap.* I can't believe I messed it up again. It was all going so well, too.

"That's the kind of loser you're into now, Shelbs?" Shane calls out loudly. He scoffs. "Good luck. You're gonna need it."

Shelby goes rigid. The shame I feel is heavier than this leather costume jacket. I move to push her behind me, to shield her from this public display of stupidity that I'm sadly the instigator of, but she stands firm. In fact, she squares her shoulders, nearly popping out of the top of that barmaid costume. Another regret of mine. I never intended for her to be in the public eye in that thing.

Before I can think of a way out of this ridiculous situation without losing any more of my dignity or getting Shelby in any further danger, she marches away from me. Straight for Shane.

I'm so stunned, I freeze, watching the scene unfold just like everyone else around us.

"Shut your lying mouth, Shane! Dallas Gamble is three times the man you could ever be! You tried to kill me with shellfish because you're too thoughtless to remember I'm allergic. Want to see what a real man's made of? Look no further than my fiancé."

Shelby's hands go to her hips, laying into the man like Meemaw when we threaten one of her chickens. I've never been more proud of her.

"He's got more class in his pinkie finger than you do in your whole worthless body. Speaking of his pinkie finger, it's bigger than your—"

Someone nearby whistles, drowning out the rest of that statement. "Ouch," someone else murmurs.

I grin like an idiot and stroll over to her, leaning down to scoop her up in my arms. She's still ranting and raving about small body parts and big trucks over my shoulder like a lioness as I walk her back to the tent to recover her clothes. As soon as we get inside what's left of the tent and she simmers down, I bend her over my arm and kiss the heck out of her before letting her go change.

I may have messed up another gesture, but I refuse to mess up my relationship with Shelby. She's a queen, and quite frankly, I don't deserve her.

She emerges from the partition with her own clothes on. I've handed over all the cash I had in my wallet to the photographer and promised to come back tomorrow with more. Shelby pulls me over to a stack of hay bales just outside the row of booths where we can speak in private.

"Humiliated enough for one day? Want to go home?" I ask, dreading her answer.

Shelby just stares at me, though, and it makes me uncomfortable. Is she going to ask me to call off this whole fake engagement thing now? My head drops just thinking about her wanting to move out. I'm such an idiot. I wouldn't blame her.

"Dallas?" she asks softly.

I lift my head, square my shoulders, and tell myself to man up. If she's breaking things off, I have to face it like a man.

"Yes?"

She reaches up and cups my face, her thumb stroking back and forth across my cheek. She's totally breaking things off.

"What's going on with you?" she finally asks. "The cow the other day? The photo booth? What are you doing, Dally?"

My head drops again, but she slides her hand under my chin and pulls me back up to meet her gaze.

"Just tell me."

I try to look away, but she just shifts so that she's in my direct line of sight. Exasperated, I decide the only way forward is to be honest. I know, I'm stunned too, but if there's one woman who can make me do things I normally don't, it's Shelby. The words explode out of my mouth. Overdue and packed with frustration.

"I'm trying to do these grand gestures you say you love so much! I've read two romance books, and they gave me ideas, but it just doesn't seem to work out for me. I'm pulling out all the stops, and they just end in failure!"

Shelby's eyes soften, but she doesn't let up on my chin. "But why? Why do all this?"

I gape at her. "Because I love you, Shelby! I'm *in* love with you! You want a man to do all these romantic gestures, and I'm trying my best, but maybe I've been correct all this time. I'm just not good enough for you. I mean, we've both known that, but I was still hoping I could be the man you said you've always wanted." I pull my chin out of her grasp, too upset to be still. My hand finds the back of my neck, and my boots kick up dust as I pace back and forth.

"I thought if I could be the man you wanted, you'd fall in love with me too. But all I've done is mess things up and prove I will *never* be the man you want."

"Dallas," Shelby says, reaching for me.

I hold up my hand. "No. It's okay. I don't say all that to guilt you into feeling something for me that you don't. I'm just telling you where my head's at, okay?"

"Dude! Did you burn down the photo booth?" Frankie's

screech interrupts my tense confession, which is just as well. I'm done making a fool out of myself tonight.

"Did you finally cuss out Shane? My hero!" My sister and her wife rush over, talking over each other about the incident that everyone's gossiping about.

Shelby, though, doesn't say a word.

CHAPTER
Twenty~Two
WELL, SLAP MY BUTT AND CALL ME SALLY!

SHELBY

"Tell me I heard wrong and Dallas didn't just burn down half the tents." A breathless Josie Mae sidles up next to me in the main thoroughfare.

"You heard wrong," I reply distractedly, my head on a swivel as I search the crowd for any sign of Dallas. One minute we were crowded in chaos, and the next he was gone.

"Thank goodness." Jo sighs in relief, pulling her thick hair up with both hands and winding it into a knot.

"He only burned one down." Where is he?

"Oh, my gosh!" Her hair slips from her hands and falls back to her shoulders. "Is everybody okay?"

"I think so. Well, physically at least." A couple of sticky-faced kids almost plow into us as we maneuver our way through the crowd.

"What does that mean?"

"It means that right after he knocked a half dozen candles onto a hay bale and rug in the photo booth, Dallas Gamble told me he's in love with me."

Jo's gasp is so sharp I worry she might have sucked down a few insects.

"I know!" I throw my hands out. "I can't make heads or tails of it, but he disappeared before I could utter a word or get an explanation. He just dropped a bomb and then scrammed. I'm looking for him now."

"I just saw him heading out the gates at the opposite end from the parking lot. Figured he was running from the cops like he was back in high school."

I grab her arm and pull her with me. "Well, come on then. I need to talk to him." Understatement of the century. When Dallas made his proclamation, I was dumbfounded. And then, with Frankie and company storming through and smoke billowing around us, I lost sight of him.

I hit redial on the phone clutched in my hand as we hustle toward the back gate. All I hear is a steady beep.

"He's not picking up, and now I'm mad I didn't think ahead and add his phone to my Find My app." Not that it would make much difference right now. This many people crammed into one spot with only one measly cell tower means crappy service.

Josie Mae keeps pace beside me, our boots kicking up dust as we double-time it. "Oh, so you had foreknowledge he was gonna burn down a tent, declare his undying love, and take off running, did you?"

"Well, when you put it like that...I just don't understand why he'd take off. That's not a good sign, is it?" If he was being serious, why would he drop a love bomb and not hang around to hear a response? Honestly, it's like ordering a pizza, paying for it, and then leaving it on the takeout counter. Who does that?

"Well, if you're hoping he meant it, I'd say no. Is that what you're hoping?" She gets ahead of me and turns to get a clear look at my face. The woman is gonna fall flat on her butt if she keeps walking backward like that.

"I don't know!" I huff in frustration. "It's all so confusing. I mean, we've been messing around a bit, but for Dallas, I figured it was just a physical thing. Same for me since he kissed me on the dance floor of Knockin' Boots that night."

She points a knowing finger in my face. "I told you that kiss knocked something loose." Then she almost trips over a denim-clad cowboy before facing the right way again.

"It appears the *something* was any sense of chastity or self-preservation," I reply in the driest tone I've got.

"Are you saying you're in love with him?"

"I don't know, Jo!" My hands flap in the air. "What's the number one rule we always repeat every time we see him with a new woman?"

"Have fun, girl, but don't get attached," we recite in unison.

"He's a good-time guy—the same kind my momma warned me about," I add.

"But what if he's not anymore?"

"Come on now, Jo. This isn't one of my romance novels."

"Yeah, he's never really had much in common with our studs from Bridgerton, has he? Although it might be fun seeing him in a top hat and a waistcoat."

"Please, if it's not cotton or denim, I'm pretty sure his immune system would shut down."

We pass by Billie from Stuffin' the Muffin on our way through the gate, and Josie Mae stops her. "Hey, Billie. Have you seen Dallas?"

She snaps her gum and nods. "Yeah. Not ten minutes ago. Looked to be headin' for Main Street."

What in Sam Hill is he doing in downtown Hornville?

Around here, we refer to Hornville as "the city," but the term is relative. Hornville is a city in the sense that it has both a Walmart *and* a Jiffy Lube, as well as a handful of fast-food joints. Not to be confused with "the big city," Oklahoma City, however. They've got more big box stores than you can shake a stick at.

We hoof it two blocks until we finally turn the corner onto Main Street, looking like a couple of meerkats as we scan the sidewalks for any sign of a flustered cowboy. No luck.

"Maybe he went for a beer," Jo suggests. "I'd probably need a drink after lighting crap on fire. Let's check out the Hornville Tavern."

We forge ahead, passing a vape shop and a realty office before walking by a jeweler with a sparkling display window. We're almost even with the hair salon next door when something catches my eye.

I stop in my tracks and back up like I'm a cartoon character getting yanked offstage by one of those giant hooks.

And then I stare. And stare some more.

"Is he in there?" Josie Mae asks, scrambling to my side and placing a hand above her eyes to look through the jeweler's window.

Since I can't find any intelligible words, I point frantically instead.

"What is the matter?" She frowns at me.

In response, I raise my left hand and nearly slap my palm on the glass. It only takes her a couple seconds to catch up before another insect-ingesting gasp escapes. "Oh my…"

My friend has apparently also lost the power of speech because she proceeds to point slack-jawed back and forth between the engagement ring on my finger and its identical twin in the display window. Right next to a tag with a dollar sign and waaay too many digits.

I start to hyperventilate.

Jo starts to choke.

"Y'all need some medical intervention over there?" a voice calls from the sidewalk across the street.

I turn to wave the person off so I can die in relative

privacy, when I see it's none other than Brad the fireman, one of Dallas's dates.

"Oh, hey! Didn't realize it was you, Shelby. You okay?" His expression is both pleased and earnest.

All I can do is nod as a grimace forms on my lips. Thankfully, Josie Mae has recovered enough to rasp, "She's fine. She just found out her fiancé loves her a heckuva lot more than she realized."

Even through my stupor, I note a downturn to Brad's expression. Was Dallas onto something and Brad was thinking he might be the Drake to my Lydia in *Burning Loins: A Tale of Fire and Romance*? One of my faves.

Huh. Now that I get a second look, Brad isn't nearly as handsome or dashing as I previously thought. He's just...a nice man on a sidewalk who likes women.

"I thought you said it was costume jewelry!" Jo hisses at me, ignoring Brad.

I wave goodbye and turn back to her. "I thought it was! Dallas even said so." Or did he? I claw back for the memory of his exact words but can't find them.

"Well, my friend, I'd say this is definitive confirmation that the man is gone over you. Old dog, meet new trick." she whoops.

"Why did he go and do a stupid thing like this?" I plead, deflating Jo's gleeful gesturing.

"Stupid's not the word I'd choose, in case you want my two cents."

"What I mean is, he can't afford to spend that kind of money on me! He needs it for the ranch. For Ryder!" Holy crap!

"Why don't you let the man decide for himself what he wants to do with his own money?" She grabs my left hand and taps the ring. "Besides, you're worth it."

Tears sting my nose. Stupid hormones. I need to find that sweet, crazy, sexy, wonderful idiot. Now more than ever.

My phone rings, and I snatch it from my pocket, hoping to see Dallas's handsome face on the screen. I guess we're far enough from the crowd to have service again. But it's Pops. Maybe Dallas caught a ride to the ranch and left the truck for me?

"Hey, Pops. What's up? Have you seen Dallas?"

"No, darlin'." He sounds agitated. "I'm sorry to bug you on your day off, but I've got a calving heifer in the west pasture struggling something fierce. Calf is breech, and I can't turn it. Been doin' this for fifty years, and I've met my match today. Ridge ain't answering his phone, and I don't want to leave the old girl to go find him."

Crap. I immediately shift into work mode. "Okay, Pops, I'm in Hornville with Josie Mae, so it'll take a hot minute, but I'll get there. Try to keep her as calm as you can, and I'll be there in thirty. Hang on."

Jo is already fishing her keys out as we haul butt back toward the fair parking lot. I'll have to find Dallas later. First, I've got a momma and baby to save.

———

"Well, that was fun." I smile up at Pops as the cow lows beside me. Her calf teeters on skinny legs, only to collapse immediately before trying again.

"You and I have very different ideas of a good time," he drawls, wiping the sweat from his brow and replacing his hat on his head.

"You best be sure to bill me this time, you hear?"

"We'll see. We're pretty much family, after all."

He crouches to rub the calf's head, the setting sun casting his long shadow on the field grass. "We can dispense with the 'pretty much' part soon, I expect."

"Pops," I scold.

"I always knew you two would end up together. You just

needed time to get out of your own ways. I like to think love always wins."

I peel off my gloves and drop them to the ground. "Look at you, you old softie. I don't think it's a lack of love that's the sticking point, just so you know. We've been best friends for so long, I just don't know if we're meant for anything more when it comes down to it."

"Well, just so *you* know, my son has known you were it for years. I reckon he's been waitin' for you to catch up."

"Are we talking about the same son? Dallas Beaufort Gamble? The guy who drained the local dating pool and had to move on to the next county before he was twenty-five?"

Pops shakes his head and stands again. "I ain't saying he was never a ladies' man. Inherited that the good old-fashioned way." He rocks on his boot heels and grins just like his boys.

"You lie where you stand, old man," I drawl. "You're the *definition* of a one-woman man. And Tessa was lucky to have you."

"I was the lucky one." His grin turns wistful. "Just like Dallas is lucky to have you."

"I'm afraid you may be reading too much into things, Pops. I'd never ask Dallas to be anybody but the man he is."

"And he's the man who's been carrying a ratty old napkin in his wallet for going on twenty years. That's who he is, and don't you forget it."

My chin jerks back, and I eye him carefully. "What are you talking about?"

A crow caws in the open sky above us like an omen as he replies, "Don't play coy with me, darlin'. I know all about it. Always have."

My eyes narrow. "Ranchin' not keeping you busy enough? You had to take up spying as a side gig?"

"No need. Don't you know all parents have eyes in the backs of their heads?"

The calf struggles to his hooves again as his mom licks his head. This time, he doesn't falter. Pops and I share a huge smile when he wobbles around in a full circle without falling.

"'Atta boy," I coo. "Time to start your new life."

"I could say the same to you," Pops says, always having to get the last word in.

Needing some headspace, I take Tango back to Dallas's house, letting the warm breeze rush over my face and whip my hair as I ride. Pops must be smoking some of Meemaw's weed, going on about the pact napkin like that. No way has Dallas been carrying it around all this time. Why would he?

When I get to the house, I tie the horse up and take the porch steps to the door. I need a good scrub-down after working with the animals, and then I'll ride back to the big house and get someone to bring me home later.

Nelly greets me at the door, tail and tongue wagging in tandem.

"Hey, buddy." He vigorously sniffs my clothes. "I'll bet you're smelling that calf, aren't you? You leave him alone, though, you hear me? He's not for supper."

Nelly ignores my instructions, snuffling away at my pant legs as I walk toward the hall. I pause, hearing what sounds like running water. When I get to the bedroom, sure enough, Dallas's jeans and shirt from earlier lie strewn on the bed, along with his boxer briefs and socks. He's home. And he's in the shower.

Nerves immediately grip my belly in a stranglehold. Why am I so nervous? I clamp my teeth over my bottom lip and glance back at the bed. "Pops, you're nuts," I mutter as I reluctantly yank Dallas's discarded jeans to the edge of the mattress and pull his wallet from the back pocket. "Old man just loves stirring stuff up, that's all," I continue to talk to myself as I unfold the leather and search the various sleeves.

It doesn't take long to find it. Tucked in the innermost pocket is the faded Knockin' Boots napkin with our handwriting on it. I pull it carefully from the wallet and unfold it. The creases are deep and worn, the edges of the napkin looking almost grungy from wear. It dawns on me then that a napkin sitting in a forgotten drawer all this time wouldn't look anything like this. It might be stiff and possibly faded, but certainly not shredded at the edges with time-worn creases like a favorite old road map.

My eyes go to the bathroom door. The shower just shut off, and I can hear Dallas muttering to himself on the other side.

With the utmost care, I refold the napkin and return it to its rightful place in the wallet—where I now know it's been living since the night my best friend and I made a silly pact while drinking and thinking about all of life's what-ifs.

Except, now it sounds like the furthest thing from silly. Now it sounds a lot like…love.

CHAPTER
Twenty~Three
HER FAMILY TREE IS A WREATH

DALLAS

"I need you to find her," I growl to my sister over the phone while my truck bounces in a pothole.

Frankie tsk-tsks in my ear, which she knows annoys the crap out of me. "I looked! Someone said they saw her with Josie Mae. I'm sure she's fine."

I sigh, exasperated and more than a little freaked out. "'Kay, thanks. Call me if you see her."

Wade called me at the fair right after I lost sight of Shelby, saying I needed to get back to the ranch as soon as possible. I only got out of him that something is wrong with Ridge before the line dropped. You'd think a town as big as Hornville could get their cell service operational as a matter of basic safety.

So here I am, driving away from the woman I just confessed my love to, after I nearly burned down the fair, and she had to defend me to her ex-boyfriend. My fist hits the steering wheel, but even that sharp sting of pain doesn't help me feel less frustrated. Ridge better be dying.

My truck skids to an abrupt halt on the dirt cut-through when I see the hulking outline of my older brother in the field that borders Wade's farmland. He's got a bonfire going, which isn't abnormal. This spot is where we often have a controlled burn, but when Ridge tips his head back and drinks something before staggering around the fire, I know something's off. Ridge isn't a drinker. Not to excess anyway.

I hustle over, checking out the fire and seeing that it's contained. My responsible brother even has a hose ready to go just in case. I swing my focus to Ridge. He takes another swig, and I'm close enough now to see it's whiskey. He wipes the back of his mouth with his wrist. When he sees me, he leans left and then staggers right.

"Whadya doin' 'ere," he slurs.

Well, great. "Coming to check on you, big bro. You okay?" I put a hand on his shoulder to steady him. Dang, he's rocking more than a canoe in a hurricane. Takes a lot to make the sturdiest Gamble boy sway on his boots.

He bats off my hand and tilts back his head for another sip. With a growl, he takes the bottle from his lips and tips it over the dusty ground. It's empty. He throws the thing in the fire, where it shatters and sparks.

"Whoa, easy there," I mutter, hoping he doesn't have another bottle somewhere on his person.

Ridge points at me, then staggers to the right. "Nothin' but a conniving she-devil."

My eyes widen. Ridge isn't exactly a ray of sunshine, but he doesn't usually use that kind of language to describe women either. "Who is?"

He grunts, kicks a pebble, and nearly ends up on his butt. He rights himself just in time to stay on his feet. A cloud of dust now hovers over our boots.

"Is this about Tiff?"

"Tiffany Grace!" he snaps, correcting me like she would. He spits, then steps right in it when he staggers left.

"Did she come back?" I feel like I'm playing the guessing game with a drunkard.

Ridge scoffs, grinning up at the sky like a maniac. "She come back?" His laugh makes me grimace.

"Okay. She's still gone, I take it?" I reach for my phone to check for a text or call from Shelby and realize I left it in the truck. I think about getting it to call Pops. Maybe he can talk some sense into Ridge.

Ridge swings his head back and nearly plows right into me, losing his balance. I barely right us both. Scratch that. Not calling Pops. Ridge is too unstable right now. He ricochets off me and bends down next to the fire. I reach for him, worried he's going to take a header into the flames. He straightens, unscathed, with a stack of papers that had been held down by a rock.

"Look at this crap," he spits. He nearly throws the stack of papers at me.

I manage to keep it all together by some small miracle, but it's the heading on the top page that has my blood running cold.

Summons: Petition for Divorce.

My head whips up to see Ridge wiping his hands over his eyes. Oh no. Is Ridge crying? Personally, I think this calls for celebration, but maybe now's not the time to verbalize how much I despise my sister-in-law.

I wave the stack of papers. "Didn't know this was coming?"

Ridge snorts and has to wipe his eyes again. He plops down in the dirt and stares into the flames. I sit down next to him, giving him enough room to take a swing and not hit me. Even drunk he could do some damage. Clearly, he's in shock. Wouldn't be surprised if he started a fight just to have something to take his mind off the impending divorce.

We end up sitting like that for close to thirty minutes without physical violence. The flames start to die down, and

I'm itching to get my phone out of the truck and call Shelby. I don't, though. My brother needs me right now. Besides, Frankie knows to look for her.

"Had no freakin' idea," Ridge finally says, voice raw. "Went out to my truck to check the cattle and some weasel in a polo shirt handed me the papers. A polo shirt. Can you believe that crap?"

He's still slurring his words a bit, but he's built like an ox. It would take more than half a bottle of whiskey to take him down. I'm not sure the polo shirt is what I'd be focused on in this situation, but I go with it.

"Total weasel, I agree."

Ridge turns to me suddenly, and I brace for impact. He grabs my shirt by the fistful and shakes. "She left to visit her parents! What kind of witch doesn't even call and just sends divorce papers?"

I want to answer that one because most of us know exactly what kind of witch Tiff is, but now's not the time. She made my brother feel guilty for all the time he spent keeping the family ranch going, as if she didn't know his responsibilities when they got married. Then she made him feel less-than because he didn't come from family money like her. When asked to help in an emergency, she'd find half a dozen excuses to get out of it. Don't even get me started on not being able to give her a simple nickname without her biting our heads off. She just…didn't fit in.

"She got some fancy lawyer."

Now that's got my attention. Is Tiff gonna try to take Ridge to the cleaners? This ranch is our family legacy. I don't know the particulars of whose name is on the deed for the land or the running of the business, but if that woman tries to take what's been in our family for generations, she's going to have to have more than a fancy lawyer. We'll all fight tooth and nail to keep what's ours.

"Women," Ridge spits. "Run, little brother. Don't get

mixed up with 'em. They'll rob you blind and leave you humiliated." He shakes his head, eyes wet. "Gave her ten years of my life and all I have are these papers." He jabs his finger into the pile of papers on the ground between us.

"Were you happy for any of those ten years?" I've wanted to ask him that since the day they got married. He's never seemed happy with Tiff, but it was never my place to point that out.

"Not sure I know what happy feels like," he muses, staring hard at the dying flames. "Momma died. I took over the ranch because Pops was a mess. Then I married Tiffany Grace because we'd been dating for four years, and it was time to make a move or cut her loose. I spent most days trying to convince her to stay on a dying ranch in the middle of nowhere, Oklahoma." He snorts. "I'm forty-five years old and not sure I ever had a day of happiness. How pathetic is that?"

Pretty sure that's rhetorical, so I don't say a thing.

His hand whacks me on the arm. "You got whiskey on you?"

I shake my head. "Nah, man. I didn't know we were having a breakdown today."

I spent my morning getting ready for my grand gesture at the fair. Not that I want to tell Ridge about that. Then again, misery loves company. Heck, he may not even remember this conversation tomorrow when he sobers up.

"I told Shelby I love her today."

Ridge's expression doesn't change. "Really?"

I shrug. "Yeah. At the fair."

"And?"

"And…she didn't say anything back."

Ridge winces. "That ain't good."

"Yeah. That's what I was thinking."

He shakes his head and sighs. "Man, you had it good too.

Best friends for years. Why'd you gotta go and fall for her and ruin things?"

My head falls until I'm staring at the dirt. "I don't know what to do now. She probably hates me. At the very least, I've made things uncomfortable. Maybe I should do the public breakup thing we always planned on. Let her move back to her place. I can't imagine she wants to stay with me and Ryder, knowing how I feel."

Ridge just stares at the smoke drifting up into the sky. Thankfully the temperature has come down as the sun sets and the flames die down. The fire is mostly gone, just a smoldering pile of ash left in its wake. There's a metaphor in there I don't want to analyze too closely right now.

"Least you didn't give her your last name and share your finances. Your house."

I wince, remembering how I offered to give Shelby a baby. That's a heck of a complication. Good thing she was smarter than me and never took me up on that.

"I always knew Shelby would be the one woman to bring me to my knees."

Ridge grunts. "Yeah, we all saw it. She's the only woman who ever meant something to you beyond the physical."

That just makes the pain in my chest ache that much more. We sit side by side for another hour. The sun starts to sink into the horizon, giving our land that golden hour glow that always takes my breath away. I could never leave this place like Houston.

Then again, now that Shelby's broken my heart, I might need to take a temporary trip. Any ol' place to get away from her for a bit. I just need some time to drop this stupid love thing. I can get back to my free-spirited ways, right? I just need a trip to the beach or something. Some sun, sand, and tanned bikini bodies. Surely that'll do the trick.

When my butt is officially numb from sitting in the dirt, I

stand up and brush myself off. "We can live without 'em, right?"

Ridge grunts, standing up and shaking his legs out. He sways once but catches himself. "Got no other choice."

I nod once, then drop the subject. "Want a ride back?"

Ridge nods too, then follows me to my truck. I drop him off at the big house, making sure he gets inside with his paperwork and doesn't detour to Knockin' Boots. The last thing that guy needs is a drunk and disorderly charge to add to his woes. Besides, if word gets out that Ridge Gamble is single again, all the ladies north of thirty will be hounding him. Shoot, maybe once the fake engagement is officially off, he and I can ride together and pull in the ladies.

That thought should make me whoop with excitement, but instead it just makes my ribs ache like I fell off a horse today. My phone dings from the passenger seat, where it's been this whole time. I see a string of messages and missed calls. I ignore them all and head for home.

It's time to face the music.

Time to face Shelby and end this ridiculous fake engagement. If I'm lucky, we'll be able to salvage our friendship when all is said and done. If I'm not lucky, I might just have to make that beach vacation permanent.

Twenty~Four

LETTIN' THE CAT OUTTA THE BAG IS A WHOLE LOT EASIER THAN PUTTIN' IT BACK IN

SHELBY

I consider busting through the bathroom door, Kool-Aid man style, but my feet are stuck to the floor, and my heart is beating out of my chest.

Dallas Beaufort Gamble is in love with me.

Let me say that again. DALLAS BEAUFORT GAMBLE IS IN LOVE WITH ME!

What kind of crazy world am I living in? This wasn't supposed to happen. We're best friends, something I've never let myself lose sight of for a very good reason. Dallas doesn't fall in love.

But he's somehow in love with me. And maybe has been for a long time, which I can finally admit is something we may have in common. I never let myself acknowledge it fully before because it wouldn't have made any difference. He was a good-time guy, not at all what I needed.

I pull my lips between my teeth to keep from laughing or screaming or who the heck knows what. I feel like I'm sixteen.

I should really go buy a lottery ticket. Or not, since they don't sell them to sixteen-year-olds.

More murmuring comes from the other side of the bathroom door, and I wonder for the briefest of seconds if someone is in there with him. But that's impossible since Dallas Beaufort Gamble is in love with *me*. A giddy teenager laugh escapes, and the murmuring immediately stops. Oops.

The door opens to reveal Dallas in all his muscular glory, hair wet, chest bare, and a towel draped dangerously low around his hips. Steam billows around him like a frickin' Hollywood movie, and my mouth immediately waters.

This man is mine if I want him. And, holy moly, do I want him.

Before I can give it another thought, I pounce, closing the distance and throwing my arms around him.

"Oh my gosh!" My voice comes out in a wheeze against his hot shoulder. "I can't believe this." I must have caught him by surprise because his arms don't automatically close around me.

In fact, he takes a step back and braces his hands on my shoulders before prying me off of him and putting space between us. My arms drop, and I smile up at him, head tilted in question, ready to hear whatever sweet or funny thing he has to say. But he's not smiling back. His jaw shifts, and his brow creases with deep furrows.

"So," he begins, voice tight. "I was thinking we should plan that public breakup. I know I haven't found you somebody, but I promise I'll still make you look like the hero."

"Very funny." I go back in, eager to kiss him for the first time knowing how he really feels, but his hands are firm on my shoulders, restraining me. "What are you doing?" My voice is tinged with humor because he's got to be kidding around. Right?

"I've kept you here long enough. You took care of Shane once and for all today, so I don't think we have to worry about him anymore. You must be dying for your own space again."

"Dallas," I begin, my smile faltering. "Please tell me you're joking."

"No, ma'am."

"No, ma'am?" I cough out an incredulous laugh. "Stop kidding around. Is this because I didn't say I love you back? You did notice the fire and the crowd of people barging in, right?"

"You don't have to say it. I shouldn't have said it. It was a mistake."

"A mistake?" I sound like a parrot repeating everything he says, but I can't make sense of this. Nelly whines from the doorway, proving he's just as confused as I am.

"You know how impulsive I am. It's one of the things that bugs you most about me."

"No, it's not."

"Yes, it is."

"No, it's not!" I insist, taking a step back. "Don't tell me what I think or how I feel, Dallas Beaufort Gamble!"

Nelly whines again, and Dallas frowns at him. "Okay. Fine. You love that I'm an impulsive screw-up." His gaze swings back to me. "Are you happy? Now, let's plan this breakup."

"No."

"What do you mean, no?"

My hands go to my hips. "We're not breaking up."

"Yes, we are. It was the plan from the beginning, and it's best we just go back to being friends. We got a little carried away, that's all."

"I didn't get carried away. I'm exactly where I'm supposed to be. And so are you."

"Oh, so I can't tell you how you feel but you can tell me how I do?" He throws his hands out, nearly causing his towel to drop to the floor. He rescues it just in time.

"I don't need to. You told me yourself."

"Like I said, that was me being stupid and gettin' a wild hair."

"I see. And the ring?" I tilt my head.

"What about the ring?" His golden eyes narrow, deepening the creases around them.

"Do you normally get a wild hair and spend *five thousand dollars* on a ring just for the heck of it?" It seems I've stumped him. "Yeah, I know it's not costume jewelry, Dallas. It's a beautiful, sweet, way-too-expensive expression of your feelings for me. You love me."

He releases a sigh of exasperation, and his dog echoes him, having come closer to stand between us. "Of course I love you. You're my best friend. And the ring looked like you."

"You're almost as bad at lying as your father."

"You deserve nice things." He reaches down and absently pets Nelly's furry brown head.

"So do you. And you deserve for someone to love you from the deepest parts of their heart and soul, Dallas. And that's how I feel about you. I always have."

He shakes his head, like doing so might make my words scatter in the wind. "You deserve someone who can give you all the things you've always dreamed of, and I'm not that guy. See how quickly I went from those stupid grand gestures to talking about breaking up right now? I can't be trusted. I don't do long-term, and you know it."

If he thinks I'm just gonna let this go, he's crazy. "Then explain the napkin to me. Why was it in your wallet all these years?"

"What are you talking about?" He crouches for a better petting position, clearly avoiding looking me in the eye while he lies. "I found it a couple months ago and grabbed it on a whim that day Shane acted a fool."

"What did I just say about you being a bad liar? Am I

gonna have to start calling you Pops?" I shift to one hip and glare down my nose at him. "Speaking of, he's the one who told me you've been carrying that napkin in your wallet."

"Old man doesn't know when to keep his mouth shut," he mutters to Nelly, whose tongue is now hanging out as he basks in his master's attention.

"I'm glad he told me! In fact, I'm ecstatic he told me. Because it proves that we're meant to be together."

He finally looks up at me. "Shelby, I already told you I can't give you what you need. I refuse to break your heart or hurt you, and that's exactly what I'd do if we tried to make a go of this. We need to break up so you can find your Prince Charming."

"I already did, and it's you."

He straightens and mirrors my pose with his fists on his hips. "I don't do romance. Haven't you been paying attention?"

"No. I've been a complete idiot and haven't paid one lick of attention to what was right in front of my face." I poke his chest. "You, Dallas, are romantic as crap."

"You really missed your calling as a greeting card writer," he drawls sarcastically.

I ignore it, too eager to express how stupid I've been. "I don't need flowery gestures and love notes and romantic getaways to Paris. I just need someone who puts me first and loves me for me. And that's been you all along."

"You may think that now, but you'll change your mind. You're not one to give up on anything, especially your dreams and convictions." His eyes trace my features. "Look at you. You're a veterinarian with a thriving practice, you've got a close circle of friends and loved ones who you'd do anything for. You've given every loser in the county a shot and have never thrown the towel in. You deserve everything you've ever wanted."

My voice cracks when I say, "And that's you, Dallas."

His tone, on the other hand, is firm. "No."

The nerve! "I love you. You're my person." I match his tone.

"I'll always be your person, Shelby, no matter what. I hope you know that." He turns and snatches a pillow from the bed before pulling a fresh pair of boxers from his dresser.

"What are you doing?"

"I'm sleeping on the couch." He heads for the bedroom door, securing his towel again as he goes.

"We're not breaking up," I tell his naked back.

"Yes, we are." He grabs Nelly by the collar. I let him take the dog.

But I bolster my voice and call after him, "If you think I'm a third-act breakup girl, you've got another thing coming, *ma'am!*" I've never been a fan, and I refuse to let Dallas write the rest of this story in the name of saving our friendship.

Twenty~Five

IF SHE'S HERE, WHO'S RUNNING HELL?

DALLAS

This ridiculous couch is going to throw my back out for real this time. I toss and turn all night, complaining out loud about the lumps to an annoyed Nelly. He joined me out here, only because I grabbed him by the collar and slid him all the way out of the bedroom, where Shelby's probably sleeping peacefully right now. He whines and buries his head under his paws.

"She deserves better, and you know it," I tell him.

Nelly sprawls over on his back, tongue hanging out of his mouth. What am I talking about? Nelly doesn't have two brain cells to rub together. The little traitor just wants me to shut up, go back in the bedroom, and curl up against Shelby's soft curves so he can get a good night's sleep.

Well, that ain't happening. I'm not going to let her get her heart set on me when I know she deserves way better. I had two grand gestures that I messed up royally. I'm officially throwing in the towel. I don't have what it takes to give her the knight in shining armor treatment. I can't write a poem, and I more often than not eat with my fingers even when utensils are provided. I can guarantee her laughs and mediocre spaghetti, which is pretty much everything I happen to look for in a relationship, but I know Shelby wants more.

I love her too much to let her settle. Besides, all I've seen is proof that love only ends in heartbreak. I don't want that for us.

My phone rings on the coffee table. Nelly whines at yet another interruption, but I sit up, wide awake. Who cares if the sun isn't even up yet? Anything is better than lying here in pain, stewing on a relationship that was never meant to be.

"Hey, Pops. You okay?"

"Your brother couldn't sleep," he says by way of greeting. Huh. Guess it's going around with the Gamble boys.

"Probably because he drank so much whiskey, he's circling Mars right now."

Pops doesn't chuckle. "He read through the whole divorce petition."

"Okay." Crap, this doesn't sound good.

Pops pauses, during which my fingers go tingly with adrenaline. I can sense the danger hanging in the air. Nelly scrambles to his feet, alert and ready to charge ahead with me.

"She wants half the ranch."

My head drops. I squeeze my eyes shut and try to breathe past the anger that's strangling my throat.

"That witch," I mutter.

Pops clears his throat. "Now let's not get into name-calling, okay, son? She spent ten years at this ranch and feels she's owed a portion of its success."

I jump to my feet. "It's success? We're barely hanging on as it is, Pops! Never once has she lent a hand when we've had a project or a crisis. She was always too busy taking pictures for her non-existent photography business. You ever think about that? She's never pitched in like a family's supposed to.

This ranch has persisted *despite* her being yet another mouth to feed."

"I ain't arguing with you there," Pops says on a sigh. "But the fact is, they didn't have a prenup, and in Oklahoma, it's an equitable division. She has a lengthy list drawn up of why she thinks she deserves half."

I rub my aching neck as I pace. "And I can come up with a lengthy list of why she deserves nothing!"

"Dallas?" Shelby's soft voice takes me by surprise.

I spin on my heels and see her approaching, hair tumbled around her shoulders. Dang it. She's so beautiful, I physically ache to pull her into my arms. Instead, I swallow hard and focus on the current crisis. Pops stays on the phone while I fill her in.

Shelby's eyes widen, but then she surprises me by snatching the phone out of my hands. "Pops? I have an idea."

"I'm all ears, darlin'," I hear him say back.

"We'll get dressed and meet you at the house. I'll call Frankie and Morgan on the way over. You wake up Skye. All hands on deck." Shelby pauses a moment, then hangs up the phone and tosses it to me. "Get your fine butt in jeans, Gamble. We got a ranch to save."

She marches away from me to get dressed. For the second time before dawn, I drop my chin to my chest and groan. Why did I have to go and fall in love with her? Why is nature so cruel as to make her perfect for me, but I'm not perfect for her?

Shelby's back out, dressed in jeans and a clingy tank top, boots on and keys in hand. I'm barely getting my jeans on. "Chop, chop, Dally."

"Go stand in the kitchen," I growl. She's too distracting.

Shelby grins and shakes her hips, walking to the kitchen with Nelly scrambling to keep up with her. I gaze up at the ceiling and think about Meemaw's chickens instead of the gorgeous woman I can't seem to stay away from. When I'm finally ready to go, Nelly runs out the door to the truck first, and I snatch the keys right out of Shelby's hands.

Just because I'm not the right guy for her doesn't mean I'm going to stop being a gentleman. She doesn't fight me on it, which is a nice change of pace. We head for the big house, bumping over potholes and gullies I'll eventually fix. If we still have a ranch once Ridge gets past this divorce, that is.

"So, what's your big plan?" I ask when we finally crest the hill and see all the lights on at the house.

Shelby's thumbs have been flying over her cell phone screen the whole time we've been driving. "Wait and see," she mumbles.

I clutch my chest. "Wow. Won't even tell your fiancé?"

That gets her lifting her head. She fires a one-eyed look of disdain my way. "Oh, now you pull out the fiancé card? After you vehemently told me last night that you're planning our breakup?"

I shove the truck into Park. Nelly paws at the window in the back of the cab, eager to get out. "For your benefit," I remind her.

She shrugs. "Then I'm not telling you about my plan. For your benefit." Her smirk is annoying. I'm about to tell her that, but she slips out the door and Nelly follows her, nearly kicking me in the face as he jumps into the front seat and out the door.

I shake my head and pray for patience. The sun is just starting to lighten the sky when I get out of the truck and look east. Part of why I didn't get into ranching as deeply as Ridge was because of the early morning hours. I'm more of a night owl myself, a habit that hasn't changed much over the years.

"Keep up, Gamble!" Shelby calls from the porch before she slips inside the house.

"I like her," Meemaw crows from right beside me a moment later.

I clutch my chest. "Jeez. Didn't see you sitting there."

She's in a rocking chair on the porch, in a dark corner like a weirdo. She's got a Silkie clutched to her chest as she pets its head. She hasn't put her dentures in yet, which I only know because she gives me a gummy smile.

"You, on the other hand…you're an idiot."

"Love you too, Meemaw." I roll my eyes and head inside.

Everyone's assembled, sitting on various furniture in the family room and sipping on hot coffee. I pour myself a cup and have a seat next to Shelby on the love seat. She puts her hand on my thigh, which makes me groan internally. Never in the history of ever have I complained about a woman putting her hand on my leg. Except today. Except Shelby. Right when I've decided I have to break up with her.

"I've been texting my little brother, Archie. You all remember him?" Shelby asks, oblivious to my turmoil about her hand.

"Does he still have reddish-blond hair?" Skye asks. "He was such a little thing. So cute with that red hair."

"Just what a man wants to be called. Cute," I grumble.

Shelby ignores me. "Well, he grew, and his hair got darker. By the end of college, he topped out at six feet exactly. But more importantly, he's a divorce lawyer in Tulsa."

Pops sits forward, putting his coffee down on an end table. "Think he'll give us a friends and family discount?"

Shelby smiles. "Better. He said he'll do it pro bono."

Ridge, who's remained a stony silent participant in the corner of the room, squeezes his eyes shut. He looks terrible. His eyes are puffy and bloodshot, and he's aged ten years in the span of twenty-four hours. I feel for the guy. He's going through it emotionally, and now he carries the guilt of the family ranch being in jeopardy because of his choice in women.

I look over at Shelby as she explains the next steps. I'm proud of her. I know, even when we officially break up, she'll be my friend. She's a good person to her core. She'd never try to lash out and hurt me like Tiff is doing to Ridge. Just one more reason to love her, I guess. Just one more reason it's going to suck trying to fall out of love with her. But to keep her in my life as my best friend, I'll do it. I'll find a way. One day, one minute at a time.

As Frankie and Skye read through the entirety of the divorce papers that were given to Ridge yesterday, Shelby confers with Pops. I steal out of the room and head for the kitchen on the pretense of a coffee refill. I stop short, seeing Meemaw perched on a stepstool, bending over the kitchen sink.

"Meemaw! We've talked about this. You can't bathe the chickens in the kitchen!"

Said chicken squawks at my interruption. Meemaw looks over her shoulder, unfazed. "He's getting bumblefoot!"

I grimace and pour another cup of coffee. "Okay, well, soak his feet in a bucket, not the sink where we prepare food."

Meemaw titters. "He's as much a part of this family as you, Dallas Gamble. You use your kitchen sink as you see fit, and I'll use mine."

I roll my eyes, but she's too busy crooning at her chicken to know. Pulling out my cell phone, I hit the contact for my twin. Houston picks up, which surprises me. Then again, phone calls this early are usually an emergency.

"What?" he says, voice so rough I can barely make out what he said.

I keep my voice low, not wanting Ridge to overhear me. "We got ourselves a situation, Hou."

He clears his throat, sounding slightly more awake. "Lost more calves?"

"No, I think Shelby stopped the spread. Thank goodness, since we already lost enough to have Pops sweating bullets. It's Ridge. He got served divorce papers."

"Halle-freaking-lujah."

"That's what I was thinking at first, but then he read the whole thing from her lawyer. She's asking the court for half the ranch."

"That little she-devil's gonna see the underside of my boot if she ever shows her face around here," Meemaw mutters not quite under her breath.

"Crap," Houston breathes.

"Yeah."

We both sit there in silence, just breathing into the phone. When he finally speaks again, there's a resignation in his voice I've never heard before. I bet most people wouldn't know the difference, but this is my twin brother. I know him just about as well as he knows himself.

"I assume with the sick calves this season, we'll have to tighten our belts?"

I shake my head, feeling a little hopeless. "Even with Shelby donating her veterinary services."

"Okay," Houston sighs. "I have a rodeo in three days I can't back out of. I'll cancel the next one since that's over a week out. I'll be home within the week."

Hope, the kind that makes you think everything will be all right even when everything's falling apart, lights up my chest. "You mean it?"

"What do you think?"

"I think my brother's coming home."

Meemaw turns from the sink at the news, a grin stretching out all her wrinkles. Thank goodness she put her dentures in.

I hang up, and Meemaw puts the chicken down, its feet bandaged up in so much white gauze it glides out of the kitchen like it's ice skating. Meemaw grabs a bowl, tucks her hand in my elbow, and we walk together into the family room. Shelby and Pops have Ridge looking a little less likely to puke right then and there. Skye and Frankie are loudly discussing options.

"I think we need to pivot. This is the perfect time to close down the cattle business and do something else with this land," Skye is saying.

Pops interjects with the question we're all wondering. "Like what?"

Four generations of Ridges & Gambles have raised cattle on this land. What else can we do with it? Become farmers like Wade? No, thank you.

"Well, I'm not sure yet. But that would solve the issue. She can't take half of nothing, right? She has no right to the land itself. That's in Meemaw's name. Tiff only has a claim on the ranching side of things. If we close it down and do something else, she loses."

Skye's not wrong, but it seems a bit crazy to shut down our entire ranch. Shelby must think so too because she jumps in, voice quiet but firm. "Let's talk to Archie first. He's a shark in the courtroom. He might be able to get her to drop her claim without you folding the ranch."

"Screw that," Meemaw says into the quiet. All heads turn in her direction. She's sitting cross-legged in the middle of the room, a small bowl on the coffee table in front of her. The thing's smoking. "I just put a spell on her. She'll drop dead before she takes the ranch."

"Good Lord," Ridge mutters, scrubbing both hands over his face.

"That seems a little extreme," Frankie whispers.

I roll my eyes, trying not to look at Shelby, who's barely holding back the laughter. "That's not a spell, Meemaw. That's just weed, and you're going to set off the smoke alarm and get us all high."

As if to prove my point, the alarm starts wailing and chaos descends.

Twenty-Six

YOU'LL NEVER CATCH THE SUNSET SITTIN' IN THE SHADE

SHELBY

"Have I told you what a lifesaver you are?"

"Don't go praising me just yet," Archie protests, slamming his SUV door shut behind him. "I've only agreed to help out. I'm not sure how much I can do in the end. Tiff has a strong case."

I take secret pleasure in Archie's use of our nickname for Tiffany Grace, even though he doesn't really know her. It's the little things sometimes. "Well, taking on Ridge's divorce case for free is already enough to win you brother-of-the-year status." I close the passenger door and head for the stairs to my apartment, stopping on the way to grab my mail. The late afternoon sun kisses the backs of our necks as we ascend to my place.

We left the Gambles to themselves at the ranch, the somber mood having somewhat lightened with Archie's arrival. Not enough to put anyone fully at ease, though. Ridge still looked hungover, even though Dallas and Skye cleared out the liquor cabinet yesterday to save him from himself. I guess beer still did the job, though, not that I blame him.

The one bright spot in this whole cluster is that Houston's finally coming home for more than just an afternoon. He stops in a few times a year when he's got a break in his rodeo schedule, but he never stays, much to everyone's disappointment. That man has a demon chasing him, and I reckon her name might be Josie Mae Turner, not that he'd ever admit it.

The apartment smells faintly of orange blossoms from my favorite essential oil diffuser, and I make a mental note to bring it back to Dallas's sometime. "Just drop your bag in the guest room, Arch, and I'll get us some drinks."

I open the fridge to inspect its contents, but it's practically empty. No surprise there since I've been staying with Dallas for so long. A pang hits me when I think of moving back in and living by myself again. If Dallas has his way, it will happen in a matter of days. I swipe two cans of seltzer from the door compartment and close the refrigerator with a little more force than necessary.

"I forgot how…turquoise this place is." Archie's eyes flit over my living space, an expression of mild distaste on his face.

"Put a plug in your talk box, little brother." I toss the seltzer at him, and he snatches it easily from the air before it can hit him in the chest. He cracks it open and wanders my living room, checking out my fabulous decor.

"So, now that we don't have an audience, you wanna tell me what's up with you and Dallas? I can't decide which of you was eyeing the other harder when your backs were turned."

I gasp in mock indignation, but it lasts all of three seconds before I sink my butt into a couch cushion and sigh. "What's up is I'm in deep, deep trouble." I crack my seltzer open and take a long pull, the bubbles tickling my throat.

Archie barks out a laugh. "Oh, I figured as much."

"I'm completely in love with the man, and I think it's mutual, but things are a little up in the air," I confess.

"How so?"

I lean forward, setting my can on a coaster on the coffee table with a loud *clack.* "He said he loved me and then took it back."

Archie's chin jerks. "Took it back? How exactly does that work?"

"He thinks he's doing me a favor." I roll my eyes. "He's under the impression he's not good enough for me or something."

"Ah." Archie's tone is knowing, and it gets my back up.

"What does that mean?" I ask his back as he bends to inspect a photo frame.

"Well, it makes sense when you think about it," is his baffling answer.

"I'm not better than Dallas! He's an amazing man. He's my best freaking friend, for Pete's sake."

Archie turns and throws his palms up in defense like I'm about to throw another can of seltzer at him. If I had another one, I just might. "I mean, as your brother, it's my right to think nobody is good enough for you."

My heart softens at that. Darn teddy bear.

"But that's not what I meant," he finishes. I cross my arms and wait for him to continue. He hesitates, probably checking for signs I might assault him, before continuing. "You've just never made a secret of your expectations of men."

Since I know he's right, I have no choice but to stay silent. Instead, I turn my head to follow him as he rounds the back of the couch.

Archie shrugs. "You can't blame a guy for thinking he can't measure up."

"This is ridiculous, though. Dallas has always been such a confident guy, and women everywhere adore him. It doesn't make sense for him to feel the least bit unworthy."

"Well, then, I guess it's your job to define what worth means to you when it comes to him." He eyes me. "If you want to be with him, that is."

I drop my head back and close my eyes. "I really messed this up for myself, didn't I?"

Archie pats my head from behind the couch like I'm a dog. "I think you can split the blame with Dallas. After all, he's been single all this time for a reason."

I open my eyes to look at my brother. He's upside down from this angle and kind of looks like our daddy. "You know, one of the last conversations I had with Momma was her telling me to watch my heart and wait for a guy who knew how to treat it right. A guy like Daddy. I guess over time, my expectations just compounded, and I felt like I had to do right by her."

"Well, I'm pretty sure she only ever wanted you to be happy, whatever that means."

He's right. Of course he is.

I sigh, and he pats my head one more time before resuming his inspection of my living room.

"I can't believe you still have this picture." Archie laughs, holding up a frame with a snapshot of our parents from the very same Knockers County Fair photo booth Dallas nearly burned down the other day. They're in sepia, dressed as outlaws and scowling at the camera with their best bad-guy mugs, both failing miserably at the effort.

"Momma never could keep from smiling, even when she was trying to be stern." I cast a wistful look at the photo, warmth filling my chest, along with the familiar shot of grief that never really goes away.

"I don't know about that." Archie grins and sets the photo back down. "She could hold a good grudge when she and Daddy got into it."

I tilt my head, my brows drawing together. "I don't remember them fighting."

"Seriously?"

"I think I would remember. I'm older than you by two years. They were madly in love."

"Maybe so, but they still fought. Oh, gosh. Don't you remember that one year when Daddy forgot their anniversary and went to play poker with the Jameson brothers?" I jolt at his words. "Momma was fit to be tied. Didn't speak to him for a whole week."

A vague memory of my daddy walking around on eggshells and my momma glaring daggers at him niggles at the back of my mind. I shake my head. "I guess nobody is perfect." Lord knows I'm not.

"Doesn't mean two people can't be perfect for each other, though, right?" Archie's got a single eyebrow raised at me and a knowing twinkle in his eye.

"Who's the hopeless romantic now?"

I lick my lips nervously, my hands worrying the paper in my lap as I wait for Dallas to walk through the door.

It's Sunday, and Dallas was a no-show at church. I spent the night at my place with Archie, and we ordered takeout from Pound Town, eating it in front of the TV and getting caught up. Tulsa is only three hours away, but with both of our busy schedules, we don't see each other as often as we should.

Dallas is obviously avoiding me, but that's okay. I have a plan. Or at least the beginnings of one. I lay awake in bed last night thinking about my conversation with Archie and about all the things I value about Dallas. It's high time I show him how absolutely worthy of love he is and how we belong together. Who am I to dictate how someone shows their love for me? I've been a complete idiot.

So, in the wee hours of the morning, I decided it was my

turn for a few gestures, though I'm not sure how grand they are.

First up, I broke into his truck this morning—which wasn't hard to do considering he never locks the darn thing when it's parked in his drive—and plugged a USB device into his radio console. I accompanied it with a sticky note reading, "Press play. P.S. Prince Charmings come in all different forms."

If things went to plan, Dallas drove around today listening to *Wrangled and Wronged by My Rival Rancher*, one of my favorite enemies-to-lovers romance novels about neighbors who fight like cats and dogs to secretly hide that they're head over heels in love with each other. My ultimate hope is to show him that romance doesn't have to be all flowery proclamations and bed-and-breakfast weekends. It can be snarky comebacks while secretly sacrificing yourself for the other person's happiness, just like Everett does for Darby.

My second project, the one that has me strangely nervous as I sit waiting on Dallas's bed, proved to be much more challenging. It turns out writing poems is hard! God bless Elias, the poetry professor, but this crap ain't for science-y people to undertake.

I hear the front door open and shut, followed by the jangle of Nelly's collar and the footfall of heavy boots across the wood floor. Dallas clears the bedroom doorway a minute later, dressed in old jeans that do fantastic things for his thighs (Oh, who are we kidding? It's his thighs that do fantastic things for the jeans.) and an olive-green T-shirt that molds to his chest like he just took home first prize at a wet T-shirt contest.

His steps falter when he sees me, his eyebrows spiking halfway to his hairline. "I thought you were with Archie." His tone is almost accusatory, but I ignore it. Nelly runs straight for me, his nose buried in my thigh while I give him a good scratch behind the ears.

"He went home. I wanted to talk to you."

His hand goes to the back of his neck. "Uh, can we raincheck it? I got a lot to do."

"Nope." I pop the P, and he scowls. Even his scowl is hot. And cute. Before he can protest again, I ask, "How are you liking the audiobook? You remind me a little of Everett right now." I can't help my grin.

He growls. The man literally growls at me.

Oh well. Time to press on. "I wrote something for you."

His expression turns suspicious now. "Shelby, I really don't—"

I cut him off. "Just let me read it, and then you can skulk away if you want to. I promise." I cross my heart for good measure, and Dallas sighs in resignation, hands landing on his hips just to make sure I can't ignore his irritation.

Welp, here goes nothing. I clear my throat and take a deep breath, straightening my spine as I perch on the edge of the bed.

"It's a poem. The working title is 'My Favorite Things.'" I bob my head back and forth before continuing, "But I wasn't exactly going for a Julie Andrews vibe, so I might change it."

The scowl is back, so I clear my throat again, lift the paper, and begin reciting my terrible poem.

You say you're not romantic

It's taken me too long to see

That your heart is gigantic

And you're the perfect one for me

I glance up to gauge his reaction, but his face is a blank mask. Maybe I should just focus on the paper before I chicken out.

We have the best time when we dance

You let me win at darts

You always look for every chance

To brag about my smarts

You know all of my favorite songs

And you're a darn great dad
You are a bit of a ding-dong
But best I've ever had

I can't help but chance another glance and am gratified to see his lips twitch just the tiniest bit.

First one to defend my honor
Never asking who's to blame
Like when you told off that guy Connor
And you punched that loser Shane
You volunteered to knock me up
So I can be a mom
You drive me slowly in your truck
'Cause you know it keeps me calm
You keep an eye on my blood sugar
Always leaving snacks around
I have to put in the word booger
It's the only rhyme I found

This time, he lets out a tiny snort, so I don't even need to lift my eyes from the paper.

You let me decorate your house
On National Spaghetti Day
You promised you would be my spouse
And I would marry you today
You make me feel like family
When I need it the most
You laugh at my profanity
And make me midnight toast
You put me first in every way
And always make me laugh
I trust you more than I can say
You are my better half
You're so protective of my heart
And say I need a prince
But I loved you from the very start
And have done ever since

You're everything I'll ever need
And now this poem's done
And I don't need Meemaw's weed
To know that you're the one.

I lower the paper and look him square in the eye. "So, what do you think? Writing poems is hard, and I swear on my truck that I'll never ever ask you to do it."

His expression has lost all irritation and impatience. His eyes have gone soft, and one corner of his mouth is hitched in that beloved lopsided grin. "You know you're ridiculous, don't you?"

My lips spread in a wide grin. I toss the paper aside and stand, ready to pounce on him. Maybe my poetry skills are better than I thought!

But before I can make a move, Ryder bursts through the door, all arms and legs, announcing to what I can only guess is the entire town, "Pizza night!!!!"

Twenty-Seven

IF YOU CAN'T RUN WITH THE BIG DOGS STAY ON THE PORCH

DALLAS

I am a coward.

It's not really the kind of realization one likes to make when they hit middle age—or anytime really—but as I busy myself with getting Ryder ready for school Wednesday morning after sleeping a scant few hours on that stupid couch yet again, I can't help but acknowledge how true it is.

I've spent the last three days avoiding being alone with Shelby because I am, apparently, a coward the likes of which hasn't been seen since the cowardly lion in *Wizard of Oz*. I know this because there was a time period when Ryder was obsessed with the movie, and we watched it nonstop on repeat until I had that whole thing memorized. Shelby has every right to waltz in here and declare I'm nothing but a great, big coward.

"Dad? What's buto-late-hydro-excito-land?" Ryder asks through a mouthful of cereal.

Shoot. He's reading ingredient lists again. I spill hot coffee on my hand as I fill my thermos. "Crap!" I put the coffee down, wipe off my hand, and try to answer his question. "Probably a chemical of some sort."

"A good one or a bad one?"

I grimace, out of my depth as I usually am with questions he throws my way. "The answer is probably the one you hate the most."

Ryder sighs, pushing his chair back and taking his empty bowl to the sink. "I know, I know. It depends."

I take a swig of hot coffee and grab his backpack. "You got it, kid. Now let's head on out."

Ryder puts on the backpack but runs the opposite direction from the truck. "We have to say goodbye to Shelby first!"

I grimace some more but dutifully follow. The boy won't leave without saying goodbye, which is freaking cute as crap, but as I'm currently playing the part of a coward, I'd prefer we just sneak out unannounced.

When I hit my bedroom door, Ryder is already up on the bed, snuggled up with Shelby, who clearly just woke up. She smiles at me like I haven't been ignoring the fact that she wrote the world's bestest worst poem for little old me three days ago. Like she actually loves me and adores the little things I do for her. I smile back, but it's forced.

"Pops is taking Ryder out for pizza tonight. Figured you and I could grab a bite at that new place, Canoodles, and have a chat?" My cowardly heart is pounding just talking to her. Why is she so dang pretty all rumpled and sleepy in my bed?

Her grin intensifies, and I know I've really messed up. "I'd love that," she answers softly.

I nod and bark my frustration at Ryder. "Come on, Ryd. We don't want to be late." Nelly blinks at me from the corner of the room, clearly choosing to stay with Shelby today instead of me. I don't think I blame him.

I walk out without a backward glance. I'm afraid if I do look back, I'll jump into that bed and spend the day cuddling up with those two like a real family.

And that's not what today is about.

Today is the day I end things with Shelby. For good.

————

Canoodles is a little dark. Almost like they're going for romantic noodles with the sputtering candle and dark wood booths. If I'd known that, I wouldn't have suggested the place. We're just about done eating, both of us sticking to light topics like our jobs and the latest town gossip. Shelby's gaze hasn't left my face all evening, like she's waiting for me to say something.

I have nothing else to say. I know she'd be settling with me, and I want more than that for my best friend. I love the woman with every fiber of my being, but so did Ridge with Tiff. And Pops with Mom. And look how happy those guys are now.

I check the time on my phone for the hundredth time. Shelby watches my every move.

"You expecting a call?" she asks.

I go to answer her but get cut off when her eyes widen, and she stares out the front window of Canoodles, distracted finally. The telltale click-clop tells me my plan has arrived. I slide out of the booth and hold out my hand to her. She takes it, still staring at the white horse that's stopped in front of the restaurant.

"What the…"

I pull her outside, where we both stare up at the guy on top of the horse. He's dressed in pretty realistic armor like a real knight of the Round Table. The chest plate piece clanks when he lifts his arm and takes off the metal helmet.

Clark is handsome in a scholarly way, hands smooth from turning pages, not wrestling cattle or sanding wood. The kind of way Shelby would find attractive. He doesn't spare me a look, which is good. I didn't hire him for me. This whole show is for Shelby. For our public breakup.

Several people have crowded closer to see what the deal is. It's not every day a knight prances down Main Street on a white steed. Mrs. Perkins pushes to the front of the crowd with her cane. She gets a little too close to the horse for my comfort, probably because she can't hear unless she's right on top of everything.

"Hello, fair lady," the knight booms, stretching his arm in Shelby's direction. "The soft morning dew couldn't be as sweet as you. No fairer place to rest one's head than in the arms of a lover, and yet does this scoundrel give you respite?" He glares at me quite convincingly. "Provide shelter through the storm? Anchor himself so he can be the tether that brings you home? I dare sayeth not!"

Gosh, this guy is good. I don't even know what the heck he's talking about.

Shelby glances at me in confusion. The knight slides off his horse with a loud *clink* and dramatically tosses his helmet into the street. Crap, I hope no one drives over it.

"Dallas! Hey!" The second part of my plan has arrived in tight jeans and a low-cut top that has me glancing away in embarrassment. One inhale too deep, and she'll be experiencing a wardrobe malfunction on Main Street. Primrose, the girl I hired to flirt with me, slides her arm through mine and presses herself against me as she stares up at me through fake lashes. She's pretty...in a way that does nothing for me. "You comin' back to my place tonight like usual, sugar?"

Shelby's mouth falls open. The knight slides his metallic arm around her waist. "Come, my fair maiden. Away from this rapscallion. My love would never find another. Let us ride off into the sunset together."

"I knew it!" Mrs. Perkins squawks and points at me. "Death by STD for that one."

I roll my eyes. Of all people, why did she have to witness

this breakup? Primrose goes up on her tiptoes to kiss me. I turn my head at the last second, stomach churning, and she gets my cheek.

Clark takes a step forward toward the horse, but ends up tipping off the curb, almost taking Shelby with him. The metal shin guards have slid higher, blocking his knees from bending. He just tips right over in slow motion, and down he goes to the asphalt in a pile of metal clanks and curses. The onlookers gasp. Shelby rushes to help the poor guy, and Primrose looks around confused.

"Oh my gosh," someone whispers. "A leg shouldn't look like that, right?"

"Wait. Is that Shelby Sweet?" Primrose asks loudly. She steps back and smacks my chest so hard I wheeze. "You wanted me to fake an affair with you so you could break up with *Shelby*?? You should have told me that! I'd never do that to my girl, Shelbs. She saved my pookie last year. My little hedgehog baby."

I groan. I should have known this wouldn't work out. None of my grand gestures did, so why would my breakup? I should have hired real actors from Hollywood, not amateurs from one town over.

"A little...help...here," the knight croaks from down below.

"Dallas!" Shelby stands, coming over and giving Primrose a side hug. "We have to call an ambulance. His leg's broken."

I already have my phone out, calling dispatch. "Hey, I have a bit of a scene here."

The dispatcher, a woman we went to high school with, cackles. "Yeah, I'm already getting calls and have an ambulance en route. Mrs. Perkins is streaming it live on her Instagram."

My head shoots up to see Mrs. Perkins shoving her cell phone in Clark's face as he wails in pain. D'Wayne slides in on Clark's other side, his orange ski cap askew. The cardboard sign he's been holding lately about the end being near blows away down the street.

D'Wayne thrusts his fist in the air. "We must cut off the leg! Here. You can bite down on my leather belt." Clearly he's getting into character right along with Clark. Crap, maybe I should have hired D'Wayne. He's pretty believable.

I hang up, look up at the sky, and pray for patience. For wisdom. Maybe even for a crater to open up and suck me in.

"See?" Shelby says, sounding way too calm. "Let's save the grand gestures for the fiction books."

Primrose whacks me in the gut again. "I can't believe you!"

Shelby shifts to stand by my side. "Don't sweat it, Primrose. He's just going through something right now. A bit of an identity crisis, I think. He was trying to put together a third-act breakup, but we all know how those end up."

Primrose rolls her eyes but thankfully appears to have stopped hitting me. "Oh no. I hate third-act breakups."

"Me too!" Shelby chirps, sliding her arm around my waist.

I drop my head back down and stare at her. "You're not mad?"

She smiles, even as the wail of a distant siren breaks up the calm night. "No. I love how much you're trying to protect me. It's misguided, of course, but it's funny as all get out to watch you try to protect me from yourself."

"This is *funny*?"

Shelby looks down at the poor knight who's writhing in agony. She winces. "Some parts more than others." Then she spins so she's directly in front of me, blocking out the scene on the ground, her hands fisting my T-shirt. She's all I can see. Has been for a while, if I'm honest. "I want *you*, Dallas Beaufort Gamble. Past, present, and all of my future. Let yourself love me. Please?"

I drop my forehead to hers, too weak to fight this any longer. "I do love you, Sweetness. So much I'm scared I'll mess it up. I would have to kick my own butt for hurting you and ruining our relationship. I've been a coward, hoping you'll come to your senses and leave me like you should."

Shelby shakes her head, jostling us both. "True courage is facing danger. Isn't that what Dorothy said in *The Wizard of Oz*?"

My eyes widen, right before my heart melts into a puddle at her feet. Of course, she remembers the month that Ryder made us watch *The Wizard of Oz* every day. She's been there for me and for him for as long as I can remember.

Terrified and hopeful, I cup her face with both hands. My throat feels like I'm being choked. "I love you, Shelby Sweet. With my whole cowardly heart."

Her eyes fill with tears. Paramedics jump out of the ambulance and swarm Clark on the ground. "That's all I want. Your whole heart. Because you've had mine since that day you accused me of stealing your cow."

And then I put us both out of our misery and tip her over my arm to kiss her. The perfect Hollywood ending to a disaster of a breakup attempt.

The kiss also gets live-streamed to Mrs. Perkins's Instagram account. My phone starts blowing up because, apparently, everyone else in Big Knob follows Mrs. Perkins.

I ignore the buzzing in my pocket and get lost in the woman who's always been mine. I was just too cowardly to see it until now.

Twenty~Eight

TIME TO BANG LIKE A SCREEN DOOR IN A WINDSTORM

SHELBY

With both of our phones blowing up and everybody asking what in tarnation that whole scene was about, I do the only thing I can think of to shut it down. I tell Norinne to text Charlene that Dallas and I were doing a bit to try out for *The Amazing Race*.

Before we even get back to the ranch, everyone in Big Knob has reached out to express their excitement and offer tips for how to get on the show. It should probably alarm me that nobody is questioning the validity of such a crazy story involving a crippled knight and a cheating fiancé, but I guess when it comes down to it, the whole town knows Dallas and I can do just about anything when we do it together.

Dallas holds my hand in the truck as he drives exactly the speed limit and only lets go long enough for us to get out at the big house.

"I like it when you hold my hand." I look up at him with a wide grin. "I think I need to add another verse to my poem."

"Please don't." He snorts when I smack his arm. "What I

meant to say is that I love the poem just as it is. Especially the part about being a ding-dong."

"No kissing in front of Isadora!" Meemaw shouts from the porch where a telltale wisp of smoke drifts from her silhouetted figure in a porch rocker.

"Dammit, Meemaw! You're gonna give me a heart attack one of these days, jumping out of the shadows like that."

Isadora squawks as if defending her mistress. "If you're looking for Ryder, he's trying to talk your dad into buying a pool. Says he wants to swim with Skye's decrepit old swine."

"Aw, crap," Dallas mutters, and we book it inside. The last thing Pops needs is to feel guilty for not fulfilling his lone grandson's greatest wish. Gosh, I hope Archie can do something about this Tiff business before the family well and truly goes broke.

"I'm sorry, but since when are y'all interested in reality TV?" Skye asks the minute we step inside. She's bent over her phone at the dining table, three notebooks and a laptop spread out in front of her. When she points the phone our way, I see Mrs. Perkins on the screen yammering on about Dallas being excellent at riding camels.

Skye and I both turn to look at him, and he throws his free hand up. "I have no idea what she's talking about. The only camel I've ever seen in person was Papaw's cigarettes."

"It's easier to just go with it," I tell Skye, and, to her credit, she shrugs and lets the whole thing go.

"What are you up to?" Dallas asks, gesturing to the mess in front of her.

"Oh, just working on a couple ideas in case Tiff steals the cattle business." She eyes our clasped hands. "The better question is what are *y'all* up to?" Her eyebrows waggle. "Don't think any of us have forgotten about Sunday dinner the other week."

I decide to let Dallas handle that one, and I'm unsurprised when his only response is, "It's like Momma always said—

mind your own biscuits and life will be gravy. Now, where's my kid? He's got school tomorrow."

We collect Ryder and use the short drive to Dallas's place to break it to him that nobody is getting a pool and to remind him of all the cool stuff he already has. It goes over about as well as any such conversation with an eight-year-old boy does.

He hugs me good night, pout and all, and Dallas takes him upstairs to tuck him in. As they climb the stairs, I hear Ryder say, "I heard Uncle Mustache is coming home soon," and I have to bite my lips between my teeth to keep from outright cackling.

We all saw a promo for one of the rodeos Houston was riding in a couple days ago, and it featured a photo of him with the worst '70s stache and matching flowing hair. We haven't stopped referring to him as Uncle Mustache ever since. I can't wait for him to show up so we can see it in person in all its glory.

But Houston isn't the Gamble brother I'm focusing on tonight. I know we need to talk some more, but I can still do that in my pjs with a beer in my hand, can't I?

Dallas descends the stairs fifteen minutes later with a sigh. "He tried telling me that the gas money I spend driving him to swim practice will more than pay for a pool. The kid is smart, but he's got a lot to learn about money."

I smile and hand him the cold beer I opened for him. He takes it with a grateful sigh and settles into the couch right next to me. His eyes travel down the length of my body in the silky blue pajamas, and he leans in to kiss my neck. Goose bumps erupt on my skin, and I sigh. Is he really mine for good?

As if sensing my question, he pulls back and studies me, his mouth relaxed and his fingers absently twirling a lock of my hair. "Hey," he murmurs.

"Hey," I echo.

We stare at one another until we're both wearing dopey grins. Then I shift in my seat so I'm sitting cross-legged and facing him. He takes a sip of his beer and watches me. I set mine on the coffee table to focus on the man in front of me.

"So, how are you feeling? About us, I mean?" I ask.

He considers my question and sighs. "Hopeful? Terrified? Excited? Lucky," he finally settles on.

"Me too. All four."

"Thank goodness. You've been sounding so confident."

I can only shrug. "We both know better than anyone that nothing's promised in this life, so I think we owe it to ourselves to dive in and appreciate every moment we have."

"Yeah. You're right." He sets his bottle down and takes my hands in both of his. "We've already wasted a heck of a lot of time."

I consider that and shake my head. "I don't know. Maybe we just weren't ready for each other until now. Maybe it's all happening the way it was meant to."

"We could have half a dozen rugrats running around here by now if I'd gotten my head screwed on straight sooner."

I can't help but lean in and drop a kiss on his lips, the sweet man. "I don't need half a dozen. The one we've already got is pretty darn great. If we happen to be able to add another one or two, that'd be gravy."

Dallas's smile broadens, and then he surprises me by vaulting off the couch and running down the hall.

Am I supposed to follow him? What is he doing?

My questions are answered a second later when he emerges from the bedroom with a box of condoms in his hand. He doesn't slow down as he struts past me to the front door and disappears through it. When he reenters thirty seconds later, the condoms are nowhere to be seen and he's making a show of dusting his hands off in a "job's all done" motion.

I can't help my laugh. "I'm afraid it might take more than

just tossing the condoms, Gamble." I sober somewhat as the truth of my words settles in.

Sensing my shift in mood like he always does, Dallas jumps over the back of the couch and pins me on my back. Our noses are inches apart, and I can smell the warm, spicy scent of his shampoo and the beer on his breath. "Believe me, I'm willing to put a lot of work into this project." He tucks my hair behind my ear and lowers his head to give me the softest of kisses. "I love you, Shelby."

"I love you too. So much."

"Now," he says, "I'll be overjoyed to never sleep on this damn couch again for the rest of my life."

"I second that."

We manage to remain clothed until the bedroom door clicks shut behind us, but just barely.

CHAPTER
Twenty-Nine

HE'S GOT MORE ON HIS PLATE THAN HE CAN SAY GRACE OVER

DALLAS

Shelby is busy in the paddock, checking out the last of the recovering calves before they get moved out to the rest of the herd. Most of them made it through their sickness, thanks to Shelby's quick medical attention, but sadly, enough didn't make it to have all of us holding our breath a bit. This season is going to be tight financially, but after Frankie ran numbers last night, we think we'll come out in the black. Barely.

"Hey," I murmur as I slide up behind Shelby and wrap my arms around her. So many benefits to taking things beyond friendship, and this is one of them.

She lets out a soft yelp, then threatens me with the rectal thermometer in her hands. That's enough to make me let go and back up.

"Whatcha need, Gamble?"

She's in work mode, and it's hotter than the midday sun. Okay, maybe not the thermometer, but her in gloves, work shirt, and hair piled on top of her head is.

"Where's Ridge? I have a couple hours before I meet up with a customer. Figured I'd offer my services."

Shelby gives me a once-over, her eyebrows wagging up and down at the boots and worn work jeans I have on. She sobers quickly, though. "Skye tried to talk to him about some business idea, and he stormed out of here. Pretty sure he took Echo so he could be anywhere by now."

I sigh and shake my head. "Alright. I'll go find him and make sure he's okay."

As a whole family, we haven't discussed losing the ranch in the divorce. Every time even a whiff of that subject comes up, Ridge goes off the deep end and spends the rest of the day either throwing things or drinking himself into early liver failure. Archie is hard at work defending Ridge and collecting proof that Tiff didn't do a thing to enhance the ranch and therefore doesn't deserve half of it. They don't even have kids together, which should have made for a speedy divorce process. Her insistence that she take half the business is asinine, and yet here we are, defending our right to our family legacy in court.

I turn to walk away and saddle up a horse, but not before Shelby smacks me on the butt. Hard. I gape at her over my shoulder. "Really, Sweetness?"

She smirks and goes back to the calf. Thank goodness we got our crap together. It's like we're teenagers again. We can't keep our hands off each other, and I wouldn't want it any other way. I want to start planning our wedding as soon as possible.

Which means I need to make that phone call I've been meaning to before I go deal with Ridge. Meemaw is trying to train a chicken to play dead on the front porch. I steer clear and head for the front room where I won't be disturbed. Archie answers on the second ring.

"My favorite Gamble sibling," he drawls by way of greeting.

"Wow. I'm your favorite, huh? What did I do to deserve that title? Was it my charm? My good looks? My great butt?"

Archie groans. "Jeez, Dallas, I don't want to hear about your butt. I just figured since you're with my sister now, I should try to have a good relationship with you."

I flop down on the love seat that's more uncomfortable than the couch I was sleeping on at my place. "To that end, maybe this'll help." I rub the back of my neck, feeling all kinds of awkward. I'm used to joking my way out of everything. This feels...important. I can't get it wrong. "I, uh, want to propose to Shelby."

There's a beat or two of silence. "Didn't you already put a ring on her finger?"

"Yeah. But that was fake. She deserves a real proposal. And I want your blessing. I would have asked your daddy, of course, but without him here, I feel like getting your endorsement would be the right move. Don't get me wrong, the proposal will probably be a complete disaster. I keep messing up these romantic gestures, but I have to try."

"Well, crap, Gamble. That just made me tear up a bit."

I flop my head back and instantly regret it when my skull meets the wood frame of the love seat. "Shut up," I grumble, rubbing my head.

"No, seriously," Archie continues, all business now. "I appreciate that. More importantly, Shelby would appreciate you coming to me. You have my full support. In fact, I have Momma's wedding ring set. After our grandparents died, they gave it to me for safekeeping. I think that was around when Shelby was dating that one vet. Anyway, I can mail it to you if you think you want to propose with it. I always assumed it would be Shelby's one day."

My heart expands in my chest. I had no idea that ring was even an option, or I would have proposed with it in the first place. "Yes. Please send it to me. I'll give her the option of which ring she wants to wear."

"You got it, brother."

———

"Thanks again for being willing to help out," I whisper into my cell phone.

Hallie is quick to respond. "Are you kidding me? I might be as excited as Ryder."

I hear the shower shut off. "I gotta go. We'll be there right before sunset."

"We'll go up now and be hidden. Don't you worry."

I end the call and shove the phone in my pocket. Shelby steps out of our bathroom, steam billowing behind her. She's all girl, that's for sure. She told me she needed an "everything shower" after her day at work, whatever the heck that is.

She's wet, her skin glistening everywhere the tiny towel isn't. She knows I'm watching her walk across the room to the dresser. Her hips have an extra sway to them that's just for my benefit. Maybe I should have planned a proposal with just her and me, so I could get that towel off her sooner.

"You're killing me," I growl.

Shelby tosses me a sultry smile over her shoulder that does nothing to help my problem. The doorbell rings, and I nearly jump off the bed. Shelby laughs and takes her time finding clothes.

"You gonna get that?" she asks when I don't immediately leave the bedroom.

I sneak another peek at my fiancée. Honestly, we don't really need food on this horseback ride. Except the doorbell rings again, and since it's my sister delivering the takeout I ordered along with the two horses all saddled and ready to ride, I know she won't go away until I answer the damn door.

"Ugh, fine," I whine like my son.

I collect the food bag from Frankie, toss her a thank you that's not nearly sincere enough for the amount of effort she's gone to, and then shove her out the door. Shelby's ready to go a minute later, her hair up in some messy bun that makes me want to fist it and drop her to the ground for a wrestling match. Preferably naked. But since I can't do that right now, I look away and try to name all of Meemaw's chickens to keep myself in check.

Nelly lies down in his doggie bed and gives me doleful eyes for not taking him along tonight. We ignore him and head outside to mount our horses. I love that I don't have to help Shelby onto Foxtrot. Whiskey is a bit feistier, so I take him, leading the way to our spot on the river.

I pull out my phone at one point and take a selfie of us on our horses, golden hour lighting in front and the wide-open spaces of Oklahoma behind us. Shelby smiles for the photo, and I see the girl she used to be, the woman she is now, and who she's going to be twenty years from now. I want to be right there to see every gray hair sprout up and each new wrinkle that forms from making her laugh every day. I want to see her stomach rounded with my baby and her arms full of all the animals she'll heal.

I'm still not sure I'm good enough for this woman, but I do know I'll love her with my dying breath. I'll never look at another woman or give her reason to doubt what I feel for her. I'll work my hands raw to provide for her and be by her side for anything she wants to tackle in life.

When we get to the river, I slide off of Whiskey and tie him loosely to a tree, then head over to assist Shelby down, even though she doesn't need the help. I catch her around the waist and pull her in for a deep kiss. She melts into me, every muscle giving way, surrendering herself to me with complete trust. It's enough to make me reconsider everything I've done in my life and find ways to be better.

"Very romantic, Dally," Shelby whispers as we come up for air. "I dare say your gestures are getting better."

I grin sheepishly, then sneak another kiss before letting her go. "When you're at rock bottom, there's only one way to go from there."

Shelby smiles patiently, like she doesn't even care how many times I messed up. She helps hold some of our supper containers as I pull them out of the saddlebags. Whiskey steps sideways, tossing his head at the interruption. We'll have to race them home, just to burn off some steam. Ridge has been a little off his game keeping up with everything around the ranch, for good reason.

We head for our favorite spot by the river, the one we come to when it's the three of us. I spread out a blanket and set down the food. I don't see Ryder and Hallie anywhere, which is good, but I also hope they made it. Otherwise, this might not go to plan.

I take Shelby's hands in mine, staring into those sapphire eyes, highlighted by the setting sun. A breeze kicks up, making the leaves shake in the trees and ripples form on the surface of the water.

"Shelby?"

She scrunches up her face, probably wondering what's wrong with me and why we aren't digging into our food right now. "Yeah?"

I drop down to one knee, and her eyes go wide. "I love you, Shelby Sweet. Have since the day we met. If friendship is the foundation for a happy marriage, then there will be no two people happier than you and me. I know we went about this all backward, but I want you to have the ultimate proposal experience. You deserve all the good things life has to offer, and I'll spend the rest of my life getting them for you."

Her eyes are swimming with tears. It's the small smile playing on her lips that has me continuing despite the fear that I'll mess this up. I reach into my pocket and pull out her momma's rings. I hold them up and see the moment she realizes what they are. Her free hand goes to her mouth, and the tears fall down her cheeks.

"Archie sent me these. I figured you should have a choice in what you wear on your finger for the rest of your life. All I know is I want that ring to mean that you're mine and I'm yours. Forever. Marry me? For real?"

Shelby nods her head emphatically before she pulls her hand down and says the words. "Yes, Dallas! Of course I'll marry you!"

I stand and pull her into my arms, sealing our promise with a kiss. A low grumble behind me has us breaking apart. I grin while Shelby tries to look behind me with confusion.

"I wasn't told there'd be kissing," Ryder says with some attitude.

We hear a shushing noise from the trees off to our left. I have to choke back laughter. I move to the side so Shelby can see Ryder approaching with a cake in his hands. He gives me a dirty look but turns an angelic smile Shelby's way.

"What is this?" Shelby whispers.

"You have to read the cake," Ryder informs her.

Shelby's gaze drops to the round cake which sports cursive writing in blue icing. *Will you be my bonus mom?*

Shelby's hand goes to her mouth again, eyes back to leaking. She glances at me, and I shrug. "We're kind of a package deal."

Shelby drops to her knees, gently takes the cake out of Ryder's hands to place it on the blanket with our supper, and pulls him close, hands on his shoulders.

"There's nothing I'd like better than to be your bonus mom. It would be an honor."

And then I'm the one choking up, watching those two hug like they were always meant to be in each other's lives. It's plain to see my boy loves Shelby and always has. Heck, he's smarter than his father. He knows a keeper when he sees one. I join the group hug and thank my lucky stars she said yes.

"Job well done, son," I whisper in his ear. He lifts his head from Shelby's shoulder to give me a grin. We've been working on his lines for a week now.

Hallie appears at my side when we finally break apart. She shoots me a wink and then gets busy pulling Ryder away so we can enjoy our engagement supper.

"Thank you, Hallie!" I holler after them. I'm one lucky man to have her support.

We wait until her SUV drives away, leaving us alone again. Just us and the river we grew up on. Shelby and I sit on the blanket facing each other. Shelby gazes at the two rings on her finger, her momma's and the one I bought in Hornville.

"It won't hurt my feelings if you choose your momma's. It makes the most sense."

She smiles at me, still glassy-eyed. "I love the ring you got me. But I also know if you can return it, that money can help your family's ranch."

I shake my head. "No way. You choose the ring you want...for *you*, Sweetness. Don't think about other people right now. I want you to selfishly choose which one you want."

She gazes at her hand, her finger touching both in turn. "I've changed my mind on quite a few things recently. I used to want a big fancy wedding ring because that's what the magazines and movies always showed. But now I want it to mean something deeper. I choose my momma's. I think it'll be nice to have a reminder of her on my hand forever. There's history there."

I reach forward and slide my fingers in her hair to cup her face. "Done. Now let's eat before your blood sugar gets too low."

It's while we're finishing our supper and before we devour some cake, that I trot out an old memory. I pull Shelby between my legs so her back rests against my chest. The temperature's dropped enough already that it feels good to cuddle up. "Remember that night in high school when Houston dared you to kiss me?"

Shelby laughs. "Oh gosh, yeah, I remember."

I think back on that night. I swear I can hear the echo of our laughter from all those years ago. "I was so mad you didn't kiss me."

She gasps and spins to see my face. "What? I thought you said—"

"I know what I said," I cut her off. "And I know I was a liar. I went home and dreamed about what it would be like if you'd gone through with it." I cup her face again and close the distance, our lips dancing across each other. "The reality is so much better than I dreamed."

Epilogue
LUCKIER THAN A PIG IN MUD

SHELBY

"Don't take this the wrong way," Archie leans in and whispers from his spot beside me.

"But I'm a little relieved you guys aren't dressed like one of Momma's bodice-ripper romance covers."

I look down at my simple silk A-line dress with its killer slit up the left thigh and bite back a laugh. No heaving bosoms in sight. "You mean my dress isn't giving you *Ravished and Returned: The Mistaken Mail-Order Bride* vibes right now?" I ask with feigned surprise. When he rolls his eyes, I add, "I don't think any of the Gambles would appreciate Dallas being bare chested during the actual ceremony."

We're standing behind a small copse of trees by the river, a late autumn breeze catching our matching copper-toned hair as we wait for our cue. I couldn't have planned a more perfect day to marry my best friend. The sun is out, the air is cool, the birds are providing a sweet soundtrack, and my groom is waiting by the riverbank for me.

"Point taken," my brother replies before extending his

bent arm for me to take. "Well, you look beautiful, sis. Momma and Daddy are smiling like crazy watching us right now."

Tears fill my eyes, but I refuse to cry today. Instead, I nod and go on tiptoes to kiss Archie's cheek. "I know." I'll always have their rings on my finger and their love in my heart. Forever.

It turns out that after years of dreaming and planning my big fantasy wedding, I found I didn't need any of it in the end. As the person who knows me best, Dallas, of course, offered to help make all my dreams come true for the big day. I thought about it, and we even sat down at the kitchen table together with all my vision boards to start planning.

But sitting across from Dallas, with his sleeves pushed up and his carpenter pencil ready to take notes, my dream shifted—just like that. The most elaborate, over-the-top, fantasy wedding paled in comparison to the reality of spending the rest of my life with Dallas.

Who needs aerialists serving champagne or a flower-crown-making station when we have all the love anyone could ever hope for? Besides, I figured out pretty quickly that planning a wedding with a Gamble would take more patience than I probably have. Dallas not only refused to believe a cummerbund wasn't a baked good, but the concept of a tablescape was way beyond anything he was willing or able to process.

So, with no big wedding to plan or vendors to book, we decided not to wait a second longer than we had to before we could officially belong to one another. Dallas has been working overtime to understand where I'm at in my peri-menopause journey to make sure we can still have the baby I want. Meemaw also declared we'd been "shacking up" long enough, and she was sick of telling her friend Phyllis to mind her own business about it.

When the first few chords of "My Best Friend" by Tim

McGraw come from Houston's guitar, my heart rate jumps with anticipation, and my hand tightens on Archie's arm.

"You ready?" he asks.

I'm smiling too hard to answer, so I nod instead, and then we're off. We round the copse of trees to see the small crowd standing to either side of a makeshift aisle. It's an intimate gathering—just family and close friends—but as soon as my eyes catch on Dallas, there's no one else here.

He stands by the river where we've spent more afternoons than I could ever count, his stance firm, boots rooted to the ground. My rock. My everything. I probably shouldn't be surprised by the tears in his eyes because I'm fighting back my own, but I don't want anything to get in the way of my view.

My groom is beyond handsome in a pearl-snap dress shirt and black suede blazer, his hair held in place by a sleek Stetson and his tanned cheeks lifted by the broad smile he's aiming right at me. The same smile that had my stomach flipping the day I met him on the street outside my momma and daddy's house over twenty-five years ago.

It's only when Ryder stage-whispers, "I didn't know she was gonna dress like a princess," that my attention wavers from my groom. I glance down to see Ryder dressed like a mini-Dallas, standing right next to his dad.

Everyone laughs, including me. Dallas's gaze locks with mine again, though, while he replies, "The prettiest one in all the land, kiddo."

Frankie "awws," and Pops coughs like he's fighting his own tears while Archie and I finally reach the front of the aisle. Josie Mae takes my bouquet of classic white roses with their turquoise ribbon, and then my hands are secure in Dallas's, his warm grip firm, telling me without words that he'll never let me go.

Houston strums a couple strangely off-key chords to finish the song, and I force my eyes from Dallas to meet Ryder's.

"Hey, Little G. You look super handsome." He stands up a little straighter at my words, and I smile at him until Dallas clears his throat and says, "Um, I'm right here."

Laughter fills the air again, just as Dallas intended.

"Here we go," Houston mutters, but there's no heat in his tone. I glance his way and shoot him a wink. How he still manages to be so good-looking with that ridiculous hair and mustache is one of the universe's great mysteries. I guess being my soon-to-be husband's twin might have something to do with it, though.

He's been home for a few weeks now, surprising all of us by not bolting back to the rodeo as soon as the crisis mode abated at the ranch and Ridge settled down. The Gambles are still in negotiations with Tiffany Grace and her lawyer, but things have been relatively quiet overall. Nobody has had the nerve to ask Houston when he's going back on the road, probably because we'd all rather he stay—even if he's been giving Ridge a run for his money in the competition for Big Knob's biggest grump.

Meanwhile, Skye is determined to save the family just like she saves every down-on-its-luck animal in the county, and she's even roped Josie Mae into her scheme. I'm betting on the two of them to show up the menfolk and kick some butt while they're at it.

It's hard to believe that in a few short minutes, I'll officially be a Gamble, even though they've all made me feel like one for years. I grin at Dallas, and he surprises me by yanking me into his arms and laying a hot one on me.

The crowd *whoops,* and the minister clears his throat while I pretend I'm trying to push Dallas away even though I'm not. It's way too easy to get lost in his kiss. When he does pull back, he whispers for only me to hear, "Hey, Sweetness. Sorry it took me so long."

My eyes flit over his features, each one as familiar to me as my own, as I catch my breath and inhale his captivating warm scent. I pause a beat, committing this moment to memory so I can hold on to it forever. And then I whisper right back, "Ditto."

———

Dallas

The second I release my wife from our first kiss and turn to walk down the aisle, two bright blue butterflies crash our wedding and take a fluttering trip down the aisle, leading the way. Shelby and I turn to look at each other with wide eyes and matching grins.

We've been reading *Shoed and Screwed by the Farrier*, where both main characters have lost their parents. They keep seeing butterflies as they fall in love, which they believe represent their parents' approval of the match. If that isn't a sign from above that Shelby's parents and my momma are celebrating with us, I don't know what is.

We race down the aisle while everyone throws flower petals at us, both of us too giddy to keep a calm pace. The reception starts instantly, a potluck with everyone bringing their signature dish. Skye puts a playlist on the speakers set up around the makeshift dance floor she's been cultivating since the moment we announced our fake engagement.

As badly as I want to dance with my wife and get those curves under my palms, I want to feed her first. No low blood sugar to ruin our big day. Not on my watch.

"Sit and eat, Sweetness. I'll get you a plate." I hold a chair while she gets settled. I pause to kiss her before getting her food from the line. Someone lets out a wolf whistle, so I take the hat off my head and shield us from these annoying family members of ours. I nibble on her bottom lip. "Think we could sneak off and make out in the field?"

Shelby slides her fingers through the back of my hair, and it feels so good I shiver. "I wish we could, but I guarantee we'd see Meemaw out there with her weed. Might put a damper on things."

I cringe. "You're probably right."

Straightening up, I put my hat back on. Sure enough, Meemaw is nowhere to be seen. She's either getting high on her medicinal weed or checking on her chickens. I make quick work of making up two plates and rush back to Shelby. We dig in best we can while holding hands and sneaking kisses every few minutes. The sun sets in the west as we all eat, a giant fireball as it sinks into the land that's been in my family for generations.

I can't believe I ever thought playing the field and remaining a bachelor was the best way to live life. Shelby and our little family are just about all I can think of these days. Which is why seeing Ridge in such a bad state about his divorce is hard. I want all my siblings to be as happy and in love as I am. Frankie winks at me from another table set up by the river, where she and Pops have their eye on Ryder for me. I give her a salute with my champagne glass. She gets it. Her and Morgan are a match made in heaven.

"Think you should go talk to him?" Shelby nudges me. She tips her head toward Ridge, where he's standing by himself next to the river, looking like he wants to jump into the brisk water and never get back out.

I put my arm around Shelby and bury my nose in her curls. "Nah. I'm too happy right now to deal with his grumpy butt."

Shelby grabs my lapel and turns me halfway around. "Good, because you might need to deal with this little situation."

She's referring to Houston and Josie Mae. My twin is reaching for another glass of champagne at the makeshift bar set up by the food table, and his old girlfriend from high school is making a beeline to confront him. Josie Mae's long black hair is flowing behind her in the soft wind, but her expression doesn't look so serene. We've managed to keep those two separated since Houston's been back, but it looks like our wedding is going to be the site of World War III.

We both hop to our feet and head over in their direction in time to hear the opening remarks.

"You keep flexing your hand. Did you hurt it or something?" Josie Mae asks, gesturing to Houston's right hand.

I frown. Did Houston get hurt at the rodeo and not tell me? He sets the champagne bottle down with a clank.

"What's it to you, Jo?" His words are a little fuzzy around the edges, telling me he's been dipping into the champagne more than I thought—or he and Ridge are sharing a flask.

Josie Mae crosses her arms over her chest, looking quite lovely in a pale teal ankle-length dress. I know she and Shelby went shopping in Hornville to get that dress, only because Shelby went on and on about how envious she is of Jo's slender waist. I had to tell her like ten times that I much prefer her buffet of curves. Actually, I quit telling her and took her to bed to show her. Sometimes my body speaks better than my mouth, if I do say so myself.

"It matters because if my ears have to hear one more wrong note out of you, they might start bleeding," Josie Mae tosses back, clearly irritated with Houston.

Shelby moves to her side and whispers something in her ear. I take up Houston's side and try to steer him over to Ridge. Maybe they can relationship trauma-bond or something over by the river. Away from me and Shelby.

Houston pushes me off of him, a strand of his shoulder-length hair falling loose from the leather strap he keeps it tied back with. Still gives me a double-take that he grew his hair out. Not sure which is worse: the long hair or the '70s stache.

"I play better than you ever will," Houston responds with

the maturity level of my son. And just a bit louder than is necessary. Heads are starting to turn.

Jo gasps. "You know that's not fair. I took lessons for years. Not my fault you have some sort of supernatural ability that other humans don't." She shakes her head and looks at Shelby. "He thinks the sun comes up just to hear him crow."

I grab Houston's arm, but he spins out of my grasp to confront Josie Mae. "You're about as useful as tits on a bull."

Josie Mae gasps. I step in front of Houston and push him backward. Enough is enough. He lets me move him, lifting his chin to give me the stink eye, but at least we're walking away.

I hear Shelby muttering behind me, holding back laughter. "We're one 'bless your heart' away from bloodshed."

Pops joins us, and I point to my two brothers and lift an eyebrow. He gets the message and engages them in conversation. I sneak away at the earliest opportunity and snag my wife's hand to pull her out onto the dance floor. Putting two fingers in my mouth, I whistle in Skye's direction. Her head pops up, and it only takes her a second to get my meaning. The song blaring from the speaker changes to "We Danced."

Shelby's head tips back, a knowing smile on her lips. Her body melts into mine while I wrap my arms around her. The Oklahoma sky is painted in a kaleidoscope of colors, turning acres of plain dirt into a legacy where love can blossom and root down deep. There's no place I'd rather be than right here, dancing with my girl under the darkening sky, just like her parents used to in the kitchen all those years ago. We took the long route to get here, but we finally made it.

As a wedding present, I finally took the napkin engagement pact out of my wallet and had it framed. It now sits proudly on the wall in our bedroom, a promise fulfilled.

I lean down and pluck a kiss from her lips, wondering if our babies will have her blue eyes or my cleft chin. Her copper highlights or my sun-kissed strands. Her curves or my muscles. Whatever they look like, I hope to God they have her brain, my family heritage, and our combined heart.

"I love you, Shelby Gamble," I whisper against her lips.

I feel her grin. "About bucking time, cowboy."

Also by Marika & Sylvie

Hot Flashes and Hockey Slashes - Hot Flash Hookups #1

Mood Swings and Hockey Flings - Hot Flash Hookups #2

Night Sweats and Hockey Nets - Hot Flash Hookups #3

Sleepless Nights and Hockey Fights - Hot Flash Hookups #4

__*Marika's Books*__:

__Sylvie's Books__:

bitly

About Marika Ray

Marika Ray is a USA Today bestselling author, writing small town RomCom to make your heart explode and bring a smile to your face. All her books come with a money-back guarantee that you'll laugh at least once with every book.

Marika spends her time behind a computer crafting stories, walking her doodle puppy, and making healthy food for her family whether they like it or not. Prior to writing novels, Marika held various jobs in the finance industry, with private start-up companies, and then in health & fitness. Cats may have nine lives, but Marika believes everyone should have nine careers to keep things spicy.

If you'd like to know more about Marika or the other novels she's currently writing, please find her in her private Reader Group.

If you want to take your stalking to the next level, here are other legal-ish places you can find Marika:

Join her Newsletter - http://bit.ly/MarikaRayNews

Amazon - https://www.amazon.com/author/marikaray

Goodreads - https://www.goodreads.com/author/show/16856659.Marika_Ray

Bookbub - https://www.bookbub.com/authors/marika-ray

TikTok - https://vm.tiktok.com/ZMJvnQ2Cv

Instagram - https://www.instagram/authormarikaray

Website - https://www.marikaray.com

About Sylvie Stewart

USA Today bestselling author Sylvie Stewart loves dad jokes, dirty rom-coms, country music, and baby skunks—preferably all at the same time. Most of her steamy contemporary and romantic comedy novels take place across her favorite state of North Carolina, and her characters never run out of snarky banter or snacks. When her laptop closes, Sylvie is a sucker for hugs from her twin boys and a good laugh with her hot-nerd hubby. If you love smart Southern gals, hot blue-collar guys, and snort-laughing with characters who feel like your best friends, Sylvie's your gal. Stay up to date on all things Sylvie! https://sylviestewartauthor.com

Join her Newsletter - http://bit.ly/s-s-nl

Facebook Reader Group - https://www.facebook.com/groups/743238732533487

Facebook Page – https://facebook.com/SylvieStewartAuthor

Instagram – https://instagram.com/sylvie.stewart.romance

BookBub – https://bookbub.com/authors/sylvie-stewart

Twitter – https://twitter.com/sylvie_stewart_

TikTok – https://tiktok.com/@authorsylviestewart

Pinterest – https://pinterest.com/sylviestewartauthor

Goodreads – https://goodreads.com/author/show/15303783.Sylvie_Stewart

YouTube – https://youtube.com/@sylviestewartauthor